BACKSTABBER

MARRISSE WHITTAKER

First published in 2024 by Bloodhound Books.

www.bloodhoundbooks.com

Print ISBN: 978-1-917214-07-0

ONE
RUN FOR HOME

I t was the mouthy girl who had been killed first, the one with *no place like home* tattooed on her arm. She'd travelled a horribly long way to find that out. She had screamed defiantly about her plans to break free and return to her mother, whereas Tanko had been so traumatised by all that he had witnessed, he hadn't spoken for a long time, not since the day of the last massacre, to be exact.

That had happened three long years ago, yet here it seemed everyone still blamed *him*. He'd had people in the street shout, 'Go back home.' But after everything that had happened, he had no home to go back to. The thought pounded into Tanko's brain along with the sound of blood pumping rapidly around his body as he hurtled along the country pathway, the killers in hot pursuit. Hearing their threats and racing footsteps closer behind him now, he skittered off to the right where the musky, honeyed smell of rapeseed, growing like a carpet of rippling sunshine, beckoned.

A mistake. It was almost impossible to fight through the tall wall of crops. He would need a machete to achieve that. Funny, the tall man leading his pursuers was carrying one. Tanko shuddered, the thought of beckoning the man over to do him a favour almost made him grin, had it not been for the fact that terror-filled tears as well as snot, was starting to run down his face, a river finally bursting its dam. Instead, he hunkered down into a tight ball, feeling a dry itch in his nose and the back of his throat. If he gave a cough or a sneeze now, he knew that he would definitely be finished.

Tanko's father had been a farmer and had told him once that rapeseed was like crack cocaine to bees, that the plant would at first attract and then kill the creatures, due to the deadly chemicals showered on them in order to enable the plants to grow. The pull of the bright lights was simply a cruel, murderous trick played on the innocent insects. Tanko knew just how that felt.

He glanced up now, pressing his tongue hard against the roof of his mouth to stop the almost overwhelming tickle, determined it seemed, to have him announce his hiding place. He'd learned to do that at school, so as not to disturb the other pupils working diligently, in a one-time peaceful life that seemed like a distant dream today. A huge combine harvester was moving across the adjoining field. Tanko wondered if the driver might be a friend or foe. Perhaps if he jumped up and waved his arms then the driver would run to his aid? But he had no voice to call for help and what if the man didn't see him in time?

The radio in the farm vehicle was loudly playing a tune that Tanko recognised, from discos that had been held at the Freedom Angels centre, when he had thought that he had finally reached his safe haven. 'Run For Home'. That was the title of the tune. Someone had explained that it had been performed by a group called Lindisfarne. The same name as the Holy Island that Tanko had been taken to visit on a day trip from the centre.

The island of Lindisfarne lay in the North Sea, just off the coast, not too far from where Freedom Angels was located. Tanko wondered if the song might be a good omen, linked as it was to people who named themselves after the cradle of Christianity.

His thought came too late. Before he had time to make any move, his pursuers had stopped, only a few feet away. So close that Tanko could hear them breathing heavily and listen to their angry curses. He felt that he might faint from the terror that enveloped him then. The tall man with the machete stepped back, looking up, so near now that Tanko caught the acrid smell of his sweat on the breeze, the glint of the blade's edge as it flashed in the sunlight. He swallowed hard, terrified that his own shuddering breaths would be heard, though the two men weren't looking his way. Their eyes were trained on a tree heavy with leaves. An English oak.

Tanko could recall when he had been excited at the thought of seeing an oak tree. It was after all, an emblem of strength. He remembered that he had learned in school that King Charles II of England had hid in one to escape the Roundheads. A Parliamentarian soldier had passed directly below it. He also recalled being taught that this famous tree supported more life than any other native tree in Britain. Hopefully that was a good sign.

Tanko took the opportunity to quickly, and as quietly as possible, fight his way in a low crawl a little further through the heady undergrowth. A gap in the rapeseed and the hedgerow inches away, opened, allowing him to see a busy road far below from his new hiding place. He'd arrived in England in a lorry such as those thundering by. The branding on the side had given the deceptive impression that it had been carrying food inside, rather than bodies.

'He's there.' Tanko braced himself, every muscle in his body tightening in terror. It was the machete-wielding man who had uttered the words.

'Where?' his comrade holding the rounders bat said.

'Up there. He thinks we can't see him in the tree.'

Tanko glanced up, his eyes scanning the huge tree. Had he moments before been a few steps further along the pathway in his escape, he would probably have skittered up the vast trunk himself and tried to hide within the wide canopy of branches and leaves fit for a king. Unfortunately, the boy that Tanko could now see, panic searing his young face, was not British royalty, free to roam unfettered across land and sea, but a fellow captor, who only minutes earlier, like Tanko, had taken the single opportunity that had presented itself to hurtle away from their prison. Whilst their captors had been disposing of the body of the girl with the tattooed arm, a few of those remaining had taken yet another dice with death to reach a place of safety. Unfortunately, it looked as though in this instance, the die that had been cast, hadn't fallen in the little fellow's favour.

The man with the machete started hacking at the lower branches of the tree. They fell, revealing the skinny boy. Tanko had heard, in whispered conversations amongst his fellow prisoners, that the lad was four years younger than him. Only eleven years old. The boy, looking like a rabbit caught in the headlights, tried to scramble further up the tree trunk.

'Get down here, you little runt,' the machete-wielding man shouted, chopping at the branches.

'I'll go and drag him down.' The second man, younger, fitter and clearly on a mission to curry favour with the other, had already started to climb the tree. Tanko could see blood on the man's hands and a picture flashed through his mind of the recent carnage, as prisoners no longer deemed worthy of the job, the frail or defiant, had been culled like cattle in a slaughterhouse. It was another horrific set of images to add to those which had already silenced him.

In response to the man's rapid movement up the tree, the skinny boy pulled his legs up beneath him and tried desperately to reach for a higher branch. As he did so, a small collection of photographs which must have been tucked safely in the waistband of his jeans, rained down like dead falling leaves. One, caught on the breeze, landed amongst the rapeseed right next to Tanko. He snatched it out of sight of the men. Glancing down, he could see the boy looking even younger in the picture, smiling to the camera, surrounded by family members. Different country, different faces and skin colours, but otherwise almost identical to the photos that Tanko had tucked inside his own pocket right now.

The man lunged up and caught hold of the boy's ankle. Tanko would forever capture the moment in his mind's eye of the boy's face as the thin branch he had been clinging to broke free. He spun around in a twisted somersault through the air, out of the man's grasp and instead downwards to the busy road far below. His scream of 'Mama!' was easy to recognise in any language. Tanko slapped his hand over his mouth as his own silent scream of horror tore through his body, merging with the sickening screech of brakes cutting through the air, as the boy hurtled into the path of a huge lorry. Tanko heard the loud thud and then horns blaring below.

'Shit. Let's move!' the machete-wielding man shouted. The younger man jumped from the tree, before both took off back in the direction they had come from at speed. Tanko was frozen in position for several moments, his ragged breath pounding in his ears, before in the distance, he could hear the sound of police sirens. In his world they didn't signal safety either.

He tentatively stood up and, looking nervously around, slowly picked his way through the sea of sun-dappled yellow, stopping under the huge English oak tree. The national symbol of strength had gone down now, in Tanko's estimation. The mighty structure might hold safe a past king of this fair country, but for people like him from far-off shores, there was no safe haven. The stories that he had been told were fake. Tanko was all alone, surrounded by only the shattered dreams and scattered pictures of the dead.

TWO
GONE MISSING

'Hold that pose, love.' A brave or misguided man holding an expensive-looking camera, shoved it into Billie's face as she strode through the corridors of Freedom Angels. She'd made some big mistakes in her life, but she didn't think that donating a substantial inheritance towards the building of this new centre, committed to helping people who had been trafficked, was one of them.

'Say *condom...*' The man exaggerated the pout of his mouth caused by the word, as Billie flicked him a murderous look.

'What?' She frowned.

'That's it. Keep that pout. Love it!' The man kept moving backwards, clicking his camera, adjusting focus as Billie gathered pace, moving past young people who were dressed up and smiling. There was excitement in the air, which would have pleased Billie had the irritating man not been buzzing around her.

'Yeah, yeah. Go on, and again, *condom–*' With a lightning movement, Billie sidestepped a pretty young girl wearing a beautiful painted-silk playsuit, and grabbed the man by the scruff of his collar, propelling him back hard against the wall.

'Say that one more time and I'll be sticking that camera where the sun doesn't shine. Got it?' Billie in heels was almost at eye level with the man. She noticed, at close quarters now, that he was wearing some sort of perfume that was no doubt expensive, yet utterly cloying.

'Okay, got it, love–' Billie rammed him against the wall again. Her stiletto pinning his fashionably sandalled toes to the floor. She hardly ever wore heels, much preferring her heavy Doc Martins, but she suddenly had a new admiration for the spikiness of the design. The man's smile dropped to a wince. 'I said okay... sorry–' Billie pushed him away and kept on walking, surrounded by more excitable people, young and old now, heading along the corridor to a spacious area, where stewards were standing at open double doors into what Billie knew was the theatre.

'Trouble is, I just can't resist a pretty face,' the man called over the heads of the crowd, with a smile and a wink as he lurched off the other way, cocky no doubt, Billie thought, in the knowledge that she was unlikely to turn back and cause a big scene on this special day for Freedom Angels. She approached a door to her right, opened it and swept inside. Her great friend and former colleague when Billie had headed up the MIT team of the local police, Boo Mensah, was sitting at her office desk. She looked up, smiled and gave a low whistle.

'Woo-hoo. Look at you, brushing up well. Not often you drop the jumper and jeans.'

Billie shut the door behind her, flicking her head back in the direction of the corridor. 'Got some questionable paparazzi out there. Guy with the paisley shirt, pimped-up Jesus sandals and smelling like a stinking corpse?'

Boo smiled. 'Ah, you've just bumped into Johnny Briggs. He's not that bad. Always upbeat, which is a plus. Volunteers one day a week. Apparently he used to be someone big in the world of design, fashion, advertising, all that stuff. Very popular, though I agree the perfume *is* a bit whiffy.'

'He's a clown. I was half expecting that camera of his to squirt water,' Billie answered.

Billie had donated part of the money needed to set up this new centre which Boo now managed. The other mammoth donator was no longer around due to a terrible accident, which Billie tried not to dwell upon. There had been a moment in time in which there had been a possibility that she and he might have been more than just benevolent patrons, even allowing for Billie's commitments to her PI agency, Wilde & Darque and her brand-new lover's international business interests. But fate had stepped in to put a stop to that idea, once and for all.

'Johnny's been giving a hand to some of the clients wanting to work in the arts. Helping to get together their portfolios, organise exhibitions and suchlike. He's been hugely supportive of Safia, assisting in getting her show polished up for tonight. She's going to be thrilled that you are wearing that dress she gifted to you. And look at me going on the catwalk too.' Boo moved her power wheelchair back to show Billie her own outfit of painted-silk top and trousers. She looked great in it and Billie had to admit that she wasn't feeling her usual discomfort when wearing a figure-skimming dress.

'Well, Safia certainly deserves all the help anyone can offer,' Billie had to agree. 'And let's face it, I've never been the best judge of men.' Though she silently reminded herself that at least she had started off liking the people that she had been wrong about before.

Safia Jamal without doubt, however, was a young woman to be hugely admired. She had been a former freelance translator for the US Army in Afghanistan, who had missed the plane to safety during the race to withdraw when the Taliban had retaken control of the country and her life was in serious danger.

The plan to escape had literally blown up in her face, due to an Islamic State suicide bomber instigating an explosion that killed one hundred and seventy Afghans and thirteen soldiers. The civilians had included all of Safia's family.

Somehow, injured by shrapnel, utterly grief-stricken and in absolute peril, she had eventually found a way out of the country, across Europe and had finally arrived in the UK via a small boat from Calais, hoping to link up with a remaining cousin, who unfortunately had moved on, destination unknown. Safia had arrived bedraggled, bewildered, clearly unwelcome and yet had still managed to pick herself up and move forward, desperate to make a mark on the world.

'He even made me look great at the photo session he led with some of his photographic students,' Boo added.

Billie gave up on further voicing her opinion of the man. It was clear that Boo was firmly in Johnny Brigg's fan club, but Billie reckoned it didn't take some allegedly ace photographer to make her look good. In Billie's opinion, Boo was beautiful enough to shame any model on the catwalk, despite losing the ability to walk after an incident at work many years before.

Not that catwalks and models generally featured in Billie's thoughts. She had been engaged once and her well-to-do fiancé's mother had dropped interest in her like a hot brick when Billie had followed her police chief father into the force rather than take up the offer from a top modelling scout to grace the cover page of a famous glossy fashion mag.

Unfortunately both she and her partner Ellis Darque, a former crack NCA operative, had been on the front cover of far too many newspapers for Billie's liking lately, due to a recent successful investigation which had a far-reaching and internationally newsworthy outcome. The coverage for Wilde & Darque had been hugely positive, which had Ellis rubbing his hands in glee at the extra work and income which followed, but

Billie preferred to be well out of the spotlight. It didn't exactly help to have photos of their faces shared far and wide when they were regularly working undercover.

'Maya's taken rather a shine to him.' Boo grinned. Billie wasn't thrilled with that thought either. Johnny Briggs looked a similar age to Ellis, if not older, and her business partner was *very* protective of his oldest daughter, who assisted Boo running Freedom Angels.

'Well I hope I'm not there when she introduces him to daddy dearest–' Billie was stopped mid-sentence due to a rap on the door. Ash Sanghera entered with his two eldest daughters, Indie and Happi, now aged seven and five. They were growing up quickly. Ash had been Billie's trusted working partner when she had ran the MIT. He was also, along with Boo, one of her closest friends in the world. Not that they hadn't been through a crisis or two, in both their personal and professional lives together, but in the end, those tests had only made their friendship stronger. Following his separation from wife Jas, Ash now lived in the basement flat of Billie's tall, Victorian era terraced house, which stood in a row of bright colour-washed buildings overlooking Alnmouth Estuary.

'We're going to be fashion models!' Happi raced across to Billie, who swept her up onto her hip.

'And very beautiful you both look too.' Billie smiled at her goddaughters dressed in their own hand-painted outfits as she pulled Indie close to her.

'Look at us, we're like a cult here,' Billie quipped. Even Ash was wearing a hand-painted silk tie from Safia's collection. She turned around to see that Boo and Ash were exchanging solemn glances. Ash shook his head. 'What's with the secret squirrel act?' Billie asked.

'Just work stuff.' Ash sighed as he watched Boo run her fingers through her hair in a look of despair, her upbeat manner from a moment before now wiped away. Billie knew that whatever operations Ash was involved with at work should technically remain confidential, but having been his boss it wasn't getting any easier for her to keep her snout out, especially as Boo seemed to be involved too.

'Anything I can help with?' she asked, raising her eyebrows as she placed Happi back on the floor.

'Nah, not really, and anyway, I've got to get the girls backstage. They're wired and it *is* the start of our holidays. I'm officially on a break from work.'

'Yes. Mum and Dad and me and Happi and Tani are all going on holiday together!' Indie announced, hopping from foot to foot. Billie knew what a big moment this was for Ash. He and his former wife Jas had gone through a lot of soul-searching before and after their divorce. To actually head off on holiday as a family to Spain, planned for the next morning, was a monumental achievement. There was no chance that they could be lovers again, but Billie desperately hoped they could make a go of their carefully negotiated friendship, for the sake of their little girls. She didn't want to take the edge off this special time, but something was clearly up.

There was another knock on the door. Safia Jamal appeared in the doorway, looking radiant in one of her creations.

'I am looking for my star models. Are you ready for the show, my little sisters?' Safia addressed Indie and Happi, giving them high fives as the girls shouted 'Yes' excitedly. 'Thank you, Billie and Boo, for giving me this opportunity, via Freedom Angels. I promise you that I will do good work with my life and give back, when I have made a success of this venture. I will never forget this opportunity you have given me, to follow my own dreams, not a life that others have chosen for me.'

'My pleasure,' Billie answered, though she didn't like the fact that her large donation to Freedom Angels was so regularly mentioned. The money had been inherited, after all, and had come from the result of less than legal actions in the first place. Billie had simply righted the wrong, she hoped, by handing the money straight on to a good cause.

As Ash shepherded the excited girls out of the room, Billie turned back to Boo. Was she wiping her eyes?

'It's one of the kids. He's gone missing...' Boo rubbed her hand over her face, leaving a mascara smudge under one eye.

'Missing? Has he not gone off to see family? Friends?' Billie frowned. Boo knew as well as her that teenagers ran off all of the time and usually turned up. It wasn't like Boo to freak out.

'Not Tanko Abubakar. He hasn't got any relatives and his friends were all here. He's suffering from traumatic mutism. Witnessed his family and fellow villagers being massacred by Boko Haram in Nigeria. He arrived by boat with a young man from the same village, which is how we know about his situation. But the other guy moved on to Sweden where he had family, so progress has been slow. He was starting to communicate a little with his therapist by nodding or shaking his head... that's why we need him back. He's only fifteen.' Boo started to chew on her thumbnail.

'But no sign so far?' Billie didn't need to ask Boo if she'd contacted all of the necessary authorities, not with her background. Boo shook her head. 'No. The trouble is he's not the first to disappear. Ash had a word in the ear of the latest chief at our old place, but no one is interested in asylum-seeking kids going missing. Let's face it, no one knows where to start looking.'

'I guess it's all this talk by the government threatening to ship people out every five minutes before processing their asylum claims? Enough to send anyone on the run.' Billie shook her head in despair. Boo nodded in agreement.

'We lost a few people when that idea was first publicised.

There were creeps hanging around outside from gangs, telling our clients that they were about to be deported so just jump in this car and we'll take you somewhere safe...'

'Like locked up in a marijuana farm in the attic of someone's house or forced labour pedalling drugs.' Billie didn't need to spell out all of the possibilities. In recent times both she and Boo had come up close and personal with the world of county lines drug gangs and sex traffickers.

'They sent a few patrol cars around here, but word is the gangs just moved out to the surrounding streets where we've got people in B&B accommodation. It's the kids' hotel that's the big problem. Tanko moved in there only a couple of weeks ago, from one of the dorms here. It's just been so overcrowded. I blame myself... I should have argued with the Home Office against the move more forcefully.' Boo reached for a paper tissue from a box on her desk.

'He might turn up. Did security on the children's hotel or any of the staff there not notice anything, have they checked their CCTV?' Billie frowned, wondering why she hadn't seen anything at all on the news about a young boy going missing. Boo shook her head in exasperation.

'That's just it. There are only agency staff wafting in and out now and then. None of them employed long enough to remember which child is which, no security, no CCTV...'

'You're not saying a bunch of kids who're alone, just arrived traumatised from a different country, are living in a hotel *by themselves*?' Billie was aghast at the thought.

'As good as. I've been complaining to all and sundry since the Home Office stuck them there, bypassing the local authority care system!' Boo almost shouted. 'But no one is listening. It's not just here. There are unmanned homes full of unaccompanied children all over the country–'

'But surely that's not legal?' Billie was astonished at the thought. Boo gave a despairing laugh.

'You are such an innocent these days, my lovely. Of course, it is child neglect on an industrial scale, but who's going to prosecute the Home Office?'

'How come I never knew anything about this?' Billie started marching back and forth across the room in utter shock.

'You have enough on your plate with the PI business, Billie. You're not a copper anymore. It's not your problem.' Boo sat back and blew out a sigh.

'It's *everyone's* problem if a kid goes missing. Especially a child who is so vulnerable, surely?' Billie hated this part of not heading up a police team, the realisation that she wasn't going to get insider information on situations such as this. But Ellis had drummed home to her that her new life and business was meant to be all about snooping and reporting back. Discovering the truth, which had been her reason for leaving the force in the first place, but definitely *not* taking action. Almost a year after launching Wilde & Darque, she was still finding it almost impossible to be what she considered a useless bystander though.

'Kids.' Boo's look stopped Billie in her tracks. 'There's more than one of them gone.'

'What?' Billie gasped.

'Tanko is by no means the first. We've lost two dozen in recent months. A couple turned up in Scotland, arrested for shoplifting – working for a gang. They've been locked up now so that's okay,' she said with an air of resigned irony. 'A handful had hitched up with distant family members. One of the girls, a fourteen-year-old, turned up in a brothel raid...'

'Two dozen?' Billie couldn't believe what she was hearing.

'Yeah, all from the children's hotel around the corner here. But as of today, from unmanned children's homes around the country, two hundred children are currently still not located. That's from the four hundred and forty that have gone AWOL in the past couple of years.' Billie stopped walking and flopped down on a chair opposite Boo, blinking hard as she took the information in.

'I can't believe it...' She trailed off. 'And all this has been going on in plain sight?'

Boo nodded. 'Yep. None of the hotels are in remote areas. Truth is nobody really cares, Billie.'

The conversation was interrupted as a young man knocked and then popped his head around the door with a cheery smile on his face.

'This is your five-minute call, ladies!' he said. 'They're looking for you backstage, Boo.' He left the door open and moved off as a group of dressed-up and chattering young people hurried by in the corridor outside.

'Imagine if two hundred British children went missing from a boarding school. Or any school come to that...' Billie mused as she followed Boo to the door.

'Yeah, well, just imagine *that* scenario on a twenty-four-hour news screen near you.' Boo gave a resigned shrug before she sped off in the direction of the backstage area. In a daze, Billie followed the audience stragglers towards a bunch of fair haired, English rose complexioned schoolgirls in local spick and span uniforms who were handing out programmes with a smile. There would be no doubt about the commotion that would be caused, quite rightly, if just one of these bright and smiley children went missing, Billie thought angrily.

As Billie inched sideways, between people already seated, to the empty chair next to Ash who was just finishing a phone call as the house lights dimmed, she glanced at the blown-up photos around the walls of the theatre of the child asylum seekers who had passed through Freedom Angels in the short time it had been up and running. Were any of those young people with shy smiles and hope in their eyes wiped off the face of the earth without anyone giving a damn too? She was itching to take action, despite no longer being in an official position to do anything.

'It's okay, Secret Squirrel. Boo told me everything... about the kids going missing. We've got to do something!' she hissed in a stage whisper to Ash as upbeat music began and a spotlight was trained on the stage.

'Yeah, well, I totally feel your pain, that's why I didn't mention it to you. I knew you would go apeshit. But missing kids aren't my department, and the latest head honcho is pretty adamant we don't go stepping on anybody else's toes. I've already stuck my neck out for Boo, putting pressure on to investigate. It's an absolute scandal what's happening, but we're way short-staffed as it is, and let's face it, nobody really knows where to go looking. Most of the kids don't have any relatives to put pressure on either – damn.' Ash stopped speaking as his mobile messaging beeped. 'Another call from work.' He sighed.

'Don't they know your holiday started at teatime?' Billie knew how important it was that everything went to plan with Ash's break.

Billie decided to try and dampen down her fury at the fact no real effort seemed to be being made to find the missing kids. She didn't need to use her imagination to guess some of the scenarios they might end up in. Many of her own murder enquiries when she had been head of the MIT had involved vulnerable children and evil manipulating adults. She was squirming in her seat just thinking about it. But it wasn't fair to labour the point to Ash. Not when he wasn't in any real position to do much about it and especially not tonight, when he was meant to be enjoying this time with his kids. He had been fighting so hard to create the best life for his own precious girls going forward.

'A couple of the guys have phoned in sick. It's that bug going around. There's been an incident apparently. Could be suspicious and they're desperate for cover...' His mobile suddenly rang loudly, just as the music had stopped and Boo had appeared on stage and had taken a deep breath to start her welcoming speech. People around mumbled and shushed. Ash took the call. 'DSI Sanghera,' he whispered, looking around sheepishly. He rubbed his forehead, as he looked down. 'Okay. Yeah, on my way,' he finally said through a sigh.

'You don't mind dropping off the kids with Jas after this?' he asked.

'No, of course not. I'll tell them you managed to see them strut their stuff and thought they were the best. I'll film them on my moby for you.' Billie had immediately agreed, though she didn't relish the thought of explaining to Ash's former wife Jas that he'd chosen work over his family yet again. Billie and Jas had once been good friends, but Ash's former wife still blamed Billie for the circumstances that had led to the breakdown in their marriage. The long hours and obsession on solving cases which had made Billie, assisted by Ash, so successful at bringing dangerous criminals to justice had been partly what had taken its toll on their union.

But that wasn't the big issue for Ash. Jas still wasn't completely aware of the full details of the catastrophic event which had so totally devastated Billie's own future plans at the same time as Jas's plans for a forever happy family life, and Billie wasn't about to dredge it all up now.

'Big shout?' she asked, wishing she was going out with Ash on the call rather than playing babysitter, much as she loved his girls. Ash tucked his phone into his pocket and reached for his jacket draped over the back of the chair.

'Yeah. A missing kid has just turned up under the wheels of a lorry.' Billie sat forward in her seat, her stomach tensing. 'But tell Jas that I'll *definitely* be there to pick them up on time for the airport in the morning.' Billie nodded in response to Ash's request, but she could already imagine Jas's scepticism about that.

'Is it Tanko Abubakar?' she whispered. Ash shook his head.

'Not from the description I'm getting. But it does sound like it's one of the kids that went missing from the asylum hotel around the corner. My money's on the missing eleven-year-old.'

'Eleven?' Billie couldn't help bellowing in astonishment. Boo, distracted, momentarily stopped speaking, glancing over at the two of them as people around made noises of disapproval. Ash had a pained expression on his face as he stood up.

'Yeah. Thanks for taking the kids,' he whispered as he started squishing past legs in the dark to more tuts of annoyance. Nobody was as infuriated as Billie was though. *Somebody* had to do something about the situation. Certainly time was of the essence to discover the whereabouts of desperately vulnerable Tanko Abubakar before his tragic journey ended on a mortuary slab too. She wanted answers and she wasn't going to stop until she got them.

THREE
HIDING IN PLAIN SIGHT

Tanko had cautiously made his way out of the field and down the embankment leading to the dual carriageway, dodging behind scrubby bushes and keeping to the shadows, his heart thumping in his chest with fear. His lungs were full of the smell of vehicle exhausts as a number of cars now snaked out along the road behind the lorry. The door of the vehicle was open, the driver holding his head in his hands as he stood upright from a crouching position on the road. Tanko heard a female voice cry out as she turned back from the inner crowd, a look of total horror and distress on her face.

'He just came flying down from that bridge up there,' the driver explained through a gasp. Everyone looked up, towards the tree from which the boy had catapulted. From this angle it was clear to see a bridge arching the dual carriageway. Tanko skittered behind a scrubby thorn-covered bush, on which a dirty crisp packet had been impaled, along with other detritus blown up from the road. He closed his eyes tightly for a moment, in the desperate hope that if he couldn't see the people talking, then they wouldn't see him.

'He looks so young.' The woman's voice broke as she said the words. 'Where on earth are his parents?'

'No houses anywhere around here,' another male voice mumbled. 'Hello! Is anyone up there?' he called as Tanko crouched down lower behind the bush, his heart hammering against his chest, feeling sure that someone was about to spot him at any moment. He wanted to run down and tell everyone what had happened, that he and the other kids had all been kidnapped, held in a building nearby. That one or two of them were on the run right now and that some, like the girl with the *'no place like home'* tattoo had been executed. If they moved quickly, Tanko thought that they might even catch the killers, free those still trapped and find the freshly dead, who he had watched being dumped in a deep muddy ditch out in the field behind the building, before in a blind panic, he had taken his chance and ran.

But Tanko still found it almost impossible to speak, not since the day that one of the world's deadliest terrorist groups, Boko Haram, had stormed the market in his little village in north-east Nigeria, killing his immediate family and neighbours. Funny that his father had always called him a chatterbox before then and not so long ago, he was able to speak English well. Now he couldn't tell anybody anything, though he desperately wanted to.

He had been a studious pupil at school, knew all about British history and had wanted to be an English teacher one day. But that was the problem, Boko Haram means 'fake education is a sin'. Fake, meaning anything western, and his school had prided itself on being open to education covering all different cultures.

Tanko had been having extra language classes on the morning when the attack had happened. He, along with an older boy learning the Swedish language, had ran away when they had seen the soldiers arrive, watching in terror from their hiding place outside, as their school had been burned to the ground, most of their teachers inside of it. Taking a short cut at speed through the dense bush surrounding their school, they had hoped to warn everyone gathered in the village square on market day, but the attack there was already underway, including within the mosque where those inside were praying for the community.

Tanko tried to wipe the soul-shattering images away. He knew that he should honour the memory of his parents by telling the truth of their demise, using his ability to speak in another language to tell the world what was happening where he came from, that people weren't fleeing to another country to make big money and buy shiny new things, but because their lives were in extreme danger at home. If that had not been the case, then he would have worked for his dream, to stay in Nigeria with his family and friends, one day have a wife and children of his own and teach English, in the village school that now no longer, like his family, existed.

Tanko had felt that if he worked really hard with the therapist at Freedom Angels, where people had been so kind to him, he would have finally found his voice. He understood that it was fear that had stricken him mute. But now he was terrified for his life all over again. He had learned that even strangers who seemed kind, were often wolves dressed in sheep's clothing. Danger lurked around every corner, even in this country where he had dreamed of finding a safe home.

Suddenly the police car which Tanko had heard in the distance only moments before, sped up, lights flashing, manoeuvring around the parked cars. They could surely free everyone still locked in the building just over the hill and catch the killers if he ran down to them and tried his hardest to speak up. But they would also catch him. Maybe blame *him* for the small boy's death? Tanko spotted a larger shrub, growing lower down the bank, as that terrifying thought popped into his head. He scampered quickly downwards, his nerves taut, keeping in the shadows, hoping that the foliage would offer better coverage, should the police start searching the surrounding area.

'Looks like he was arsing about on that tree up there and fell off,' Tanko heard one policeman say to another. Tanko was screaming the truth in his head, willing it to somehow transmit through the airwaves to the law enforcers. He desperately wanted to help those left behind, even if nothing could be done for the young boy under the wheels.

Even if they didn't arrest him and, instead, took him back to the hotel where he had moved, having stayed for a short while at Freedom Angels, then the bad men would simply catch him once more, bundle him into the back of a big van as they had the first time, and bring him back to that prison. Make him pay for running away. The thought filled him with a terror that made his stomach churn. Nobody seemed to see what was going on around them in this country. Perhaps all of the people born here thought that they were safe, when murderers and slaves were all around them, hiding in plain sight? Or maybe they didn't care if the bad things were happening to people who had started life far away, with different skin colours and a mother tongue unlike their own?

An ambulance sped up, though it was clear from the demeanour and shocked whispers of those he could hear now that he was closer to the scene, that no medical intervention could bring the boy back to life. The police were unravelling crime-scene tape and moving cones across the dual carriageway. A long line of vehicles had built up and it looked to Tanko as if the stationary traffic was about to move around the tragic scene, via a coned-off lane.

He could feel his anxiety levels rising to exploding point.

He didn't want to stay here, all alone, so near to the place where he had been kept prisoner, but the only safety he had ever felt since arriving in this country was inside Freedom Angels. He had no idea where he was or how to get back there and maybe find his therapist, or the head lady, called Boo, who seemed to be kind and understanding.

As two or three lorries in a line moved forward, Tanko scrambled down the embankment. When he had been sleeping in woodland with his friend near Calais, towards the end of their terrifying journey to safety, many other asylum seekers had attempted to jump onto lorries in order to bypass the heavily policed tunnel to Britain. It wasn't easy however, and both Tanko and his older friend had been too scared to try it for themselves, after one young man from Albania fell and had crushed both of his legs under the huge wheels of the vehicle. He had felt sorry too for the lorry driver, the fearful look on his face as he had been swamped on stopping, by people desperate to hitch a ride. Tanko had been brought up to always be polite to strangers, never to take anything which was not first offered.

That was just before English men had approached them, offering the journey on the small rubber boat across the Channel. First, he and his friend had to give them every Euro that they had saved from selling their family's belongings when they had crept back into their empty homes in Nigeria, the balance to be paid once they got to England. The men knew exactly where Tanko and his companion would be taken by the authorities when they were intercepted on an English beach, and that is why, as soon as Tanko had been moved to the hotel, they came quickly to take him to their workhouse.

On arrival, the men told him that now he had to work until his labour would one day cover the cost of his voyage over the water. That is why Tanko's older friend had fled immediately to Sweden as soon as he got a chance. He knew they would be coming. Tanko had been told by his captors that he would therefore be working to pay for both of their journeys, with interest. He wasn't a stupid boy, simply desperate. He knew that in reality, that meant that there would be no way out for him, ever. Not alive.

As the lorries started to follow the traffic being waved around the area where his young fellow prisoner now lay, Tanko slid down the embankment to the side of the road, his limbs shivering with fear.

'Did you see someone just come out of the bush there?' one of the police officers called to his colleague.

'Hey, is anyone there?' The other police officer began to head in Tanko's direction. An explosion of utter terror coursed through Tanko's body, propelling him forward. Pulling his hoodie over his head, he rushed onto the road, weaving past the nose of a lorry. The huge vehicle brushed his arm. Tanko felt his heart slamming against the wall of his chest. Through the framework he could see both police officers together now, their eyes searching the scene where he had just been hiding.

He hesitated for a moment, frozen with fear, before snapping out of his panicked state. Feeling sick at the smell of the exhaust fumes, he started to dash alongside the lorry. He knew which bit on the structure he needed to head for – the area between the driver's cabin and the cargo-carrying box-like refrigerated unit behind. A huge leap was required to grab hold of the framework whilst avoiding being crushed by the unit, as the lorry turned to the right to access the opposite carriageway where the traffic was being directed.

Tanko sped up a little, stumbled as he lost his footing for a moment on the uneven, grassy strip of land adjoining the road, wincing as his ankle twisted. A second lorry was moving ahead now. He quickly gathered himself, made a final decision and launched into a sprint, despite the weakness in his ankle. He spotted the section of the framework that was vital to reach in order to cling on limpid-like to the lorry, as he judged the correct distance needed to attempt a flying leap, his heart hammering once again. His fate would be decided in the next second there in the dark shadow between cab and unit. Would he be heading for another chance of making something of his life, or about to be flung down under the huge wheels in a cold and agonising death like his small friend lying only metres away? Swallowing hard, he took a leap of faith.

FOUR
OVER HIS DEAD BODY

E llis hit the floor with a bang as he rolled out of the bed, reaching for his ringing phone. He was way more asleep than awake, his head feeling as though it had been packed with cotton wool. He squeezed one eye open, trying to focus on the pink clock with the cartoon princess motif, on the wall. It said 6am. Maybe it had stopped? He'd only managed to get a single hour's shut-eye if it was correct.

Connie, his five-year-old daughter, had refused to settle until he'd lain on the top of her small, narrow bed, the duvet printed with pink fairy figures, and read her one story after another. He reckoned that her disgruntlement was due to her building up to starting school for the first time or maybe getting some bug or other. Kids seemed to get them non-stop at this age, but in truth, what the hell did he know about these things?

'Yep?' he managed to mumble, after attempting three times to engage the green answer swipe.

'Is that Wilde & Darque Private Investigators?'

'Um, yes that's right,' Ellis answered, immediately opening both eyes and blinking hard. He usually checked before answering, to deduce whether he was receiving a personal or work call. So much for being an ace PI. 'Can I help you?' His voice sound dry and croaky.

'This is Graham Harper, CEO of the Porkie's Big Eats chain. I wish to arrange an urgent meeting over a very delicate matter. Can you come in within the hour?'

Ellis coughed and rubbed his face, forcing himself to brighten up. The Porkie's Big Eats chain would be a lucrative client, and though Graham Harper didn't know it, his outlets selling freshly baked goods, drinks and sandwiches, seemingly on every corner across the north-east of England, were regular lifesavers for Billie and Ellis whilst working. Billie could practically mainline their cheese pastries. Ellis couldn't help smiling at the thought of her, all tall, long-legged, slim and stunning with her wild red hair, stuffing stodge down her throat, like it was about to go out of fashion, spilling crumbs all over every top she wore, without a care for her appearance.

'That was the key to the feeding of the five thousand,' she had answered when Ellis had the first time pointed out the major flakes of pastry fall out of her munch on the run. 'Porkie's Big Eats pies. They got the loaves and fishes bits wrong in the Bible. I'm sure they had an outlet in Bethsaida. With these things, the crumbs are twice the volume of the original pie.' Ellis had known right then and there, the first day that he had joined Billie's MIT team as a crack NCA advisor, that they were definitely going to get along.

'I'm afraid we have another meeting about to start, right now.' Ellis was only partly lying. He had glanced over his shoulder and Connie wasn't actually in the bed. The door was slightly open. He jumped up and headed towards it. 'But we can be there at nine thirty,' he offered, finally sounding like he was a crack professional, eager to get on with the job in hand.

'Well if you really can't get here earlier,' Graham Harper said through a worried-sounding sigh. He clearly wasn't used to having to wait. 'But you must agree to *absolute* confidentiality over the matter that I am about to share with you.'

'I can guarantee that, Mr Harper.' Ellis was on the landing now and by the open laundry cupboard. He could see a trail of sheets winding down the steep stairs. It didn't take a crack PI to work out the direction Connie had been moving in. His heart leapt into his mouth. He had been told many times that he was being a way too overprotective father, but one wrong step and his precious little daughter would have tumbled straight to the bottom, breaking her neck.

'This is a life and death matter, Mr Darque, life and death. I'll see you at nine thirty sharp.' Graham Harper cut the connection, as Ellis hurried downstairs.

In the past year he'd had sole care of Connie, after his former wife, Storm Benbow, had gone AWOL. Any day now, that would be signed and sealed by the courts, making it legally watertight. Storm had been mixing with seriously crooked types and had gone on the run, or alternatively was dead in a ditch somewhere. To be honest, Ellis couldn't care less if she was. There had been no love lost between them, even by the time Connie had been born and his former wife had done everything in her power to stop Ellis's court-approved weekly access to his daughter. However, he couldn't say that being a single dad was proving to be easy.

His eldest daughter Maya had taken over nannying Connie for the past few months, having dropped out of training to be a police officer, though she had already proven herself to have had huge potential, doing work experience on Billie's MIT team. She had instead juggled the care of Connie, with assisting Boo setting up Freedom Angels, though Ellis had strongly advised against it. He was certain that she had become involved in the new organisation as a knee-jerk reaction to the traumatic time she had endured whilst volunteering abroad last summer. But in the end, he hadn't been able to convince her to stay on course with her police training and now she had made it clear that she wasn't going to be around full-time caring for Connie, seeing as her little half-sister was about to start school. She hadn't arrived home last night for starters, which had Ellis worried sick.

As he arrived at the ground floor, still following a trail of sheets, he rubbed his head and yawned. The truth was, he didn't really know either of his daughters well, though he was absolutely thrilled to have them both move in with him. Maya had been conceived during a short-lived relationship twenty years earlier. Ellis hadn't even known his lover was pregnant when they had parted company, but following her mother's death two years earlier, Maya had come looking for the dad that she had never met and who had never known that she had existed, until the truth had been revealed.

Maybe both had been trying too hard to please the other, during their getting-to-know-one-another period. Things were starting to get a little bumpy now that they were more relaxed in one another's company and dropping their Sunday best behaviour, when maybe they had been viewing one another through rose-tinted specs. Maya had started complaining that her dad was too controlling, but all Ellis wanted was to keep his two girls safe and sound.

'Connie, where have you got to, sweetheart?' Ellis called, heading towards his kitchen. He finally spotted his tiny daughter kneeling up at the kitchen table which she had covered in one of the bedsheets. She was surrounded by upturned cereal boxes and a jar of honey on its side, trickling over the sheet and onto the floor, in a pool of stickiness. The whole scenario, including Connie, was covered in white flour, from a bag which she had upturned on the table, mixed with thousands of coloured sugar strands from her cake-making play set. She had a wooden spoon in her hand, stirring something in a large crock pot. On seeing Ellis, a wide smile crossed her sweet face, which also featured various formations of honey and cereal around the mouth area.

'I'm making pancakes for your breakfast, Daddy!' Connie shouted, waving the wooden spoon in the air. A large dollop of the dubious-looking mixture glued to the spoon dropped on her head, causing her to giggle. Ellis didn't know whether to laugh or cry at the scene.

'That's lovely, but we've got to get a move on, Connie. Last day at nursery.' Ellis didn't quite know where to start his crisis management but thought he should maybe turn the jar of honey upright first. He grimaced as his bare feet stuck to the gummy widening pool already on the floor.

'But I've made it, Daddy!' Connie pulled a grimace as Ellis tried to wipe her face with a dishcloth. 'I don't want to go to nursery. We can play chefs.'

'Not today, baby–' Ellis stopped mid-speech as Connie started to wail, a technique she had perfected recently in order to get out of doing anything she didn't want to do, seeming to sense that he was a novice at this full-time parenting stuff.

A sudden rap on the front door had Ellis glancing at the kitchen clock. It was still only five minutes past six. Who on earth could be knocking on his door at this time? His stomach lurched. Maya hadn't come home last night. She'd left a message saying that she was staying with a friend. He hoped to God that she was okay. Swinging Connie up onto his hip, he headed for the door, ignoring her tearful eyes and upturned lower lip.

'Hello?' he called, pulling the door open to be faced with his lawyer Edward Twyford, a tall, dapper man, with salt and pepper hair and wearing an expensive pinstripe suit. He was costing Ellis an arm and a leg, but hopefully he had finally successfully won the legal arguments required for Ellis to have sole parenting responsibility for his little daughter. 'What's up?' Ellis moved back to allow Edward to step inside of his hallway.

'Disagreeable news, I'm afraid. I have some work to do in the office before court today, hence the early call, but I thought I should alert you to the fact that there may be a fly in the ointment regarding your final court hearing later this week.'

'As in?' Ellis was already almost at the end of his tether with meetings with the various officials needed to check that he was suitable to look after his own flesh and blood. Funny how nobody seemed to worry about Connie's mother, when she was in bed with a major criminal.

'Ms Benbow has emerged, I'm afraid, as if from the grave and has made an application to the court to adjourn the final hearing. She wants the child arrangements order amended to be in her favour once again.'

'What?' Ellis couldn't believe what he was hearing. 'She can't do that, just come out of the woodwork after being AWOL for nearly a year and expect to take Connie back. She never bloody looked after her anyway. I paid for end-to-end nannies and childcare. Anyone can see that I can look after the kid better!'

Ellis noticed Edward Twyford blink slightly as his eyes took in the scene of Connie covered in food and now tapping Ellis on his bald head with the wooden spoon. A drip of honey ran down his temple. Looking down at the floor he could see the lawyer tracking his honeyed footprints on the wooden floor from kitchen to doorway.

'Ms Benbow has stated that she has been ensconced in a domestic violence support location, in fear of her life with regards to her former partner and also claims to have child protection concerns regarding your own ability to care for Connie.'

'You are *joking*?' Ellis gasped. 'Connie is perfectly safe with me.' He yanked the wooden spoon covered in the glue-like concoction out of Connie's hand as he did so, before she could tap him on the head again. She started to wail once more.

'I want my *mummy!*' Tears started to spurt out of her eyes, worthy of an Oscar winner.

'Shush, baby.' Ellis quickly kissed Connie on the cheek. She started to squirm from his arms, kicking out. He put her down on the floor, whereupon she raced back up the stairs wailing loudly, climbing over the trail of discarded sheets tangled down the steep staircase like a death trap.

'She means Billie.' Ellis turned to Edward Twyford in way of an explanation.

'Billie?' He raised an eyebrow. 'Really, Mr Darque, I thought that we had gone into great detail about the need for disclosing all relevant relationships. Is this Billie female or male or otherwise inclined? You also need to inform me immediately if this is a live-in relationship. As I explained, such details are highly important to the court.'

'She's my business partner, that's all.' Ellis rubbed his hand across his head. It stuck to the honey concoction left by the spooning.

'Well, I'm sorry to be the bearer of such bad news. I'll leave it with you for now. My secretary will make an appointment to speak later this week. But I must warn you, Ms Benbow claims to have gotten her life back on track and has engaged a formidable legal team. She is demanding full custody of Connie.'

As Edward Twyford made his way out of the gate and towards his expensive car, Ellis shut the door, leaning hard against it for a moment. He opened his eyes and looked at the devastation around him, before heading upstairs where he could hear Connie crying in her room. He knew that she would cheer up within moments. Just like most kids of her age, she was simply desperate to have his full attention at all times. It was nothing to the tears that would be shed, should Storm Benbow actually be successful in her shock return and attempt to grab full custody rights.

Ellis absolutely knew that if she got her claws back into the child who was so precious to him, she would do another disappearing act, this time with Connie, just to spite him, and no one would see them for dust. Ellis was adamant she would only achieve that one way – over his dead body.

FIVE
A MATTER OF LIFE AND DEATH

The small boy was lain out on the gurney behind a glass screen, sheet covering his body, sweet face largely intact, which was lucky, Billie reflected, as apparently nothing else of him was. At least this way, a definite identification could be made, should a relative ever eventually turn up, or go online via the Missing Persons Unit, looking for the boy. They would then get to know the bad news, rather be left wondering forever if he'd made a bright new life for himself.

'I'm guessing it was all pretty quick, if that helps.' The mortuary manager, who was unknown to Billie, attempted to offer words of consolation to Boo who was quietly sobbing at the sight before them. Both Boo and Billie were no stranger to the freshly dead, including children, but the isolation of the tiny figure waiting for the appointed pathologist to dissect him even further, was particularly poignant.

'I'll just take these records through to help with identification, though you seem pretty positive.'

'Yep. Niko Zefi. No doubt whatsoever. One of our staff took him to the dentist only last week. He still had one of his baby teeth...' Boo trailed off for a moment, trying to gather herself. '...

at the back. He had it removed to enable his adult one to push through. The pathologist will be able to see that. He lost one of his front teeth when the rubber dinghy he was travelling on overturned in the Channel on the way to the UK.' Boo squeezed her eyes shut in distress. Billie could see the remaining front tooth, too large for his small face, resting on Niko Zefi's pouted lower lip. 'His big brother drowned,' Boo whispered, blowing her nose as she tried to get a grip. Billie shook her head in distress. Even she was beginning to feel tears prickling the back of her eyes.

'Shame the police liaison officer hasn't turned up. I was hoping we could get more background on the circumstances surrounding the death,' Billie said to the mortuary manager.

'He was here earlier, but when he heard that you were coming from the refugee place, he said there was no point waiting around. It's not like there are any relatives...' He trailed off mid-sentence, possibly registering the flash of anger in Billie's eyes. 'But I heard him talking to the pathologist and the word is that the kid was larking about on a tree hanging over the road and just fell off in front of the vehicle.'

'That's bollocks for starters,' Boo snapped. 'No way would Niko have willingly climbed up any tree unless his situation was desperate. He was phobic about large trees. Both his father and mother were hung from the one outside of his house, hence coming here to seek asylum. He was being treated by the therapist for severe post-traumatic stress, phobic about large trees in particular. Impossible for him to have been playing on one. Make sure that the pathologist knows that.' Boo had wheeled in front of the morgue manager, blocking his route along the corridor, to make sure that she had made her point clear.

'Yes. Well, I will pass that information on,' he answered,

sidestepping Boo and moving away along the corridor, the boy's dental records tucked under his arm.

'Hung?' Billie glanced from the small figure laid out on the gurney to Boo, wondering how unfair life was that such a shocking catalogue of tragedy could have befallen one so young. Boo moved back towards her.

'Blood feud apparently. It's still a major cultural situation in some northern regions of Albania, like Niko's home in Shkodër. An eye for an eye thing. The social obligation to take blood from an offender or member of their family to salvage another family's honour. There's real pressure to follow through, even when a slight is generations old or involves distant relatives. In Niko's case, a long-dead great uncle seduced the woman of another family and killed her parents, as they took steps to prevent them from marrying. We're talking fifty years back. His great uncle and his new wife moved away, so the debt for committing the murders was never considered repaid. Then Niko's family moved back to the area last year, not even aware of the historic scandal, until the great nephews and cousins of the murdered couple, Niko said, came to finally seek *hakmarrja* – revenge.

'So there's no way out of such situations, other than making a run for it?' Billie had a twisted family background, but this made hers seem like a fairy-tale scenario.

'Nope. But the Home Office have just decided not to recognise blood feuds anymore, so anyone seeking asylum with that excuse is sent back. I'm guessing that's why, in Niko's case, they weren't in any rush to place him into local authority care. Also, there's a shortage of foster parents.'

Billie felt anger rising inside of her again. 'Regardless of the reason he was here, the fact that he is only eleven years old should have been enough for him to have been given protection.'

'Yeah, in a perfect world. Most people have no idea what is really going on,' Boo said through a sigh.

'I'm guessing with the lorry damage it's going to be difficult to see if there is any additional cause of d–'

'Oh what a marvellous surprise. Good morning, my darlings.' Billie and Boo turned around in reaction to the familiar voice of Josta King, who had once ruled the roost as top-dog pathologist in the local area, working full time with the police and regularly with Billie when she had been head of the MIT. Now that she was running her own independent forensic service centre, the very glossy and cutting-edge King & Beech Forensics, Billie hadn't expected to encounter her here in the bleak and bare-walled police mortuary.

'Thank God, Josta. You were the last person I expected to be handling this case.' Billie perked up at the sight of their old friend, as well as colleague.

'One likes to step into the breach when one's colleagues call for assistance, my dear. My fellow pathologists are proving to be rather thin on the ground at the moment what with holidays and these endless bugs doing the rounds, and it sometimes does one's spirits good to take a trip down memory lane.'

Billie smiled ruefully. She and Josta had certainly been through some grizzly cases together which had taken their toll personally as well as professionally, but that was all water under the bridge these days. Only recently, Josta's expertise had helped Billie and Ellis get to the bottom of a huge case for Wilde & Darque, for which Billie would always be eternally grateful.

'I'm so pleased that you will be taking care of Niko.' Boo had visibly relaxed, knowing that the child would finally be in expert hands.

'Poor mite. Thank you so much for putting a name to him. It's astonishing that a child should have no relatives rushing to report his being missing but thank goodness you've explained the situation.' Josta squeezed Boo's shoulder. 'I assure you, dear, that I will leave no stone unturned in deducing what the sweet child can convey to me of his final journey.' Boo clenched Josta's hand for a moment in gratitude.

Billie gave a quiet exhalation of relief. She was in absolutely no doubt at all that Niko was in the safest hands he could possibly be in at this heartbreaking stage. Josta treated all of her deceased clients, but especially the children, as though they were her most precious guests. If anyone could give more information on how Niko ended up in a strange area under the wheels of a huge lorry, then it was Josta.

Boo spent a few minutes going over the details of everything that she could impart to Josta about Niko's life until he had disappeared from the children's hotel. As she did so, Billie got more and more exasperated at the tale being told. She paced the floor in distress, aware that she was booked in to walk around a park that morning, taking photos of someone being unfaithful to his wife, rather than organising a team to catch the people responsible for kidnapping children such as Niko. What on earth had happened to all of the others? The questions and answers spun around her brain, none of them resulting in pretty images.

Lamenting heavily at the story so far, Josta prepared to get on with her job. All present paused for a moment to watch Niko Zefi being wheeled away by the mortuary assistant to the suite in which Josta would conduct her examination.

'I'll arrange a celebration of his life at Freedom Angels when his body is released for burial,' Boo said thoughtfully, as she and Billie headed away towards their respective cars. 'Otherwise, it'll be a bog-standard local authority send-off, probably in the communal grave over at the cemetery.' Billie grimaced at the thought of the child getting the burial once known as a pauper's funeral.

'I'll take care of the cost. Flowers, casket, give the poor mite the full works,' Billie advised. She had been through a lot in the past couple of years, but fortunately what she didn't have was money worries. Not that she needed much in the way of material things. Circumstances had led her to inherit a large sum from more than one benefactor, much of which had been donated to the creation of Freedom Angels.

Her mobile suddenly rang. 'Better get this. See you later.' She lifted her phone from her pocket.

'Having a lie-in, are you?' She heard a rather irate Ellis over the sound of Connie being cantankerous in the background. 'Been ringing you for ages. It's like trying to awaken the dead.' Billie could have made Ellis feel bad about his unintentionally dire choice of words, due to the location she was leaving, but decided against it.

'It's only eight o'clock. Billie checked her watch in case she was mistaken. Her date with the unfaithful man, his amour and her camera wasn't due for another hour yet. It all seemed particularly trivial after the scene that she had just witnessed.

'Well, some of us have hardly had any sleep,' Ellis moaned.

Billie refused to be drawn on the subject. She had met plenty of single mothers who survived on little shut-eye without bleating on about it. She sometimes wondered if dad care was like man flu. She, like Boo, and Ellis's older daughter Maya had all gladly mucked in to help with looking after Connie, bearing in mind that Ellis had taken over sole care of his small daughter so unexpectedly. They all adored her, just as they all adored Ash's kids and loved hanging out with them too. But with Maya now keen to get on with her own life, Billie hoped that Ellis would finally heed her subtle hints to move forward with a paid nanny to offer regular structured childcare for his smallest daughter. But so far, the idea had fallen on deaf ears.

'Thought any more about hiring that nanny?' Billie's mind's eye flashed up a picture of Niko. She tried to wipe away the vision of what she knew would be happening to his body right at that moment. She'd had her own crazy family experience, still had flashbacks to some incidents she would much rather forget and knew first-hand how important it was to feel safe, secure and loved, growing up. Billie was in absolutely no doubt how much Ellis loved his girls, but this hands-on father stuff was clearly taking some getting used to.

'No one can take care of my kid better than me,' Ellis snapped defensively. 'We've got an urgent meeting. Nine o'clock. I'm texting you the details now.'

'But I've got a date in the park–' Billie started to remind Ellis, who clearly had other things on his mind.

'Drop that. This is a matter of life and death, apparently.' Billie could hear Connie's feet coming across the wooden floor of the hall towards Ellis. By the sound of the footsteps Billie guessed that she was wearing an old pair of stiletto shoes that Billie had been about to throw out. She had decided that even the one extra pair was too many, when Connie and her tiny feet had taken ownership. The little girl had hardly removed them since. The thought of her clomping around in them made Billie smile.

'Is that Mummy?' Billie heard Connie ask. Her heart suddenly sank. She was going to have to have another serious chat with Ellis about the habit. It wasn't the first time that Connie had called Billie by that name. She still persisted, though Billie had gently tried to put her right several times now.

'We're going to have to talk about that–' Billie began before Ellis cut over her words.

'Yeah. I'll settle it once and for all, if she comes anywhere near,' Ellis announced, shocking Billie with his tone of voice. He was usually careful to be genial dad whenever Connie was anywhere near.

'What?' Billie frowned, confused.

'It's Storm. She's turned up...' Billie was shocked into silence for a beat, '...yeah, go into the kitchen, sweetheart. Daddy's going to make you boiled eggs and toast soldiers.' Ellis softened his voice, holding the conversation for a moment as Billie heard Connie shout, 'Yay' and heard the clip-clop of her old shoes in the direction of the kitchen.

'You're joking,' Billie gasped. She would never have put her money on Ellis's ex turning up again like a bad penny.

'Do I sound like I'm laughing?' Ellis hissed down the phone in a stage whisper. 'But if she tries to take Connie away from me, I swear I'll fucking kill her.'

SIX
A NEEDLE IN A HAYSTACK

Finish it off, before we do. Billie found herself alongside Ellis, peering at an A4-sized photograph featuring a Porkie's Big Eats Breakfast Pie with a large syringe sticking out of it. She struggled not to lick her lips, despite the printed threat. She still hadn't managed a coffee that morning and she could hear her tummy rumbling, despite the sickening scenario at the morgue first thing. Nor had the vision of a syringe, half-full of a liquid, presumably depicting poison, wedged at an angle in the crust of the pie, put her off the idea of heading straight to the local Porkie's Big Eats, to neck one down as soon as the meeting was over.

'So this isn't the first threat that you've had?' Ellis called over his shoulder to Graham Harper, who had slid the photo out of an envelope and laid it on his desk before striding briskly over to the door of his office, to check for the second time that it was locked. He had already told his secretary to hold any calls.

'No. This one is the third. As I said, damn the expense. I want to get to the bottom of this ASAP...' Graham Harper headed back to his desk and unlocked the bottom drawer. His desperation had been clear to Billie by the fact that he hadn't even flinched for a second when Ellis had quoted nearly triple their standard hourly rate to take on the job, despite Billie doing a double take. Graham Harper laid two other similar-sized photos on the desk. One read **Kill it. Porkie's Big Eat's is dead.** In this photo a large gun was positioned pointing at one of the outlets. The threat, just like the first, was printed in bold ink.

'Kill what?' Billie questioned, musing that anyone wanting to kill off a Porkie's Big Eats Breakfast Pie would have to get past her first. Her eyes scanned across to the third photo.

Death to the family. Kill Porkie's Big Eats. You have one month to close all outlets or people will die.

The third photo had a pile of Porkie's Big Eats food products piled on a table, surrounded by various bottles filled with liquid or pills. All were labelled 'poison'.

'I received this too, only this morning. It was posted through the main letter box here. Security found it whilst doing their rounds.' Graham Harper grabbed a memory stick from his desk top making Billie wince at the fingerprint opportunities lost by him handling the item. Ellis exchanged a glance with her. He'd obviously been thinking the same thing himself, but it was too late to stop the mishandling. Graham Harper clicked on his desktop PC and then turned it around for Billie and Ellis to view.

A figure heavily disguised in a black padded jacket wearing ski goggles and black balaclava, to leave only the mouth exposed, was standing by a stacked tray of Porkie's Big Eats pies. One by one, the figure started to pick each pie up, spitting on the product, before rubbing the saliva across the crust, then replacing it. The image faded, before appearing again, clearly shot from a hidden viewing spot. An unwitting staff member could be seen sweeping in and taking the pastries to a counter in the front seating area, where customers were queuing to buy. The video faded to black. Billie immediately started to consider an alternative breakfast.

'Just leave the memory stick in situ, Mr Harper.' Billie dug in her pocket for her emergency pack of gloves and evidence bag. 'There might just be a tiny chance of retrieving some DNA evidence. We'll bag up the photos too.' She hoped that she didn't sound too judgemental, but thanks to Josta King's cutting-edge forensics unit only a few miles down the road and a contact that she could have a quiet word with in her old place of work, it might just be possible to pin down a suspect quickly.

'You have pinpointed the outlet?' Ellis questioned. 'We can have a word with that staff member for starters. See if she remembers seeing anything unusual. Looks like an inside job. Any pay disputes going on, or disgruntled employees that you are aware of?'

'None at all. It's the shop on the high street, right here. Our flagship outlet. I collared that worker first thing, hurtled down there as soon as I opened this. She's the supervisor there. We bake throughout the night in each of our premises, but she claimed to have seen nothing amiss recently. That said, our shops are family friendly and do a roaring trade all day long. The staff aren't looking for people spiking food, they're concentrating on the job in hand. She did say that the staff exit door is often open at that venue, to cool down the room, with the ovens having been on all night. I've put a stop to that with *immediate* effect. It backs onto an alleyway.'

'Apart from staff, are there any other individuals or organisations who might hold a grudge against you?' Billie asked, carefully bagging the evidence. Graham Harper shook his head in an exasperated fashion.

'I run a multi-million-pound business. We have outlets right across the region and we are preparing a big national launch. We'll be finished if this gets out. Yes, of course we run afoul of one group or another now and then. At the moment we have animal rights activists protesting regularly outside of our various shops, especially since our award-winning vegetable products are about to be released. They are piggy-backing on the PR campaign, demanding we go totally meat free across our whole range of produce. I certainly wouldn't put it past that lot to be doing this. Some of them have been pretty aggressive. Recently my wife was unwell and they barricaded my car on the road when I was trying to race to the hospital.'

It was on the tip of Billie's tongue to ask if she had just eaten one of Porkie's Big Eats pies when she had fallen ill but thought better of it.

'Your wife hadn't just eaten one of these had she?' Ellis asked. A look of horror crossed Graham Harper's face. Billie rolled her eyes.

'Absolutely *not!*' he exclaimed. 'My wife had been seriously unwell for some time... Of course, one wishes that one had been more attentive, noticed the signs earlier... but we have been so busy with expansion plans within the UK this year, preliminary talks about locating outlets in Europe too...' Graham Harper took a deep breath, his face full of sorrow. 'Then she suddenly passed away so quickly. I couldn't get there in time, thanks to those *damn* animal rights hooligans...' Billie and Ellis exchanged glances. Graham Harper was clearly at breaking point. 'My poor daughter was heartbroken and all alone by her mother's bedside when I finally arrived, too late to say my goodbyes. It has had a huge impact on her mental health.'

'I would suggest closing this venue down for the time being,' Billie said gently. 'It looks like food has already been contaminated.' Her mind was racing, trying to remember the last time that she had eaten an item from the local branch. She didn't have to wait too long, as a vision of her tucking into a bag of doughnuts only the afternoon before skittered through her mind's eye. Ellis had shared it. He wasn't looking like his usual self, come to think of it, but there were extenuating factors in his case, which she hadn't had a chance to go over with him.

'No, out of the question. That's the reason I'm speaking to you–'

'Have you contacted the police–' Billie continued.

'No police!' Graham Harper shouted before correcting himself. His secretary had flicked her head up from her position at a desk, in alarm, catching Billie's eye through a viewing window. 'No police. I must have guarantees that this will stay completely confidential.'

'You do, of course,' Ellis assured Graham Harper, shooting a warning look at Billie. She wasn't the slightest bit deterred.

'But you simply can't put the public at risk. At the very least close this particular outlet for the time being and trash any remaining products at that spot. If someone does suffer before we can get to the perpetrator, your brand will be damaged beyond repair, and you will end up behind bars, Mr Harper.'

Billie couldn't stop the latent police officer in her coming out, even a year after she had left the force. She knew that it annoyed the hell out of Ellis, who had a long history of going undercover with the NCA and other rather secret organisations before that, and had without doubt, been called upon on occasion, to carry out not exactly lawful acts to get a job done. He had once explained that he had learned to separate himself from such actions, were they to be called upon to tie down a case. Billie simply couldn't do that.

'I suppose I could have it closed under the pretext of having new extractor fans fitted now that I've insisted on a no-open-door policy in the baking area. But surely the perpetrator will just move on to one of the other outlets if they aren't already active in those already?'

Billie guessed that whoever was doing this wouldn't risk being caught by dressing up in such garb and licking produce so close to such a busy area again, not now that they had got their message over. She safely bagged and now tucked away the memory stick for further perusal.

'The third photo appears to be giving you a month's warning at least, so that allows us time to crack on. When exactly did you receive it?'

Graham Harper suddenly looked sheepish. 'Um. That one would have been, um... three weeks ago...' He glanced up at Billie expecting her to react. Instead, she hoped that she was holding her poker face. Over the CEO's shoulder however, Ellis's slap to the head in disbelief said it all. They had only one week to catch the perp and put a stop to the march of the killer pies.

The trouble was that Porkie's Big Eats produce was so popular that it was like looking for a needle in a haystack. It wasn't just Billie who had, until today, something of an addiction to their entire stock. People from small children to grannies could be seen all day long queuing to buy the freshly baked goodies at their numerous outlets. There seemed to be a shop on every corner. In fact, in that particular area, people were practically tripping over Porkie's Big Eats pies.

SEVEN
AMONGST THE RUBBISH

A black bin liner filled with rubbish inside of the skip toppled over Tanko, spilling out a mixture of household rubbish. In the middle of it was a half-eaten and discarded pie, inside of a takeaway box marked *Porkie's Big Eats*. Tanko blinked, then was wide awake. His heart hammering against his chest once again. He felt as though he was still moving, though he had jumped to safety from the framework of the lorry hours ago. He squinted his eyes against the sunlight as he tried to get his traumatised brain cells to make sense of the situation, immediately recalling the horrific scene of the boy lying on the road. Scattered pictures of the terrifying scenario had broken his dreams during the hours of his fitful sleep since he had found this hiding place.

Tanko focused on the pie, suddenly feeling ravenous. It clearly hadn't been to the taste of the householder, but Tanko immediately recognised the smell of one of the pies he had seen in all of the high streets here in this part of England. The company even had a café in Freedom Angels. His mother had always been a stickler for hygiene back home in Nigeria. She would have been horrified at what he was about to do. But as he tried to quell the panic that washed over him every time he recalled the last massacre in his homeland and then the events of the night before, he grabbed the pie and started to eat it like a starving animal.

Suddenly he felt himself lurched almost upside down, the remains of the pie falling from his hands, disappearing deep amongst the other rubbish below him, as household detritus rained down upon his body. Tanko had thought this to be a safe haven, having discovered it after jumping down from the lorry which had whisked him away from yesterday's horrific scene on the road, but had he entered yet another nightmare?

He had travelled on the lorry for two hours or so, clinging on to the framework for his life, shivering from the cold, his knuckles numb from gripping the icy metal so tightly. When the vehicle had turned right or left, he had squeezed against the driver's cab, fearful of being crushed by the container behind him, flattening his body against the cabin also, when the lorry had slowed next to a car, lest the driver to the right or left spotted him in the shadows and alerted the lorry driver that Tanko had hitched a ride.

He had seen the look of anger and fear on the faces of so many of the lorry drivers when he had been in Calais trying to reach the UK and couldn't blame them for their feelings about people such as him. He too would have been terrified if he had been driving a vehicle, surrounded by those so desperate to start a new life that they would do almost *anything* to get on board. Tanko had tried to put himself in the place of those drivers, though few people in western countries seemed able to imagine themselves in the horrific situations *he* had encountered. Instead, they often claimed that people like him simply made scary stories up, to get a free and easy life.

The lorry had eventually started to move more slowly through a built-up area. Larger buildings loomed in the distance, lighting up the sky as day slowly melted into night in streaks of crimson and purple. A church clock and office blocks rose above him, tall and bright. To Tanko's relief, the town appeared to be familiar, though he'd had little experience of the many towns around the UK. For all he knew, they all looked the same. He desperately hoped that it was the place where Freedom Angels was located, that he could somehow communicate to Boo the head woman, what had befallen him and the other children and beg her not to put him back in the hotel where his kidnappers had been waiting to snatch him and so many other young people away.

The lorry had approached a gate and idled the engine as a security guard ran out to open the way into a secure loading bay. It was here that Tanko had jumped to the road, his knees buckling as he scampered into a scrubby roadside shrub. He had stopped to catch his breath, before starting to wander down the surrounding streets of terraces. He had desperately needed to find a safe haven to rest before he decided what to do next.

After a few steps, he had winced in pain. His sprained ankle hurt with every step, as he limped along, looking into the windows of houses with lights on inside. It seemed that so many happy families were gathered together, taking for granted that no danger could possibly sweep in without any warning and smash their happiness to smithereens. He sometimes wondered if people in this country knew just how lucky they were. Maybe this was why so many found it hard to accept that asylum seekers such as him could seriously be running away from the horrors that he had faced, even though his country was not officially at war.

The big yellow skip that he had finally found at the kerbside outside of a house, had seemed like a gift from the gods, when his ankle had been hurting so badly. Plump black bin bags had cushioned his fall as he had pulled himself up and dropped inside, finally resting his head on a door carpet with HOME printed on the prickly coconut fibre, An old child-sized patchwork quilt, half spilled from an overflowing bag had been his saviour from the chilly night air. He wrapped the throwaway around him. Two discarded items together, Tanko had thought ruefully. The quilt was worn in patches with a little stuffing hanging out, but just like him, still had so much warmth to give with the help of a little loving care.

Tanko was hanging on to the quilt now for dear life, however, as he tumbled in terror amongst the rubbish. The place that he had considered to be a safe refuge was now moving upwards and swinging precariously through the air. He realised that the noise that had at first awoken him had been the sound of chains being attached to the sides. As he looked up, hugging the small patchwork quilt tightly around him, he could see that a double crane, arms painted bright blue and attached to the back of a different type of lorry, was lifting the skip up high above the ground.

'Wait a minute!' a man's voice had called as the skip hung in mid-air. 'I need to chuck this inside!' A wooden chair with one leg missing hit Tanko hard in the face, making his eyes smart with tears of pain as well as fear. He pushed it away, trying to quickly pull himself both together and upright as the skip moved across towards the back of the lorry and lowered down. Each time he did so, he slid down once more amongst the bin bags. Eventually, as the driver stopped what he was doing to have a word with the other man about the weather, which Tanko noted was such a British thing to do, he managed to catch hold of the edge of the skip and having climbed onto the upturned chair, his ankle crying out in protest, he swung himself out and onto the lorry bed, quickly jumping down, the small quilt still fastened around his shoulders, due to the knot he had secured it with last night.

'Hey! What are you doing?' The skip driver and householder stopped mid-sentence as Tanko landed in a crumpled heap in the gutter.

'He's nicking one of my things!' the man shouted, as though he had suddenly remembered some hidden value of the trashed child's quilt. 'Catch him!' But Tanko had scrambled to his feet now and skittered, half running, half limping, backwards into the road, causing a white van to screech to a halt.

'Got a bloody thief rifling,' the skip driver explained to the van driver, thankfully not giving chase, Tanko noted as he glanced back in panic, weaving his way as speedily as possible, like a startled and injured animal, between cars to the other side of the road.

'Looks like one of those asylum seekers to me. I knew there'd be trouble when they built that place for them up the road,' the van driver replied.

'He's stolen my kid's quilt. It was an heirloom that was,' the householder lied.

'Sooner they send that lot back where they come from the better,' the van driver bellowed. 'Get my vote anytime.'

'I'm going to report that to the police,' the householder shouted for Tanko's benefit, as the boy winced in pain, his ankle in agony, terrified that he was going to be arrested for his theft of the quilt and the half-eaten pastry and taken straight off to the centres he had heard all about, ready for immediate deportation back to Nigeria and the Boko Haram killers, or maybe some other country across the world. He hopped around a corner into an alleyway, full of bins filled sky high with rubbish, and sank down once again, his arms over his head to hide his tear-stained face, feeling both guilty and grief-stricken there amongst the other unwanted items which nobody seemed to care about.

EIGHT

MY WAY

Billie was trying to get her head around poisoned pies, as she brought her car to a halt, to allow a lorry to finish securing a big yellow skip that appeared to have just been loaded onto the back of a blue lorry. It was amazing the stuff people threw away nowadays, she mused, suddenly seeing a picture of Niko Zefi in her mind's eye. A throwaway child, it seemed, that someone had no more use for. She shivered at the thought.

It was then that her attention was caught by something else further up the road. Safia Jamal, clearly having a row with a tall man, his back facing Billie. He placed his hand on Safia's arm which she shrugged off. Then suddenly he had grabbed her more forcefully and started to propel her off the main walkway and into one of the alleyways that spread out in rows right and left, backing onto terraced houses that ran at right angles to the main road.

Billie jumped out of her car and hurtled up the street to the point where Safia had now disappeared from view. Swiftly turning into the alleyway, Billie all of a sudden realised that the man was Johnny Briggs. Though he appeared to be trying to force Safia against the wall, she was doing a good job at fending him off even before Billie intervened.

'Get your filthy hands off her!' Billie yanked Johnny's arm behind his back, propelling him away from Safia before pinning him up against the dirty red-brick wall. He looked momentarily startled before seeming to catch himself.

'If it isn't Wonder Woman herself,' he suddenly leered. 'You just can't seem to keep your hands off me, can you? Always desperate to pin me up against walls.'

Billie stepped back. Everything about him made her want to throw up, particularly the bad smell he was giving off, just like the night before.

'You okay, Safia?' Billie glanced across to the young woman. She looked shaken, but defiant.

'I am fine, thank you.' Safia tilted her chin up, looking sternly at Johnny, who turned his slimy smile in her direction. It wasn't reciprocated.

'Safia and I were just having a difference of opinion as far as business is concerned.'

'*My* business,' Safia emphasised.

'Simply a bit of creative tension. I guess having been a flatfoot and now a snoop you don't understand passion the way we do, Billie, my girl.' Johnny turned back to Billie now, that smirk still on his face, except for a sudden wince as he tried to flex the arm Billie had just twisted behind his back. It looked like her sudden move had bruised more than just his ego, not that she was going to lose any sleep over that.

'I'm *nobody's* girl.' Billie emphasised the words.

'Nor I,' Safia agreed.

'Got my car. Jump in, I'll give you a lift,' Billie said to Safia.

As they turned to walk away, Billie suddenly swung back,

overcoming her revulsion to being close to Johnny. 'If I *ever* see you touch one hair on her head again...' she threatened, her face almost in his. His smirk dropped for a second, before he moved away and started walking off in the other direction, turning to face her again as soon as there was space between them.

'What? You'll jump me? Now wouldn't that be a treat?' He ran his tongue across his upper lip. 'Thing is, you think you've got big balls, Billie Wilde, but when you're trying to rock that intimidating woman routine, all men are thinking of, is that you'd be a lively ride in bed. Once they've managed to pin you down and clamp that sexy little mouth of yours shut, that is.' He started walking backwards, beckoning her in a mocking way. 'So come and get me, sweetheart, next time you fancy jumping a guy. I'll have my arms out wide, waiting.'

Billie wanted to tear his hideous smirking face off his head, but she could hear car horns beeping out on the road now and someone shouting.

'Fucking female drivers.' No doubt because they couldn't get past her car. She so much wished at that moment that she still had her police identity card to shove in a few faces, starting with the total jerk sauntering off up the alleyway, albeit with a stiff arm he couldn't quite disguise.

Billie gave the swearing man, stuck at the head of the queue of cars, the finger as she joined Safia and got back behind the wheel. The skip lorry had moved on now, but she hadn't been aware of any abuse being shouted in the burly male driver's direction when it had been blocking the road minutes earlier.

'You sure that you are okay?' Billie asked Safia, once she had confirmed that she wanted to be dropped off in the centre of the city.

'Yes. I am used to dealing with trouble.'

That was a major understatement, Billie mused, considering the young woman's history. 'Has that creep ever touched you before?' Billie felt furious when she remembered the way in which Johnny Briggs had grabbed hold of Safia on the street corner.

'No. It will not happen again.' Safia tilted her chin in defiance once more. 'He has been very kind to me until now, as has everybody I have met in this area.' She looked out of the car window to all of the people walking by. 'But my dream is to be a fashion designer who also gives back to this community that has accepted me, by working with local people, to create my company. I want to pay fair wages and initiate good working conditions for everyone, with a share of the profits going back to local charities. I have been invited by a business angel who saw my show last night, to discuss how I can move things forward. That is where I am going this morning.'

'That's brilliant news.' After all of the negative events that morning, Billie felt uplifted, and overwhelmed with admiration for this amazing, talented young woman who was grabbing a new chance at life.

'But Johnny wants me to do things very differently, join forces with him and make big bucks. So now things are turning ugly.' Safia gave a deep sigh.

'Controlling men often work this way, Safia,' Billie advised. After all, didn't she know it herself? 'They try to dazzle with their charms and then things turn nasty if you don't let them take over.'

'Yes. But like in that old song, I intend to do it *my* way.' Safia chuckled. 'Johnny Briggs won't stop me. That's for sure. The Taliban could not end my dreams, after all. Only death will ever do that.' Safia smiled and patted Billie's hand in thanks, as she pulled the car to a halt in front of an imposing city centre building.

As the graceful young woman got out of the car, Billie watched Safia walk up the steps. She turned and gave a dazzling smile as she waved. Billie hoped that the door was just about to open to the brilliant future that Safia envisioned and that she had given up so much to realise. She suddenly thought of her own plans for this afternoon. Might she have taken a wrong turning as far as her own destination in life was concerned?

NINE
DEFINITELY DEAD

'I 'm binning this.' Ellis dumped his bacon sandwich back onto his plate. Billie was sitting opposite him on a Formica table in a booth at a greasy spoon type of café. Out of the large window to one side of their table, a Porkie's Big Eats café faced them on the other side of the road. Billie made a grab for the remains of Ellis's sandwich just as he was standing up to head for the bin with it. She'd never been one to let good food go to waste, or bad food either, for that matter. Ellis slumped back down again. He was still looking out of sorts.

'I see you haven't lost your appetite,' he grumbled, as he reached for some of the ketchup sachets in a container on the table and pocketed them. Billie stopped mid-bite. 'Connie loves these. Uses them in her play kitchen. Anyway, seeing as you are scoffing that rubbish and I'm not going to get my money back, this is my refund.' Billie finished chewing as she watched Ellis sit back in his seat and sigh. She knew that it wasn't just the lacklustre breakfast that was bugging him. But so far, they had been concentrating on the Wilde & Darque jobs in hand, rather than the elephant in the room.

A couple of former police associates, now retired from the

force, sometimes came on board to help out with investigations, especially since the most recent big case that had received so much press attention. Wilde & Darque hadn't exactly been short of work recently. Billie had spotted Safia on the way back from a quick meet-up with the freelance investigator who had taken her place in the park, where she had originally been due to work that morning, confirming a man was, as suspected by his wife, having an affair with his PA. Another payment in the bag, another heart broken. Billie didn't want to dwell on that fact. She'd been in that position herself, more than once. It would be her job to go around and break the news to the client later. Suspicion was one thing. Finding out the truth in such situations was never a cause for celebration. She would remember to take a pack of paper tissues along for the ride.

'Shame about that little kid.' Billie broke away from her thoughts as Ellis spoke. He hadn't responded in any sort of positive fashion earlier when Billie had arrived at the Porkie's Big Eats head office for their meeting, still agitated about the missing children. 'But don't you go thinking you can turn all Pied Piper and lead them all back in a neat parade,' had been his warning then. 'You can't save the whole world and we've got enough on our own plates right now.'

Billie had bristled at the warning but had been unable to respond, due to Graham Harper suddenly appearing on the scene. She knew that Ellis was a warm and caring guy and funny too, at least when he had first arrived from the NCA to give her and her MIT team expert assistance on a serious drug investigation. But his personal life had been thrown into such a spin with an eruption of both delightful and devastating events since then, that the pressure was beginning to take its toll, even on someone like Ellis, who had a reputation for not crumbling under the most intense professional strain.

'Yeah, heartbreaking,' Billie agreed, finally dropping the

remains of Ellis's bacon sandwich onto the plate. 'People trafficking... if I could get my hands on those sickos–'

'Yeah, like Storm. Let's not pretend that you live with a major sex-slave trafficker and know nothing about it.' Ellis's face darkened. 'Why else would you dump your kid and go on the run? She's claiming she was scared, coerced. That's absolutely bollocks!'

Billie guessed that Ellis's assessment of his former wife was accurate. She had only come across Storm Benbow once, by chance on an investigation for a client, but once was enough to see that she was unlikely to be the sort of woman to be easily controlled. However, Billie also knew that Ellis would have a hard time proving that in court. Storm's former lover, a major criminal, was no longer around, as proof of the dangers of little Connie being cared for by her mum. Though when he had been alive, he had caused untold damage to Maya's life plan to follow her dad into the police. She had totally changed direction as a result of her harrowing experiences. One of the reasons that Ellis refused to have any connection with Freedom Angels. The memory of how the centre came to be, was just too painful.

'I got back on the blower to my lawyer when I was waiting for you to turn up. I was so shocked when he came around to my place and dropped the news like a bloody bombshell, that I didn't take in everything he was saying. Turns out she's claiming that she's been in hiding for her life. Arguing that she hadn't made contact with Connie simply in order to protect her daughter. Total lies!'

'That's why I'm so worried about these missing kids. Out there with no one to protect them–' Billie started to say, but Ellis was on a roll now.

'And now Maya's giving me grief. I mean, she said that she wanted to nanny Connie in between doing this Freedom Angels thing, but last night she didn't come home, said she had a date. He's not someone from that place, is he? Have you met him?'

Billie shook her head, seeing a picture of Johnny Briggs clicking away in her mind's eye. She batted the picture aside, silently answering, *I hope not.*

'But that offer was made a year ago, Ellis, when Maya was particularly vulnerable and was probably keen to stay safely at home. Connie's starting school now and Maya's done a great job, but maybe she's reached the point where she needs some independence—'

'I created that lovely flat for her on the top floor of my gaff, didn't I? That cost me an arm and a leg. I hope she's not thinking of moving in with this guy.' Ellis had gone to take a sip of coffee from his mug but had now slammed it down, so that it splashed in a tidal wave onto the table.

'I think you're jumping the gun a bit.' Billie reached out and patted his hand. He caught her fingers and held on tightly. Billie could see how the latest news was affecting him and didn't want to see her dear friend as well as colleague so stressed, not just as his life was finally getting back on an even keel. 'You've done a great job with the flat, but then that was in lieu of wages. Maya has been a full-on nanny to Connie—'

'Well, she's her stepsister, isn't she?' Ellis argued. Billie slid her hand away, ostensibly to reach for her mug of coffee, but also to free herself from Ellis's grip. 'I thought she was happy, that we were all one big happy family. Now she's getting all antsy.'

Billie smiled ruefully. Until the past year Ellis had never had full custody of Connie. In fact, he'd had to fight Storm for every access period, despite a court order. The year before that, he hadn't even known that his oldest daughter existed. He'd had a huge upheaval in his life.

'Ellis, Maya absolutely adores you. But you have to let her

grow up and be her own woman. I really think you should look into the professional nannying thing—'

'No! I've said to you like, a thousand times, I don't want strangers hanging around my gaff. I just want family.' Billie gave up on the argument. She checked her watch.

'Best get to work,' she said through a sigh. 'Our shift starts in five minutes.'

They both glanced over to the Porkie's Big Eats outlet across the road. They were about to go undercover as working staff. Billie guessed it was going to take more than the bright-orange uniform, hairnet and peaked cap to cheer up Ellis's grim demeanour. She certainly didn't relish the thought of being a customer facing him off if they were unhappy with an order. Right now, his looks could kill at twenty paces.

As it turned out, even Ellis couldn't help giving a little chuckle as he emerged from the staff changing area inside the Porkie's Big Eats outlet to face Billie wearing a similar bright-orange and truly unflattering uniform.

'You look like newcomers. Take this mop and do the floor,' a tiny and miserable-looking woman with a badge labelled '*Supervisor*', who Billie immediately recognised from the footage sent to Graham Harper, shoved her mop into Ellis's hand and walked on for a few steps before swivelling around to look at Billie. 'And you, shove that strand of hair under your net.' The woman stomped off, mumbling under her breath, 'Can't get the staff these days.'

'Power complex.' Ellis was grumbling again.

'I don't know about you, but it's the glamour of being a PI that took me away from my top copper job,' Billie quipped cheekily to Ellis. He rolled his eyes and smiled.

'Move it!' the tiny supervisor barked.

'See you at tea break.' Ellis blew through his lips as he started mopping the floor, scanning the location and other staff members as he did so, whilst Billie was put firmly in her place behind the counter on serving duties.

'Get a move on. You're handling that pie like it's a bloody bomb.' The supervisor had been eyeing Billie up from the moment she had started serving. Little did she know the truth, that the pie just might be hiding something inside, just as deadly. The truth was that Billie felt conflicted about handing over produce that could be someone's last supper. Especially as so many families with kids were queuing for food. Her mind briefly slipped back to the desperately sad scenario in the morgue that morning, the memory of little Niko Zefi laid out, ice cold and all alone on a mortuary gurney.

'Here, let Lil take over and go around the back. The queue will be out of the door and down the street at the rate you're moving,' Billie's new nemesis barked out in a voice way too loud for such a tiny frame. Little did she know that in different circumstances, Billie would have her pinned up against the wall now for her attitude. It certainly was an eye-opener working undercover rather than as an acclaimed head of a top MIT.

Billie buttoned her lip and dutifully headed backstage, as she thought of the set-up, with customers facing front of house and a completely different vision of people beavering away, sweat on their brows out of sight around the back. So far, she hadn't spotted anything untoward, bar her own sadly under par serving skills. Billie couldn't help thinking again that this was like looking for a needle in a haystack. She hoped that Ellis was having better luck.

Suddenly her mobile, tucked away safely in her pocket, pinged. She squeezed into a corner, as various staff members came by, holding trays of fresh pies to feed the hungry mouths outside. It was a video message. Ash suddenly loomed into view, framed by palm trees. He burst out laughing at the vision of Billie in her orange uniform.

'Well, that sight has made my day.' He chuckled.

'What's wrong, holiday entertainment boring you already?' Billie answered, pleased that Ash had made it to the airport in time to catch the flight that morning. As Billie had guessed when she had dropped the girls off the night before, Ash's ex was less than thrilled to discover he had changed arrangements and headed back to work.

'Just checking that the ident went okay this morning? Definitely Niko Zefi, one of Boo's kids?'

Billie nodded in agreement. ''Fraid so. Josta's taking care of him. I can't believe this is happening, Ash–'

'I know how you feel. I didn't want to leave the poor little mite until you and Boo got there, but I was late for the airport. Fell asleep on the plane over, so I'm already in the dog house–'

The conversation was abruptly curtailed as Billie's mobile was suddenly swept out of her hand by the tiny supervising terror of Porkie's Big Eats and clicked off.

'No mobiles at work. Have you even read the rules, or maybe you need specs?' The woman glared up at Billie as she pointed towards a list of rules attached to a door facing them. It was true that *no mobiles at work* was number one on the Porkie's Big Eats rules hit parade. Billie was champing at the bit to retort in an even more aggressive fashion, but professional decorum sadly stopped her. 'Health and safety, dearie.' The woman bent nearer to make her point. She still didn't come up to Billie's chest height. 'Put that away immediately in your locker.' She was already stomping off towards Ellis, who Billie could see dolefully mopping the floor. 'Look, you are *still* missing that stain!' she barked. 'Dearie me, management have sent over the dregs today!' She cut a swathe through the pie carriers, who turned away and looked busy lest they caught her eye.

Ellis mopped his way over to Billie and whispered in her ear, 'They do say that poison usually comes in small bottles.'

'Bearing in mind our reasons for being here, that comment doesn't exactly make me feel better,' she answered, as she watched one of the pie makers looking shiftily over his shoulder before walking across the room at an angle, lifting four pies and then quickly tucking them out of view as he headed in their direction.

'Aye, aye, what's all this then?' Ellis was looking in the same direction as Billie. He busied himself mopping as Billie rearranged her cap. The pie carrier brushed past them and then into the staff changing area. Billie and Ellis exchanged glances.

'I've just been ordered to go that way.' Billie peeled away and followed the man's direction of travel, into the changing area. It was empty. A short and narrow corridor of lockers ended with a door at either side. He entered the male changing rooms. Billie did a quick sweep of the ladies changing area. No one was inside. She emerged just as Ellis entered the corridor. 'He's all yours.' Billie nodded to the male changing rooms, just as the door to that area opened and a huge cartoon-pig-like figure wearing a Porkie's Big Eats cap, pushed out, pinning them both against the wall as it waddled by and out of the door into the main area. Ellis entered the men's changing area and did a quick sweep of his own. He came back towards Billie holding an empty insulin syringe in his hand. 'Nobody else in there.'

'Must be him then.' Billie thumbed the cartoon figure, her foot holding the door open so that they could see that the huge cap-wearing cartoon pig was now carrying a tray of pies out into the front area where people were queuing.

'Time to upset the apple cart, I think.' Billie moved fast, passing the tiny supervisor, who by the look on her face was just about to reprimand her for something else. Ellis was hot on her heels. As they caught up with the man in the giant pig outfit, people had already started crowding around him, lifting pies from the tray he was offering around.

'I'll be taking that, mate.' Ellis grabbed the tray from the costume-wearing figure, holding it above his head, though many of the pies had already been grabbed and people were still reaching out for the others. Billie snatched a pie out of the hand of a toddler in a pushchair, who was just about to take a bite.

'Hey. Give that back to my kid!' the child's mother shouted in protest, though Billie had already thrown the half-eaten pie back onto the tray that Ellis was fighting to stop anyone else from accessing. The hope was that they could get most of the pies over to Josta's forensics labs to check which ones might have had poison administered via the syringe, for prosecution purposes. Billie could see the angry supervisor fighting her way through the scattered customers even as she grabbed the costume-wearing man by the scruff of his pink furry neck and propelled him backwards against a wall.

'Got any more stashed in there?' She nodded to his suit.

'Wha–?' the giant pig replied in a voice filled with panic.

'I said unzip and spill,' Billie commanded, pulling back the giant baseball-capped pig's head, to reveal the man who had taken the pies and entered the staff changing area only minutes earlier. His hair was already stuck to his head with sweat, due to the heaviness of the suit, his face bright pink.

'What on earth is going on?' The tiny supervisor was now hopping up and down beside them furiously, looking like an orange-uniformed Rumpelstiltskin. Billie spotted the zip on the costume and still pinning the man up against the wall with one hand, pulled the zip down with the other, to reveal the man's pink flesh encased in an orange vest and greying white boxer shorts. Four pies tumbled out from the folds onto the floor.

'Mummy! Porkie Pig's just been sick,' Billy heard the child who she had just robbed of her pie, call out.

'What's inside of those?' Billie held her hand out in warning, should the supervisor come even one step closer.

'Two are pork and pickle, the other two cheese and ham. It's for the kids' tea. I'm on zero-hours contract with this job and with the leccy and mortgage going up, we're skint—'

'And the syringe?' Billie still had the man pinned by the scruff of the neck against the wall. He was turning even pinker.

'It's for my diabetes. I always have to have a shot before I put this thing on. It's boiling in here. Starts to bring on a hypo, but everyone's got to take their turn to be Porkie, so—'

'That's it. Ladies, gentlemen, I'm sorry for the temporary disruption. Can everyone leave the shop for a short while whilst we clear up this mess.'

Despite the collective groan of annoyance and disappointment, the supervisor was suddenly all eyes and teeth as though on stage addressing an audience, which she was, Billie thought in a way, as she ushered the customers out. She had been aware of people taking photos on their mobiles, no doubt about to find their way onto social media. Not good for a business that was supposed to be working under the radar.

Graham Harper was going to be less than pleased, but for all Billie knew the man in the ridiculous suit was, well, telling porkies. The pies would still be going to King & Beech Forensics to be checked out. Far rather that scenario, than the child in the pushchair behind her, munching into a poisoned pie. A picture of Niko Zefi hopscotched through her mind's eye for a second time that afternoon. She didn't want another child heading in the same direction, whatever the CEO of the company insisted upon.

'You are dismissed!' the supervisor yelled at the sweating man in the suit. 'And you two can follow him out of the door!'

Billie heard a thud and then sensed the crowd who had been sullenly moving towards the exit collectively stepping back. The mother of the child suddenly gasped.

'Move out of the way, I'm a nurse!' Billie released her hold on the man as she turned to see an old lady who had been in the queue, now lying on the floor, her rheumy eyes open and staring. She immediately moved across to the frail figure, bending down to take hold of her birdlike wrist to check for a pulse as the nurse, now kneeling opposite, held two fingers to the woman's neck for identical reasons. Billie could already hear Ellis calling the emergency services.

'Did anyone see her eat anything? Did she sample any pies?' Billie had been aware at the time she had been serving, that staff members sporadically moved down busy lines, offering small samples to customers in order to whet their appetites and stop them from moaning about the length of their wait.

'Let's get her moved to the staff area, so that we can continue serving.' The supervisor shot a dagger-like glance towards Billie, before turning to give a simpering smile to the customers, who seemed to have collectively lost their appetites.

'Anything?' Billie addressed the nurse. She couldn't feel any pulse at all. The nurse shook her head as she looked up.

'Nope. She's definitely dead.'

TEN

A STARVING ANIMAL

A rat, recently deceased and now being visited by flies, faced Tanko as he had cowered for hours now, nerves on a knife-edge, amongst the dustbins in the alleyway, still clutching the child's quilt around him. He checked that no one was passing and then, feeling nauseous and still limping a little, he scuttled along the lane, weaving in and out amongst rubbish and stuffed black bin bags, some ripped open with stinking detritus spilling out. The smell of rotting food compelled Tanko to cover his face. But as he made his way along the alley, the aroma changed to the warm smell of pies baking. Tanko felt his stomach rumble, this time in hunger rather than revulsion.

As he hobbled towards the smell, allowing himself to imagine for a moment how such an aroma might translate to taste, he suddenly heard the sound of a siren and quickly hunkered down next to a huge industrial bin. The siren got louder. Had the police discovered where he was hiding and come to drag him away? He found himself shivering in fear, tucking into a tiny ball in the shadows, his head bent down, hoping that he wouldn't be found.

When the noise got so loud that Tanko had to slap his hands

over his ears, it suddenly stopped. Hearing a door open then rapid footsteps, he looked up in terror, then dropped his hands in relief. The sound had been an ambulance, not a police car, stopping at the edge of a square that he could just see beyond the back lane. The emergency vehicle sirens seemed to sound so similar to him, in this country. Two paramedics were racing towards the front door of what might perhaps be a bakery, Tanko thought, licking his lips again.

Suddenly his heart leapt. A person speedily appeared through a gate right next to where he was hiding behind a bin bag. She was a small woman, wearing some sort of overall and carrying a large rubbish bag. Tanko hunkered down as she stood on tiptoe, opened the huge lid of the industrial bin and hurled the bag onto the pile already peeking out of the top. She looked quickly around, as though to check that she hadn't been seen either, Tanko thought, and then moved back inside the gate, slamming it behind her. He heard a bolt firmly locking the gate shut. The aroma of freshly baked pastry was almost overwhelming, as Tanko reached up and caught the edge of the bag. It toppled down beside him, warm and inviting as he ripped it open. Lots of small pieces of filled pastry were stuffed inside, as though a large pie had been cut into tiny pieces. Tanko scooped them up in his cupped hands and ate them like a starving animal.

ELEVEN
A PROPER LITTLE HAREM

'So I'll be at the animal rights activist gathering at 7pm.' Billie ran through the plans for that night. The protest had been well publicised and was centred on the town square opposite the main Porkie's Big Eats outlet, so Billie was going to infiltrate the protesters to see if Graham Harper's suspicions were correct that one or more members of the group might be involved in the threats being made. But before that, as soon as she had dropped Ellis off, Billie was planning to head to the one regular commitment set in stone, that she had in her life. It was an early evening date, on the same day every week, that only a dire medical emergency would compel her to pull out of.

'I would cancel the footie tonight, to cover the protest with you, but I don't want to let Teddy down.' Ellis had glanced at Billie as she followed him up his garden path to say a quick hello to Connie before she headed on her way.

'It's okay. It doesn't take two of us to scope out a crowd,' Billie had answered. She was still quietly of the opinion that the threat to such a big business should be handled by the police rather than a PI and if it turned out that the old woman *had* been poisoned, there would be absolutely no argument about that. However, the deadline, if the threats were to be believed, hadn't been reached yet, and the elderly woman had looked desperately frail even before she had toppled over. Poisoned pies might have had absolutely nothing to do with her downfall.

'I'll do the husband-shagging-his-boyfriend night shift when I get back from the match. If I get the evidence, I can drop the photos off with his wife first thing, wind that case up.' Ellis ran through their outstanding investigations. The football tickets for the match tonight had been an extra reward from a pleased client and Billie had been happy for Ellis to take his cousin with him to the event. She knew how important family time was, though she no longer had any blood relatives of her own – that she was aware of anyhow. Nothing would surprise her after the last few years of bombshell shocks. Relaxing at the football match would help chill Ellis out too – take his mind off the Storm Benbow situation, at least for a few hours.

'Maya texted to say she would pick Connie up from pre-school, so I've got childcare covered.' Ellis opened his door to see his very beautiful daughter Maya coming down the stairs towards him. She was wearing only a long white shirt.

'You *have* picked Connie up from pre-school?' Ellis was instantly alert.

'She's playing out the back.' Maya smiled. Ellis craned his neck, looking down beyond the hallway, squinting. The kitchen door was open to the back garden.

'She *is* out there?' Billie could see that he was going to be hyper alert about Connie's whereabouts now his ex-wife was back on the scene.

'Yeah, she's on her swing.'

Billie had spotted the child. She waved towards Connie, who looked thrilled to see her, waving enthusiastically back.

'She's growing up fast.' Billie said the words out loud but Ellis was looking Maya up and down.

'It's just that you look like you've been upstairs having a kip–' As he said the words, a man's jean-clad legs appeared at the top of the stairs. As he wandered lazily down, the rest of the man's body came into view. He wasn't wearing any shirt. Billie felt her eyes widen with horror and repulsion.

'I think that might be mine.' Johnny Briggs smiled widely at Maya, brushing his hand down her arm. She giggled, flushing pink as she looked up at him.

Billie braced herself. Ellis certainly wasn't smiling. In fact, he was stricken silent for a moment. 'Hi, long time no see,' Johnny Briggs said with an ironic smile, raising his eyebrows, having clocked Billie. *Not long enough,* she had wanted to retort before slinging him with some force out of the door, but Ellis was already looking ready to kill. 'This must be grandad,' Johnny Briggs quipped as he continued walking to the bottom of the stairs, his feet bare. He wrapped one arm lazily around Maya's shoulders, holding out his other to Ellis.

'Maya's father,' Ellis corrected, steel in his voice. 'And who exactly is *this*?' He was looking at Maya now, having refused to accept the handshake. 'You are supposed to be looking after Connie.'

'She's okay, she's with Tina,' Maya answered huffily now, rolling her eyes in annoyance. 'This is my friend Johnny, by the way, as at least *I* am being polite.'

Connie suddenly rushed in and flung herself at Billie, who lifted her into her arms, pleased to have the distraction. 'Mummy!' she shouted happily, as Billie perched her on one hip.

'No. Remember, I'm Aunty Billie, sweetheart,' she replied, smiling firmly. She wished Ellis would drum the fact home to

Connie. She'd already mentioned the situation several times, but right now wasn't exactly the moment to continue the confused naming scenario. A strawberry-blonde-haired girl, with curls nearly as wild as Billie's own, wearing spectacles and a cheery smile, had followed Connie in from the garden. She came to a halt beside them.

'Hi, Billie Wilde, I'm Tina. I saw you last night at the fashion show at Freedom Angels–'

'Yeah, Tina took all those huge photos that you loved on the wall, Billie,' Maya added. 'She's like, so multi-talented. She can do any sort of design stuff. You name it.'

'Says you, Mrs Supermodel,' Tina answered, grinning at Maya, before turning back to Billie. 'I would have recognised you anyway, from all the social posts that you were starring in from Porkies this afternoon. Good show.' She chuckled. 'My dad was incandescent. Graham Harper, I believe he's got you working for him on some secret squirrel project. I'm guessing workers with their fingers in the till again.'

Billie thought of the poor employee, sweating inside of the huge pink Porkie Pig suit, having to steal pies because he was paid so little in wages. Clearly Tina hadn't spent too much time worrying about that angle. In fact, she looked a lot more upbeat than Graham Harper had described, when he had told Billie about his precious daughter.

'Dad's closed the outlets early, thanks to all that, which is a win-win, for me. He's coming to see my latest mixed-media design show over at the exhibition centre tonight, rather than working all of the hours that God sends, like he usually does.'

Johnny Briggs leant over and kissed Tina on the forehead gently, stroking her hair back from her face before he brushed his hand down her arm, glancing slyly towards Billie as he did so. He was still squeezing Maya's shoulder with his other hand.

The action made Billie's stomach turn, so she could only imagine how Ellis was feeling.

'And so your dad should, drop everything.' He winked at Maya, then looked back towards Tina. 'You are such a talent, baby, a truly unique talent.'

'Johnny's been a total inspiration with my work.' Tina glanced at Johnny like an actual love-struck teenager. Billie suddenly inhaled a waft of Johnny's strange perfume. Her stomach flipped in protest again, as a picture of him meanly propelling Safia into the alleyway flashed through her mind. Billie could hardly bear to keep schtum on her feelings about the man, or her urge to get him as far away from the two girls as possible.

'Yeah. I'm definitely going to catch up with you both over there later.' Maya stroked Johnny's back, looking even more loved up than her friend was. 'Sorry, but Connie's all yours tonight, Dad. I had rung a babysitter I found in the local paper to come over. But she's just cancelled, and I've got other plans myself now. Once I get dressed, that is.' Maya smiled coquettishly at Johnny. Billie thought Ellis might explode, though she considered it possible that she might do so first.

'But, it's all arranged. I told you ages back that I'm taking your uncle Teddy to the footie tonight,' Ellis argued. 'And I don't want Connie being looked after by some stranger, who's put adverts in the newspaper.'

'So take her to the football. At least I've made an effort to find alternative care,' Maya snapped back, turning on her heel and storming back upstairs.

'Kids today, eh?' Johnny winked at Ellis and turned to follow Maya. Ellis moved to make a grab for his arm.

'I don't remember inviting you into my gaff, mate.' Ellis was almost nose to nose with Johnny. 'Maya!' he shouted up the stairs. 'Bring that poxy shirt down with you!' Johnny pulled away calmly, an annoying smile playing on his lips. He caught Tina's hand and pulled her to the open door.

'Come on, baby. Tell Maya we'll wait for her in the car.' Johnny winked at Billie, as he walked out, not in the least perturbed by his undressed state or the fact that Billie was looking like she could happily kill him. Certainly she wished that at the very least she had broken his arm that morning. Ellis turned to her, his face like thunder.

'Friend of yours too, is he? Got a proper little harem on the go by the looks of it.'

'Nope, and I take that as a personal insult. The further Maya stays away from him the better and I will definitely be trying to convince her of that, when I get her alone. But she's twenty years old now–'

'And bring his damn shoes. I don't want that stinking slimeball coming back in here for them!' Ellis clearly wasn't listening, he was wafting his hand in disgust, clearly feeling as attracted to Johnny's aroma as Billie had been. 'You'll do me a favour and take Connie with you? I've got to pick up Teddy and get on the move–' Ellis grabbed his football scarf and hat which had been slung over the stair post, clearly thinking Billie's answer was going to be a foregone conclusion, but she cut him off mid-sentence.

'I'm working later, and you know I always meet up with Boo tonight, early doors.'

'Yeah, so I'll give her a quick bell. You can hand Connie over to her there.' Ellis's voice took on a pleading tone, as Maya came racing down the stairs holding Johnny's shirt, shoes and an overnight bag.

'I was going to tell you this when you were in a better mood, but I might as well tell you now, as you've made my friends so unwelcome. I'm looking for a place of my own,' Maya announced to Ellis.

'What?' Ellis was clearly shocked. 'So I'm meant to be thrilled when you're bouncing around with no kit on upstairs, with some oily piece of work who looks older than I am, when your little sister is downstairs?' Ellis argued. 'Not to mention that I've just spent a fortune on that flat of yours. Got it exactly how you wanted it.'

'But strictly on *your* terms. Tell you what, why don't you convert it into a nursery? The way you two are always hanging around playing mammy and daddy with Connie, it's you two who need to get a room!'

Billie was taken aback. She had noticed Maya having the odd difference of opinion lately with Ellis, but until this moment, she had always gotten on amazingly with the girl that she so admired. She had thought the goodwill was mutual. But as Maya had angrily stormed out, almost taking the door off its hinges as she banged it closed behind her, Billie reminded herself that she knew nothing, after all, about giving birth and bringing up kids.

The bigger worry for Billie was that Maya didn't have a clue how ugly Johnny Briggs could get when things didn't go his way either. Not that it looked to Billie like Maya was in any mood to take any advice from her direction these days. Ellis rubbed his head in exasperation, before turning back sheepishly to her.

'I can't let Teddy down. It's the final, he's been looking forward to this for ages. She's got some pyjamas over at Boo's place. You love staying overnight with Auntie Boo, don't you, sweetheart?' he said, turning to Connie. He tried to pull an encouraging face, avoiding eye contact with Billie, clearly unwilling to discuss Maya's parting statement about the nature of their relationship.

'No! I want to stay with Mummy,' Connie declared, pointing a small finger at Billie before she snuggled in tightly to her neck. Billie sighed. It was possible sometimes, to see the bright side of having no blood family left at all.

'Have you learned all of your numbers ready for big school yet?' she asked Connie, accepting the unescapable. 'Because where I'm taking you, you are going to need them.'

TWELVE
BABES IN THE WOOD

'Bingo!' Connie waved her small arm in the air, almost spilling the long glass of orange juice that she had been sipping from a straw, at a table in the ex-servicemen's club.

'Well done. You recognised that number six quicker than me!' The old man sitting next to Connie held out his hand in a high five motion which Connie enthusiastically returned. Boo and Billie exchanged amused glances as other bingo players, pipped to the post, looked over disapprovingly. There was a certain etiquette involved in such sessions, Billie had long ago realised. Children on site, especially at this time of the day, was *definitely* seen as seriously bad parenting, especially when the five-year-old had just won the elderly man twenty pounds.

'Drinks are on you, Jimmy,' Boo quipped.

'Why not send Connie up to get them, we couldn't be more frowned upon than we are right now,' Billie whispered as the bingo caller checked that the card was correct.

Billie and Boo's once-a-week, early evening regular date with Jimmy The Hat, for a bingo session here, where few people these days were, in truth, ex-servicemen, had been set in stone for the past ten years. During that time he had seen both females rise through the ranks of the police before they had each broken free to embark on new adventures. Regardless of their new timetables, both Billie and Boo were determined to keep up their double date with the elderly man for as long as he was still around.

They had first come across Jimmy, always wearing an old army beret and sitting on various street corners, whilst they were out on police calls. He was a former soldier, who had spent time living homeless after leaving the forces. That's how he had met Hilda, at the local soup kitchen. Love had blossomed over vegetable broth and a joint background having served in His Majesty's army.

The reason that Hilda was without a roof over her head was that she had found herself with an unplanned pregnancy due to a forcefully amorous sergeant major who had battled forth despite rejection. It had resulted in immediate dismissal for Hilda, being made homeless at the same time, though the sergeant major happily soldiered on. The shock and stress of finding herself unceremoniously dumped on the streets, had unfortunately caused her to lose the only child that she had ever carried. Jimmy said that she never really came to terms with that fact, despite the less than joyful conception scenario. She had always wanted to be a mother and after all, the child would have been innocent. But having got together later in life, they had helped one another get back on their feet and into a small bungalow provided by the local council.

Boo and Billie had often stopped for a chat back in the day, when Jimmy had still been dossing on the streets, slipping him a hot drink and a bacon sandwich during that time when he was down on his uppers. He had rewarded them with VIP invitations to his tiny wedding to Hilda, which had been followed by fish and chips and drinks in this very bar.

But an even bigger show of gratitude towards his two good

Samaritans, had been Jimmy's regular feeding of information on criminal comings and goings. People tended to be careless when they were stepping over those living rough on the streets, imagining them to have no interests in life other than cadging the next fag, or a smattering of change for their probable next fix. But Jimmy had been a Special Observer in the Royal Artillery, back in his army days, working covertly behind enemy lines, to track and report enemy movement across the battlefield, so nothing much got past his wily eyes. At one time, lives had been dependent upon his hawk-eyed skill.

Jimmy seemed to have had a knack for being in the right place at the right time in order to convey tiny pieces of information that could be game-changing. Billie was of the firm opinion that it wasn't the fact that her father had once been the local chief of police, that had resulted in her securing such a high rank at such a relatively young age, it was information that she had gleaned from those friendships she'd had with eyes and ears on the street, particularly those belonging to her oldest street friend, Jimmy The Hat. Neither Billie nor Boo had ever seen Jimmy without his army beret of midnight blue, complete with brass cap badge. He had even worn it on his wedding day.

As soon as his council bungalow had become available to buy, Billie had circumnavigated Jimmy who had immediately refused the offer of money and had instead accompanied Hilda to the council offices to sign the documents, ensuring that neither could ever end up on the streets again. Hilda had taken little persuasion. She had already had a dire medical diagnosis confirming that her own time was soon to be up. But this way, she wouldn't have the added stress of worrying about Jimmy having a forever roof over his head.

'Mummy,' Connie called over to Billie.

'Aunty Billie, sweetheart. Remember we had a little talk

about that?' Billie tried to correct Connie for the second time that day and the umpteenth time that week. Of course, she had felt momentarily flattered and loved up, when the little one had at first mistakenly labelled her. But now it was becoming a worrying habit.

'Aunty Boo...' Connie avoided Billie's eye, turning instead to Boo.

'Is Jimmy my grandpa?'

Billie felt her heart sink at the desperation in Connie's eyes to have a storybook normal family. It just reminded her how the child needed structure and certainty now she was taking her first steps into school life, especially now that Storm Benbow was back on the scene and seemingly determined to have access to her daughter once more.

'I'm Jimmy the Magician, my lovely.' Jimmy suddenly lifted a pound coin from his pocket, clapped his hands together and made it disappear. It was an act that Billie had seen often, but Connie was thrilled. 'You can be my magic assistant if you like,' Jimmy added. 'I can do that with bad people as well. So you just come to me if anyone is upsetting you,' he said conspiratorially, 'and I'll make them disappear too. All right?' Connie nodded. He opened her tiny fingers and popped the coin into her palm, closing it tightly. She looked thrilled.

'Can you make Maya's boyfriend disappear? He's called Johnny,' Connie asked, leaning close to Jimmy.

'Out of the mouths of babes,' Billie whispered to Boo. She had already recounted both the incident with Safia and the confrontation at Ellis's house on a quick bathroom break. Boo had been shocked but had immediately agreed to wind up Freedom Angels' association with the odious Mr Briggs, for which Billie was hugely grateful.

'I'll see what I can do, luvvie. But for now, you just hang on to this magic coin and think of Jimmy the Magician, whenever you're feeling a bit scared. Okay?' Connie nodded, with a wide smile, as she held up the pound coin for Billie and Boo to see. Billie checked her watch.

'I've got to run. Connie, Aunty Boo is going to read you *Babes in the Wood* tonight when you stop over, won't that be nice?' Billie encouraged Connie to put on her coat as Boo took a call on her mobile. Her face was suddenly a picture of horror and sadness.

'What's up?' Billie crossed to Boo, whilst Jimmy, immediately alerted to the upset, started to tell a gripped Connie about his racing pigeons. Boo turned her mobile around to face Billie.

'They've just found three more of the kids. Back to the morgue again first thing in the morning, to confirm identification. But see the girl with the '*no place like home*' tattoo? That's Katya.' Billie stared at the photo. The young, bloodied bodies lay in a tangle of limbs, leaves and mud scattered over them, in a communal grave. On top was the pale body of a girl, her arm outstretched as though fighting until the bitter end. 'Katya was a feisty girl from Ukraine, and brave too. If *she* couldn't stand up for herself, then none of them could. There's no mistake these kids are our regulars, living in the damn children's hotels.'

Billie felt bile and fury rising in her chest in equal measure. The communal grave was in a clearing surrounded by trees. These young broken souls were sadly real babes in the wood. Alone and abused and just as in the traditional tale, these poor mites clearly hadn't had a happy ending.

In the work of fiction, the uncle who had abandoned the babes had to face God's wrath. Billie wasn't sure that any God existed, not one who could allow this to happen. But she didn't need the help of any deity, because despite not being the head of the local murder investigation team any longer, she was determined to find a way to bring the perpetrators of this horrific scene to justice. God had nothing on the wrath they were going to suffer at her hands when she managed to do so.

THIRTEEN
WILD BY NATURE?

Death to the animal eaters, read the first banner that Billie spotted on arriving at the animal activists' protest in the town square. Billie moved closer to the two women holding that particular banner, though many other plaques on poles being held aloft had similar sentiments scrawled across them. Another read **Pies to die for**, featuring Porkie's Big Eats pies alongside slaughtered animals. Graham Harper had been correct in his assessment that he didn't have many well-wishers amongst this particular cohort.

Billie had quickly tucked her wild red mane of hair under a dark wig at Boo's house, along with having changed into a black sweater and jeans, in order to merge in with the crowd of activists. Now nearing the group, she slipped on a dark face mask and pulled up her hoodie, in order to further disguise herself.

As it happened, the animal activists were a colourful bunch and though she seriously hoped that no one within this collection of people really did intend to harm anybody because of the food choices that they were making, Billie did take a moment to rethink her own, eat absolutely anything tendencies.

She certainly would never have the words '*picky eater*' carved onto her gravestone.

But having been so busy in her personal life, doing mostly what other people had wanted her to do, she did sometimes wonder who she *really* was. Was her Wilde by name, wild by nature reputation a true reflection of her personality? Or had her notoriously headstrong manner of working been in reaction to her easy-going nature in her personal life, pandering to other people's whims, at least until a couple of years ago?

Her world had been turned totally on its head since then. She had been faced with some shocking revelations in relation to her family ties, as well as the true nature of some of her closest friendships, yet through it all, she had thrown herself into one major murder case after another. Now she had embarked on her new PI working partnership with Ellis and that had not long ago unexpectedly resulted in another murder investigation too.

She hadn't given herself any head space to really think about the crazy journey that she had been on. Had that been a subconscious attempt to block out any inward thoughts about her true persona? Of course, if anyone had tried to talk to her about such things she would have swept the conversation aside as the sort of pathetic and self-indulgent behaviour that she had no time for, not when people were facing real hardships, like serious disability, or living rough on the streets.

But right now, for example, two very pretty girls wearing short, pale sweater dresses, smeared in blood, were jointly carrying a dead lamb, half-skinned and badly damaged, in response to the cruelty that they were claiming was due to the processing of Porkie's Big Eats Lamb Mince Pies. Billie swallowed hard at the sight, feeling there and then that she, for one, would never eat one of those again.

Other activists, in animal design onesies, were lying in the middle of the road, as though dead, thick white chalk lines around each individual body in a parody of those that had been a common sight for Billie during her time heading up the local MIT team.

As cars edged ever nearer, irate drivers honking their horns in fury, Billie couldn't help feeling a little stab of admiration for those who felt so passionately about animals that they would do almost anything to protect them. She felt the same way about the missing asylum-seeking children. **One life is no more important than others**, another poster read. Billie had to agree with that sentiment. By and large, the protesters gathered around her right at that moment appeared to be a peaceful group, despite the spectacular show that they were putting on.

But suddenly, a more formidable figure burst out of the crowd, as though making an entrance on stage, as they jumped up onto a stone plinth opposite the door to Porkie's Big Eats. The figure was also clad in black – a bulky padded boiler suit on their tallish frame. The boiler suit also had a hood pulled over the wearer's head, face totally obscured by a sinister plastic white skeleton mask. Dark leather gloves ensured that not an inch of skin was left on show. Billie's mind immediately turned to a similar figure featured in Graham Harper's threatening video that she had watched earlier.

The figure pressed what must have been a mobile app or something similar, inside of their pocket, which began a forceful speech on animal rights. The words fed through a sinister voice synthesiser, loud but distorted, so that there was absolutely no way of working out the gender, or any identifying accent traits, whilst the dark-clad figure emphasised words as though a mime performer.

The feel of the crowd suddenly changed, as some young teenage boy hecklers left Porkie's Big Eats, biting into lamb mine pies, holding them out, taunting the girls holding the bloodied lamb. One of the girls stepped forward carrying the broken animal, before a tall boy grabbed it from her outstretched arms and threw it onto the pavement, where another boy kicked it. All hell broke loose as animal rights protesters and boys started to scrap with one another.

Billie held herself back from wading into the crowd to separate the two warring sides, feeling a now familiar frustrated sensation that she was, albeit through her own choice, no longer a police officer and was, in any case, undercover and needed to make herself scarce, now that she heard police sirens in the distance, but moving closer, clearly alerted to the situation kicking off around her. It really wouldn't do to get arrested.

As Billie forced herself to step back towards the edge of the crowd, she glanced upwards to where the dark boiler-suited figure was unravelling a banner and holding it high above their heads. Printed in bold, it read **Kill Porkie's Big Eats**. The intimidating phrase was identical to a section of one of the threatening letters sent to Graham Harper. Had Billie just found the perp, a quest that she had feared would be like searching for a needle in a haystack?

Pushing her way speedily now sideways through the crowd towards the plinth, she was suddenly punched in the face by one of the teenagers. Startled for a moment, she had been tempted to grab him, pin back his flailing arms now aimed at another person and march him with force up to the police car now speeding to a halt at the edge of the square. Instead, she was forced to watch him laugh and push his way backwards, kicking out, before he turned with his mates and started to run down the street.

Billie glanced back up to the plinth. It was empty save for the banner draped across the top. The boiler-suited figure had jumped off, onto the wall of Porkie's Big Eats and was hurtling down the side alleyway. Billie broke into a jog as she pushed through the madness, in hot pursuit.

The masked figure raced down the alleyway, knocking dustbins over as they passed, the garbage entrails spilling out across the lane, in an attempt to slow down anyone chasing, but Billie had already sprinted around the corner, leaped over the stinking rubbish and was gathering speed behind.

A scuffling movement to one side, in the shadow of a huge industrial bin, made her swerve sideways. Perhaps a cat or a giant rat feasting on the leftover food, was the thought that flashed through Billie's mind before she continued to sprint along the alley. The masked figure turned briefly to look at her and then skittered sideways into a backyard. Billie followed, pushing the gate painted with scuffed green paint closed behind her. The boiler-suited figure was crouched between some household dustbins, still masked and gloved.

Billie felt the sweat running down her back, due to her body being so covered. She imagined the other person was at least as hot as she felt, especially under such bulky clothing and still wearing the plastic mask. She hoped that she had been considered a friend not foe, a fellow protester, and so the face covering could be about to be removed. Might Darque & Wilde's seemingly impossible job to reveal the sender of the threatening letters be over so easily?

The two bodies sat opposite one another for a moment, Billie trying to appear to be watching the gate and listening, rather than staring hard at the person sitting opposite in the hope of any identifying features slipping into view.

'I'll just see if the fuzz has gone.' Billie was using her best fake accent, to disguise her natural voice, as she pulled herself upright and made a show of creeping to the gate and peeping out. Luckily they had no other followers, either police or protesters, and the night animal that she thought she had caught a glimpse of behind the industrial bin, had either merged into the shadows or been a figment of her imagination. 'All clear,' she said in an attempt to sound like she and her backyard mate were comrades in action.

But as she turned to give a thumbs up sign, she realised that the dark figure had already pulled themselves upright and jumped onto one of the bins, about to leap over the wall. Billie only had a second to reflect that she never had been very good at judging friends, before she decided to drop the best-buddies-fighting-against-the-world idea and instead make a grab for the masked figure. She managed to whip her arm out and grip one ankle of the heavily-studded boot, clinging on like a limpid.

The masked figure had their knee on the dividing wall of the terraces and rocked back, unbalancing for a beat, before reaching down to try to yank Billie's hand off their leg. Billie grabbed the dark leather glove, tussling to keep a grip. But she was hit by a heavy smack on her arm, as her target snatched a dustbin lid, using it as a weapon. They brought it down again, heavily on Billie's shoulder as she fought to keep a grip. Filthy dust billowing out from the cover stung her eyes and made her want to gag as the taste of decomposing garbage clung to her lips. The final smack, this time on the side of the head, had Billie dropping to the ground, momentarily dazed.

Her eyes regained focus to see the figure disappearing over the wall into the adjoining yard. A loud clatter rang out as bins were upturned in the neighbouring property, followed by the sound of footsteps running fast. As Billie sat up, pulling the mask off her face, she looked at the small silver charm logo in her hand that had ripped free from the black glove she'd been hanging on to. It seemed to be a design of two letters entwined.

Suddenly, the back gate slammed open. Billie tucked the charm up her cuffed sleeve as a uniformed police officer appeared and stood looking down at her. The back door of the house opened, and a middle-aged woman marched out, mobile phone in her hand, looking angry and brave now that an officer of the law was present.

'There! Just as I told you.' The woman spoke to the police officer whilst pointing to Billie with her mobile phone, venturing closer now, rather than viewing from behind the net curtains, Billie imagined. 'The other one went off over the wall. Dregs of society, this lot. I saw them kicking off in the square earlier when I went to get my Alf his Porkie's pie. You want to lock this reprobate up and throw away the bleeding key.'

'Hello, ma'am.' The police officer had recognised Billie immediately. She had, after all, once been the pin-up girl of the force. Billie dragged the dark wig off, rolling her eyes. 'New job not quite panning out the way you hoped?' he asked mildly.

'Doesn't look like she's got a job, or she wouldn't be arsing around causing trouble would she? Sponger. Lock 'em all up and throw away the key.' Billie sighed, holding out her hands, wrists together.

'It's just plain Billie now, Darren,' Billie answered as the woman rattled off more abuse at ever closer quarters. 'It's a fair cop. For God's sake, just get me out of this place, or you might have to arrest me for murder.'

FOURTEEN
ON THE RUN

Please, Lord, please don't let me die. Tanko repeated the words in his head over and over, feeling himself shaking, as he crouched down behind the industrial dustbin, pulling the child's quilt tightly behind him. He had been fitfully snoozing due to distress, exhaustion and the fact that his body was suddenly having to cope with the broken pie feast that he had ravenously eaten after the woman had thrown away the samples that had been passed around Porkie's Big Eats, earlier. There was a chill in the air too, now that the sun had gone down, and dark shadows filled the alleyway.

Tanko's first feeling was one of nausea, as though the pies hadn't actually been fit for consumption. He wondered if perhaps that was the reason the woman had thrown a whole tray full of food away? But then he realised that something else had caused his heart to start beating fast – the noise of people shouting, of police sirens ringing out.

Half awake, but only in that mode for seconds, his mind was suddenly full of images of the massacre in his village, the screaming in terror and pain that he had witnessed, which had merged into images of the girl with the *'no place like home'* tattoo. Once again, he relived her ear-piercing shrieks as the man had borne down on her with the machete. That horrific vision had been broken by the ongoing police siren. Flickering images came into his mind instead, of the small prisoner who had broken free with him, dead under the wheels of the lorry, his body destroyed, scattered pictures of his family raining down on Tanko and the police car racing along the road, too late to be of any assistance.

But then he had been wide awake, reacting as though he were about to be struck as he had heard shouting in the big square next to the alleyway and then police sirens again. As he had awoken, he had thought that they had been in his dreams or memories, but no, they were right here, loud and clear. Had they come looking for him? Had someone spotted him slumped behind the bins in the dirt and discarded wrappers and told them to come and take him away?

He closed his eyes tightly, slapping his hands over his ears at the noise as one person ran past, kicking some of the bins nearby over. Then he had scuttled sideways, trying to squeeze behind the big full industrial bin, that stank with assorted rubbish and the smell of the pies which were now making his stomach churn. There had been another set of footsteps, also running, which had made him even more terrified for his life, causing him to almost cry out in fear as he desperately tried to shroud his body in the shadows. As they had passed, the alleyway had stood silent for a moment, save for the noise he could hear in the square, which had changed from shouting and screaming to people singing a song about suffering animals. Tanko seemed to sense they were singing a peaceful song, as though the danger was over. He breathed out a sigh of relief.

Suddenly though, there had been another clatter of bins at

the end of the alleyway and footsteps running back towards him. He had managed to tuck himself completely behind the big industrial bin now, crushing his lungs in an attempt to flatten himself between wall and rubbish container, as the figure stopped running only inches away from him, so close that Tanko could almost reach out and touch their leg. He held his breath as the person stepped back against the wall, in the shadow of the huge bin, breathing heavily as they quickly pulled off the big dark boiler suit that they had been wearing and other clothing too. Tanko peeped up and almost let out a squeal of horror as a skeleton face turned towards him as though the devil himself had come to get him. But then the mask was taken off and thrown into the bin along with the big suit. All he could see now was the shadow of the person moving close to him.

Tanko felt that he couldn't hold his breath much longer, silently crying out as he spotted a rat scurry out from behind some rubbish, starting to sniff at his foot. He didn't know if the person who had been wearing the skull mask had seen it too, as they moved off quickly, walking normally now instead of running, as though they had shed one persona and taken on another.

As Tanko gingerly slid out from his squalid hiding place, he noticed that the gloves that the person had been wearing had tumbled to the ground from the industrial bin. He picked them up. They were leather and warm from the heat of the wearer's skin. He pulled them on, seeing the glint of some sort of metal charm on the right-hand glove. He didn't know what it meant, didn't want to take something that wasn't his, but it seemed that in this country people discarded all sorts of things, not seeming to care whether anyone else could make use of them or not, so his decision was made.

He suddenly felt so very grateful for the immediate feeling

of warmth that the gloves brought him, as though he was holding hands with another person. It was a good sensation. It made him think of his mother. He felt his heart slow as he gingerly stepped out into the middle of the alleyway, legs shaking. He looked up and down as he tried to decide which way to safely turn next. That choice was taken away from him immediately as a police car turned into the far end of the backstreet. The headlights shone brightly. Would they see the upturned bins, the lane in a mess and think that Tanko had created this damage? He wasn't going to wait to find out.

He skittered quickly into the shadows of the opposite wall, grateful that his sore ankle was much less painful now, sadly turning when he realised that he had left the comforting child's quilt behind amongst the rubbish, but not daring to venture back for it. Instead, Tanko rushed back out of the lane and curved away from the busy square, breaking into a limping run. He didn't know where he was rushing to, but right at that moment, it felt like he had been on the run non-stop since the moment that he had been forced to leave his beloved home village in Nigeria.

After a few minutes and feeling his sore ankle aching, Tanko desperately hoped that he had put enough distance between himself and any further danger. He looked nervously back over his shoulder, to check that no one was in hot pursuit, before slowing down. There wasn't anyone in sight behind him, yet he still had to struggle to calm his fast-beating heart. Ahead, he could see empty streets and a large park to one side. It appeared peaceful and quiet, the way that he had always imagined England to be. Everyone else on the boat that he had crossed the English Channel with, seeking a safe haven, had thought the same thing. He wondered where his fellow frightened, yet excited sailors were now.

As he neared the park, Tanko could see some boys were in

the playground area. They were laughing, just as he had so often done when his family and friends in the village had played football together, when peace had prevailed in his homeland. He had shouted noisily enough then and laughed out loud. Tanko wondered if perhaps the happy faces of the boys ahead were a sign that he was heading towards friends at long last?

FIFTEEN
GHOSTLY FRIENDS

E llis caught his reflection in the car mirror. He wasn't exactly putting on a happy face, that was for sure. The footie match had been cancelled at the last minute due to a wildcat strike amongst ground staff, over a disagreement about pay and working conditions.

He guessed that the workers did have a point. The big game money in high level football wasn't exactly shared evenly amongst the football club staff, finalists in a major tournament or not, with players earning millions whilst the other essential workers lower down the pecking order had to live on meagre take-home pay. The strike meant that those protesting had a way of making their case via the media present tonight when all other avenues of negotiation had fallen on deaf management ears. Ellis couldn't say he wasn't disappointed though.

Teddy had suggested that they go on a pub crawl and then on to a club for late-night entertainment, but Ellis had made his excuses and pulled out. He might have appeared to most people to be a totally happy-go-lucky type of guy, but he had a serious work ethic, born out of many years working as a top undercover operative for first the Serious Organised Crime Unit, then the

National Crime Agency. He had promised Billie that he would do the night shift tonight and that meant no alcohol on workdays. That rule had probably made the difference between life or death on one or two occasions.

Yes, tonight he might just be hanging out, hopefully getting proof that someone's husband was shagging another man, but the rules stayed the same, whatever the less risky game he was playing in his working life today. He had to be on his mettle. He wouldn't let himself down, nor Billie. No, he would never, ever let Billie down. At least, he hoped not.

Scattered pictures momentarily skipped across his mind's eye of the one night they had spent together. Both had been rolling drunk and drowning sorrows over a lost work colleague and friend. They had woken up in the same bed the next morning, totally hungover and embarrassed, claiming that they could remember nothing whatsoever about the night before, then had speedily scooted off in opposite directions. The subject had never been mentioned again.

Ellis didn't know if Billie actually *didn't* remember the nitty gritty of that night. He half laughed at himself for the thought. It didn't say much about his prowess with the ladies if she truly *couldn't* remember a thing. But he could perhaps take his drink better than her, and that night wouldn't be one he would forget in a hurry. Not even on his death bed in fact. She had certainly played up to her Wilde name, that was a fact.

But for Ellis it had been more than that. He had never met a woman quite like Billie Wilde. He had actually fallen hook, line and sinker, the very first moment that he had set eyes on her, with that mane of red hair and the not-to-be-messed-with manner, in a grimy holding cell under a magistrates' court, Billie not realising at first that he wasn't a con at all, but that he was, in fact, working undercover.

She was gutsy and brave, rocking a sometimes uptown girl

air, but with very down to earth values. Not only that, but she was both serious and witty, kind with the kids and yet a she-devil with any lawbreaker who crossed her. Christ, she was so very sexy, without even realising for a moment the effect that she had on men. Sexy in bovver boots, jeans and jumper, spilling crumbs all down her front, sexy pinning some low life on his face and cuffing him with astonishing force, and on the odd occasions when she slipped into one of the two slinky dresses she owned, Ellis could feel himself almost losing control.

When Connie called her mummy, it made his heart lift. Despite assuring Billie that he would set the child straight, he had to admit that he hadn't exactly discouraged it. The sooner Storm Benbow was wiped from his tiny daughter's memory the better, was the way he saw it. She'd never been any sort of loving mother. He was going to move heaven and earth to ensure that the bitch didn't just think she could turn back up and sink her claws into their daughter after doing a bunk to escape being dragged into a major criminal enquiry.

In a perfect world it would just be him, Billie and his girls, business and personal life all linked together. Maybe have another little one. He was done with his crazy dangerous life always on the move. That was in the past. He was ready to settle down now and maybe, just maybe, if he kept schtum and waited long enough, Billie Wilde would relax and feel the same. God knows, she'd made some dire choices with men in the past. He couldn't be worse than that bunch, could he?

Way things were looking, his Maya was also going to be useless with guys. But he'd soon give that greasy oik she brought home tonight short shrift. Would have picked him up by the scruff of his neck and sent him on his way, with a smack, if the girls hadn't been present.

Suddenly, Ellis's musings stopped in mid-thought. There had been some movement at the house he was watching, the home of the alleged lover of the husband. Ellis lifted his camera. Through the powerful zoom lens, he identified the man and started clicking. A frown crossed his face, however. The information he had was that the lover would be visited at home by the wayward husband. The agreement was that their client would ring as soon as hubby had left home that evening, claiming he had an unforeseen work issue as seemed to be the excuse he had been regularly using. Ellis would be waiting, camera at the ready when he turned up here. The client seemed to know exactly what was going on herself, but didn't want a big showdown in the street, hence calling in Wilde & Darque. Being early, Ellis had been expecting a long wait, but maybe there had been a change of rendezvous?

Ellis quickly slid from behind the car seat and out onto the road, staying a safe distance behind the lover as he headed down the street and around the corner. There was a big park to one side, long shadows now falling from the trees fringing the edge of the open ground as nightfall started to cloak the area.

The lover suddenly turned to the right, through an open park gate, slipping inside, heading across a wide expanse of grass towards a cricket pavilion over in one corner of the park. Ellis snuck through the gate, paused to watch the lover's direction of travel and then, skirting around the edge of the grassed area, followed him via a perimeter pathway. The man was standing outside of the building, under a roof awning, checking his watch as Ellis concealed himself behind a wide-trunked tree.

It was at that moment, another figure appeared from the shadows of the roof overhang. Was this the wayward husband? If so, then Ellis would capture the moment. If not, then what went on with the lover behind closed doors, not to mention open spaces, though Billie might argue that point, was absolutely nothing to do with him. He smiled at the thought of Billie once again. In truth, though he would die before admitting it to anyone else, she was never far from his mind.

Ellis lifted the camera to get a closer look at the two men, who, believing to be out of sight of anyone else, were making no bones about being more than just passing friends. Ellis started clicking, unable to get a clear picture at first, because of the rapidly lowering light. Once the deed was speedily done, the man who Ellis expected to be the wayward husband moved away from the cricket pavilion and in his direction.

Ellis slipped back into the thicket of hedge, keeping his camera trained on the figure. Hopefully he would get a full face shot which would wind up this case, earning another few pretty pennies for Wilde & Darque's pockets. God knows his new home refurbishments and particularly Maya's top-floor flat, had cost him an arm and a leg. He hoped she was just having a stroppy joke about moving out.

He pushed that thought aside as the figure came within inches of where he was standing. He clicked, before his brain fully registered who he was looking at. The man caught in the act definitely wasn't his client's wayward husband. But Ellis certainly hadn't expected to see Wilde & Darque's newest customer, quickly making himself scarce as he scurried along the perimeter path before leaving the park.

Tanko had been hiding behind a thorn-filled bush, watching the boys larking around, for a while now. They looked about the same age as him, playing similar games to those that he had enjoyed after school with his pals. If he should ever get a chance to go back home at some time in the future, then though he knew that his friends no longer existed, he would forever see their ghosts playing in the clearing outside of their homes. Different scenery, here, but same activity.

His mother had once told him that nobody truly dies until the last person left on earth with a memory of the deceased also passes away, so Tanko would kick a ball and imagine his friends kicking it back to him. If he concentrated really hard, then maybe one of his ghostly friends, knowing how much he was willing them to be alive once more, might just be able to do it.

As Tanko's thoughts turned to his lost friends, a football bounced to a halt before him. Tanko glanced up. The group of boys were looking his way.

'It's somewhere in those bushes,' a tall boy shouted.

Tanko couldn't help suddenly kicking the ball back. He had always been a star of the school football team, had once harboured dreams of being a player for the national side, stepping up to take the Africa Cup of Nations in his two hands and holding it up high to an applauding crowd. The ball fell neatly at the feet of the tall boy.

'What the fu...' The tall boy frowned, looking to the others. Tanko held his breath, his muscles tensing as he leaned back against the bush. The thorns dug into his skin like tiny razor-sharp arrows. Why on earth had he done such a stupid thing?

'Must be someone in there.' One of the other boys with blond hair and the face of an angel announced, taking control of the ball, then kicking it into the bushes. Tanko heaved a sigh of relief. Surely this meant that he was amongst friends? He stopped the ball with one foot and then kicked it back.

'Might be a ghost,' a smaller boy, just finishing off a Porkie's Big Eats pie, discarding the branded bag in an otherwise pristine flowerbed, had grabbed a tree branch from the grass and poked another of the boys with it, laughing. The victim jumped and then, finding his own combat implement amongst the fallen twigs and branches from the many trees surrounding them, stabbed his assailant in retaliation, beginning a battle that was now full of laughter, but had the air of a play fight that would soon end in tears as the jokey blows became harder.

The large boy, however, followed by his friend with the angelic face, was moving forward towards the thicket of bushes that Tanko was secreted within, squinting into the semi-darkness.

'Hey, who's in there?' he asked, picking up a large branch of his own and pushing the foliage aside to reveal Tanko, who couldn't, of course, answer, though he desperately wanted to tell the other boys of his footballing prowess. The words just wouldn't come out after the massacre, though the therapist who he had started seeing at Freedom Angels had explained and Tanko had nodded to show that he had understood, that his voice would most likely come back in time.

He could actually hum tunes to himself when he was all alone, tunes that had been passed down through his family for generations, even sing a few words to himself. He had intended to try hard to murmur a favourite song, which had told a story of happy village life, for his therapist at his next session, had he not been kidnapped. She had been kind and patient and didn't make him freeze up in fear, wondering what might happen to him next.

She had explained that his condition was more about the people and less about the place. Once he realised that he was safe and amongst friends in his new country, he would no longer have the strain in his throat, his heart beating so fast that it might burst out of his chest or experience his eyes starting to water as they were right now, when someone was staring at him like he was the crazy kid.

'It's some big cry-baby kid,' the angelic boy sneered, beckoning the others over.

'Come out here and explain yourself.' The tall boy tapped

Tanko on the leg. 'Skulking in here spying on us.'

'Maybe he's some sort of perv,' the angelic boy piped up. 'Are you a perv, squirt?'

Tanko shook his head nervously. He didn't know what the boy meant. Maybe he was alluding to some tribe or other. He wanted to say '*I'm from Baga, a town in north-eastern Nigeria. My people are Kanuri. Boko Haram came to my local market, tied up my family and all of my friends and slit their throats*', but his own throat was now drier than ever.

'Spit it out then. You don't look like you're from *round here*,' the angelic-appearing boy persisted.

'You can say that again,' one of his stick-battling friends joined in, alluding to Tanko's dark skin.

Tanko felt himself shaking, his mouth drying as though it was suddenly full of sand. Though they were boys of around his own age, they weren't smiling like his own footballing friends. Their eyes were filled with hatred. It reminded him of the looks on the faces of the Boko Haram terrorists on that horrific day of the first massacre. Different scenery, same feeling of danger.

Adrenaline finally kicked in and instead of being frozen to the spot, Tanko pushed his way out of the bush and tried to run as fast as he could, just like he had on that first fateful day, if only his weak ankle didn't let him down.

'Get him. Teach him a lesson. This is our turf, perv kid!' the angelic-faced boy shouted as the others gave chase. Despite Tanko's past fitness, the horrors that he had experienced since leaving Nigeria had taken their toll on his body as well as his mind. His ankle twisted over again before the tall boy easily overtook him. Jumping back and forth, goading, arms outstretched like a goalkeeper ready to catch a ball.

Suddenly Tanko's legs were kicked away from beneath him. He lay on the ground, trying to shield his head as the angelic-faced boy kicked him in the side of his body. Tanko attempted to struggle to his feet, but the tall boy pressed his shoulders down hard towards the grass. He was on his knees as the small boy hit him with his stick. The other boy used his own stick, even harder, on the back of Tanko's head, pushing him with his foot as he did so.

'Want to get back to where you came from, scum,' he shouted, his small face screwed up in anger. Tanko felt as though he might be sick from the panic. Would he have travelled all of this way, endlessly, it seemed, running for his life, just to have his throat slit by these unexpected foes?

As one of the tree branches snapped due to a particularly vicious blow and the other boys cheered on the attacker, Tanko took the split-second lack of attention to leap up and try to run as fast as his racing heart and weak ankle could take him, towards an open gate that he could see at the other side of the flowerbeds across the park. The boys immediately took chase, screaming racist and cruel chants at the fleeing child. When the tall boy came alongside Tanko once again, he grabbed him by the scruff of the neck and kneed him in the stomach. Tanko doubled over in a ball, winded and coughing as fists and kicks rained down upon him.

'Hey! Get off him.' Tanko heard a man's voice shouting loud and forcefully. He glanced up to see a tall, broad man, camera slung around his neck, striding fast towards them. The boys stopped what they were doing, backed off a little, save for the angelic-faced lad who gave another hearty kick to Tanko's kidney area. He cried out in pain.

'Back off or I'll do to you what you've just done to him.' The man was speeding towards them now, anger etched across his features.

'Bog off, Baldy,' the tall boy shouted, though mercifully, all of the boys had moved away a few feet now from Tanko.

'You okay, son?' The man crouched down on one knee, his

warm hand on Tanko's shoulder. Tanko wanted to say that he felt hurt and desperately sad but had felt worse. He also wanted to tell the man that he was grateful for his intervention. It appeared as though so many people in this country didn't realise how very thankful those in his situation were. How grateful he had been for the chance of a new start in life. He didn't want people to think all he wanted was to take from them. He wanted to explain that one day, when he could talk once more and finish school, he wanted to be a teacher, help children to grow up seeing all that was good in the world.

'Hey, the bloke's got a camera. Worth a mint that. Let's mug him,' the small boy taunted.

Ellis Darque looked up. 'I don't fancy any of your chances if you try it, lads. Now like I said, skedaddle.'

'Free world. We can hang around a public park if we like.' The smallest boy waved the stick he was still hanging on to. 'What you going to do about it, Slaphead?' He stepped back as he shouted the taunt, nevertheless.

Ignoring him, Ellis lifted Tanko to his feet asking if he was okay once more. As Tanko nodded, the first stone ricocheted off his head. He ducked, pinning himself to Ellis. More stones were picked up and thrown in their direction before Ellis moved forward.

'Right, I warned you.' Moving at a lightning pace, he grabbed the arm of the tall boy who had lifted a large stone from one of the rockery flowerbeds and was clearly about to hurl it in their direction. The boy tried to pull away, before Ellis deftly pinned his arm around his back. He dropped the stone on his own foot.

'Aggh, my effing foot. Ow, you're breaking my arm,' the boy said in a pained voice.

'That's an offence. I'm gonna ring the coppers. You've just assaulted a child, Grandad,' the angelic-faced boy shouted.

'His won't be the only one, if you don't all make yourselves scarce,' Ellis answered in a steely voice.

'He's probably a paedo, that's why he's been lurking round here taking pictures,' the stick-wielding lad shouted, still backing away.

'Yeah, I'm gonna ring Childline and tell them he's shown me his dick,' the smallest boy called out, getting his mobile phone out of his pocket. It was at that moment that two special constables wandered into view on the road outside of the park.

'Hey, over here. There's a paedo trying to drag me into the bushes,' the tall boy yelled in the direction of the two uniformed special constables. They stopped and looked across, before walking fast to the open gate, heading in the direction of the warring group.

Tanko broke out into a cold clammy sweat. He wasn't sure where safety lay so he decided on his usual course of action, turning away from the melee, before starting to run fast, despite his bruises and painful ankle.

'Yeah, miss. He was with that black lad. He tried to nick our ball, so that the man in the bushes could grab us.' The angelic-looking boy had his hand up in the air as though he was top scholar in class, as Tanko glanced over his shoulder and sprinted even faster towards the shadow of the trees on the outer perimeter and then hopefully freedom from this latest version of hell. He hoped that the police would see that the boys were lying, that the man had been a good Samaritan.

As he shot through the open gate and peeped back through the metal rungs of the fence, his hands gripping the bars to stop his body from shaking so desperately, he watched the police approaching the still-mouthy boys. Tanko felt guilty for leaving the man there. But he was in no position to tell the police officers what had really happened. It seemed that few people in this country, that he had heard so much about being free and welcoming, believed anything that people like Tanko told them. For all he knew they might arrest him and the man together. What if he was locked up again and then immediately sent across the world to another place, one that he had heard was not much safer than his home country? He felt sick at the thought.

'You're nicked, you're nicked. Paedo, paedo!' Tanko heard the boys shouting and clapping as though in celebration as the man, flanked by the two police officers and looking irate, headed towards their waiting car. Tanko leaned his head against the cold railings, grateful for the dark leather gloves, like a warm hand holding his, though the rest of his body was still trembling. He could barely forgive himself for stupidly kicking that ball. He desperately hoped that the kind man didn't have family, children perhaps, waiting at home. What would happen to them if their innocent and kind father ended up locked away in a jail cell?

SIXTEEN
ON THE WRONG FOOT

'Y ou were nicked by the police, having discovered Graham Harper *in flagrante* in a park?' Billie shook her head lest she was still half asleep. 'Tell me I'm not still dreaming.'

Ellis handed her his camera. She started looking through the photos that he had taken the night before. 'So, he's hooking up with men in questionable locations?' She raised an eyebrow. 'Not illegal, but it's a shame he didn't mention that yesterday. It certainly opens up the field of suspects in the Porkie's case.'

Billie reached for a clear bag on a side table, to show Ellis the silver charm logo from the gloves. 'But hopefully it's simpler than that. The phrases used on the animal rights banner were identical to the words used on one of the threatening letters and I at least managed to get a souvenir from my tussle. I'm guessing that this won't have much useful DNA on it, but it's an unusual design, so if we find out who sells the gloves locally, we may find a shop assistant who remembers someone who looked a bit suspect buying them.'

'Good luck with that in the time we've got,' Ellis said with a sigh. He was holding a kettle, pouring hot water from it into a bowl. 'Shame Darren didn't actually nick you, we could have shared a coffee in the custody suite.'

'What are you doing with that?' Billie shied away, as Ellis headed towards her holding the bowl, having dabbed a cloth into the warm water.

'Bathing that black eye of yours. It looks like you did ten rounds with a cage fighter.'

'It's okay.' Billie pushed him away. She hadn't actually gotten around to looking in the mirror to check out her injuries. 'I've had worse beatings in my time.' She grinned, amused at the look of concern on Ellis's face as he had approached her. 'And it's a bit creepy looking at you, rocking your inner Florence Nightingale, so stay back,' she joked.

Ellis's face fell. 'Don't *you* start labelling me a creep.' He shook his head in disbelief. 'Bleeding so-called *special constables*, think they're some crack MIT squad, rather than wannabe beat bobbies.'

Billie had to admit that she had been surprised when Ellis had come home first thing, explaining that he had intervened in a kids' fight and crazily been booked in at the station. But the truth was that she had been lucky with her own police intervention. The vast turnover of staff in recent times meant that fewer and fewer police officers recognised Wilde & Darque PI as being manned by former crack officers from the Murder Investigation Team, so they had to go through the motions, should they be apprehended whilst carrying out their PI investigations, just like any other member of Joe Public.

'I wouldn't care, but the kid I stepped in to protect, ran off, so he couldn't verify my story that I'm not a kiddie fiddler. He was probably tucked up in bed with a mug of hot chocolate watching *Spider-Man* on the telly with his loving family by the time I reached the nick. Whereas I'm trying to keep *my* family together...'

'Come on, you know it won't go any further,' Billie said, trying to calm Ellis's anxiety. 'Chill out,' She had desperately wanted to tell him the reason that he had come home to find her asleep on his sofa, nearly jumping out of her skin when she had woken up to find him kneeling down beside her, stroking her sore face, but the subject matter was strictly off the cards with Ellis. Knowing that Boo was absolutely distraught about the discovery of the murdered children and with another early-morning appointment at the morgue on the cards, to identify victims who had once been associated with Freedom Angels, Billie really didn't think it was fair to leave her dear friend to look after Connie overnight. So instead, she had headed back over to Boo's after her skirmish, scooped Connie up, sleepy in her PJs, and taken her over to her own bed at her dad's home.

It wasn't that Billie thought that Ellis wouldn't be upset over the fate of the missing children. After all, he was a big softy at heart, but Freedom Angels was still a major sore point with him, therefore it was easier not to mention it at all. He had made his views loud and clear at the time, that he believed that part of the donated funds to build the sanctuary for young people seeking asylum, was dirty money.

Ellis didn't like the major donor to the project – nor the fact, Billie had noted, but not discussed with anyone else, that she had been in danger of falling for the man, who had died in a shocking accident, soon after donating. Only Billie was aware amongst their friends, that had she not already been committed to helping Ellis with a party for Connie's birthday, then she would likely have been with him when he had died.

Ellis, more importantly, in Billie's opinion, blamed the place for Maya's decision to leave her police training, to assist Boo running Freedom Angels instead. No matter how many times Billie, Boo and even Maya herself had attempted to broach the subject, Ellis had closed the conversation. He made no bones about the fact that he was blaming Freedom Angels for Maya's increasingly rebellious nature, avoiding the fact that he had never been one to exactly toe the line himself.

'It's not going to look good on the dad CV, is it? Lifted, after an accusation of trying to drag some kid into a bush, when Storm's back on the scene causing havoc and wanting custody.' Ellis had still been marching back and forth as Billie had returned downstairs, having gotten Connie up and dressed, hoping he might just have calmed down a little.

'Have you messaged Graham Harper, to get his sorry arse into work ASAP for a debriefing, if he doesn't mind the terminology?' Billie had decided to change the subject. 'I just need to nip home first and get a change of clothes as soon as we've dropped Connie of at–'

Billie's words were cut off in mid-sentence as a small voice called from the hallway, 'Coming. Watch, Daddy!' Billie leaped up and peered around the door as small footsteps could be heard carefully negotiating the bottom stair from her bedroom above. Even Billie's heart was doing a little flip at the sight before her, so she couldn't imagine how Ellis was going to feel at any moment.

'Well done.' Billie held the door open for Connie to walk under her arm, smiling proudly at Ellis.

'Look, Daddy. I fastened my shoes all by myself!' Connie was dressed in a sweet red-and-grey tunic, short white socks and shiny T-barred black shoes, on the wrong feet. Billie looked up to see tears filling Ellis's eyes. He rubbed his face, unable to speak for a moment.

'Your daughter is ready for her very first day at school,' Billie announced, patting Connie on the head as she skipped towards Ellis. He swept her up in his arms, a wide grin now spreading across his face.

'That's my girl. I'm so proud of you, baby.' He headed back

towards the hall when the front doorbell rang, still holding Connie, her arm around his neck, head nestled against his cheek. Billie was relieved to see Ellis relaxing a little at last. She had never been the mothering type and probably never would be, but she loved being an auntie figure to Ash's children and now Connie too. She was beginning to understand how Ellis was happy to give up life in the fast lane, content to snuggle down with his two girls, whereas Billie, in truth, was still struggling to fit into life at a more mundane pace.

'Mr Ellis Darque?' a woman's voice in a rather booming tone, could be heard enquiring.

'Yeah...?' From her spot in the doorway, Billie saw Ellis's face fall into a frown again.

'And this must be young Connie.' The woman gave a perfunctory smile towards Connie, as she attempted to step inside. Ellis put out his arm to block her way.

'Er, who exactly are you?' he asked without any attempt at a polite retort.

'Ethel Rutherford, CAFCASS,' the woman answered, fishing out a business card from the top of the clipboard she was holding.

'Eh?' Ellis grunted.

Billie smiled inside, noticing that Connie was also frowning, looking very much like a tiny hair-plaited version of her dad.

'Children and Family Court Advisory and Support Service,' Billie offered, as Ellis moved his arm to hitch Connie further onto his hip and the woman took the opportunity to march past him and into the lounge. Clearly she'd had practice at circumnavigating uninvited entry.

'Top marks, young lady. And you are?' the woman, who had sharp beady eyes and a birdlike nose, addressed Billie.

'She's my mummy.' Connie pointed a small finger in Billie's direction.

'Actually, I'm Mr Darque's *business* partner,' Billie corrected.

'Here rather early are you not?' Ethel Rutherford craned her neck to look beyond Billie to the pillow and sofa throw she had bedded down with for the night.

'Hey, why exactly is this any of *your* business?' Ellis barked as he followed Ethel.

'Billie was in a fight, in a street,' Connie advised Ethel, pointing now to the bruise on Billie's eye. 'She brought me from Auntie Boo's, cos some of her children got killed.' Billie made a mental note never to discuss such things again in front of a seemingly sleeping child, even in whispers, as she had done with Boo the night before.

'Eh?' Ellis looked as shocked as Ethel now, who flicked her birdlike gaze from Billie to Ellis in disbelief.

'Daddy was out in the park playing with a little boy. Then the policeman took him to the station.' Connie was talking to Ethel now as though they were neighbours gossiping over the garden fence.

'Hang on. Can we just start this again,' Ellis demanded. 'This is my daughter's first day at school, so I haven't got time for—'

'Your daughter's welfare, Mr Darque?' Ethel Rutherford raised an eyebrow. 'As a court-appointed officer, it is my job to advise the court officials about the well-being of children caught up in a parenting conflict and to help advise on a solution that is in *their* best interests. The welfare of the child is paramount. It will be my job to spend time with Connie as your custody hearings move forward with your former spouse, Ms Storm Benbow.'

'Eh? I haven't agreed to any of this.'

'I'm afraid the family court isn't interested in your needs, Mr Darque. I will report back and then it is for the judge or magistrates to decide if, as Ms Benbow claims, you are using alienating behaviour to obstruct Connie's relationship with her mother. Connie's wishes are paramount.'

'Connie wants to stay with me.' Ellis looked fit to kill.

'And my mummy. I want to be with my mummy too,' Connie announced loudly. Ethel Rutherford started noting the conversation down on her clipboard. Billie wanted to say, '*I think Connie means me,*' but as Connie had just associated her with a fight in the street and murdered children, she wasn't sure if she would just make bad matters worse.

'I want *Mummy* to take me to school.' Connie started to spurt tears as only a five-year-old can, seemingly at will. Billie blew out through her lips as she glanced at Ellis, his face like thunder. Right now, she wasn't sure that things *could* get much worse.

SEVENTEEN
TAKES ONE TO KNOW ONE

W*as Porkie Taking Home the Bacon?* the local newspaper headline read, as Graham Harper held it up in front of Billie. *Pigging the Pies*, the subheading underneath read. The accompanying photo featured the company's mascot being searched by her, pies tumbling out of his unzipped suit.

'So much for confidentiality, Ms Wilde!' Graham Harper was red in the face, spittle flying from his lips in fury, as he waved the paper in front of Billie's face. 'Together with Mr Darque, you may as well have carried a loudspeaker into my flagship outlet announcing the threat. I see that he has left *you* to face my wrath.' Graham Harper slammed the newspaper down on the desk in front of Billie.

Billie scanned the story in seconds, completely unmoved by Graham Harper's temper tantrum. He was lucky Ellis wasn't with her, considering his mood when Billie had been forced to leave him with Ethel Rutherford, attempting to investigate in forensic detail, his relationship with Connie as well as his feelings on his former wife.

'The good news is most people thought it was simply a theft issue and it also looks like a false alarm,' Billie said, deciding on the upbeat option in way of response. 'Overnight fast-track tests at King & Beech Forensics had shown the pies confiscated from Porkie's to be free from any noxious substances. The sample of scattered samples on the floor, though we couldn't retrieve them all, have also tested negative as has the search for DNA on the threatening photos to date. But the employee was acting suspiciously and with your reporting of this situation to us so late in the day, it left us with little choice.' Billie still felt a stab of regret and sorrow towards the poor employee playing Porkie, who had been paid such a tiny salary that he had felt compelled to steal a supper for his family.

'And I have now just received *this* in the post!' Graham Harper wasn't in the mood for listening as he grabbed a large envelope. He took out an A4-sized photo of the old woman who had died on the shop floor, in a body bag, being shipped out of Porkie's Big Eats. Stamped across the photo were the words, **P1ES TO D1E FOR. YOU HAVE BEEN WARNED**.

Billie narrowed her eyes at the shot. Had the person making the threats been watching from outside or picked up the photo from an online source? So many people had been around at the time, with mobile phones in their hands. Like the other photos, she guessed that this one too would turn out to be devoid of DNA, but she took out her gloves, slid them on and bagged the photo and envelope up, reflecting that Ellis had been wise to charge so highly for this job. Forensics tests didn't come cheap.

Josta had stepped in again, the evening before at the police mortuary, conducting the old woman's post-mortem. She couldn't, of course, officially divulge confidential information with Billie, now that she wasn't a serving police officer, but a simple thumbs up emoji answer from Josta to Billie's question via a text message, which had read, *Old lady, Porkie's. Natural causes?* had put Billie's mind at rest on that front.

'Still, having to shut down your shops earlier yesterday

meant that you managed to get to your daughter Tina's design exhibition last night. I believe that she was really looking forward to you attending.'

'What has that got to do with–' Graham Harper was about to continue, when Billie stopped him in his tracks by holding up the clearest photograph of him, taken by Ellis the night before, beside the cricket pavilion in the park.

'Was that why you needed to hurry out of the park last night after this rather *dangerous* liaison?' Billie watched the blood drain from Graham Harper's features. 'Whilst I accept that the public attention yesterday wasn't ideal, not giving full disclosure about the possibility of enemies made, due to casual hook-ups in a park, where children, by the way, were playing nearby, doesn't exactly help us narrow down the pool of suspects.'

Graham Harper sheepishly tried to break eye contact, but Billie was staring him out. He had been keen to wipe the floor with her, after all, so now it was time for him to take responsibility for his own actions. 'Has anyone threatened you after a *date* such as this one?'

'You've been following me?' Graham Harper grabbed the photo from Billie's hand.

'No, you simply walked into another enquiry, which only goes to show how much you need to big up your security all round. I hope you took my advice to do that in each of your overnight bakeries and also on every shop floor from this morning.'

Billie wanted to make it crystal clear that she had been firm on that point. As far as she was concerned, the protection of the public, which until this situation had emerged, had included *her* on most days, overrode any need to keep things running smoothly with a paying client.

'Indeed, at great cost, I might add. I promised my late wife that I would expand and leave the business in great shape when

I finally hand over to my dear daughter. She'd be turning in her grave at this. The original Porkie's Pies was started by her great-grandfather, passing through her family line. My daughter is the one who will take the company forward unless this mess puts a major spanner in the works. I've seen food companies go bust with this sort of malicious food-tampering threat.'

Graham Harper indicated the photo in his hand, before pulling out the top drawer of his desk and placing it inside. 'You will at least keep this confidential... my daughter is very fragile, Ms Wilde. She has a lot to take on her young shoulders learning about the business side of things. She doesn't need any extra stress. I want her to know nothing about these current threats, nor anything to do with my private affairs.'

'Agreed,' Billie shrugged, 'though Tina might have noticed something, if she's doing work experience on the shop floor.'

'She's the *CEO* in waiting, Ms Wilde. She doesn't need to do any work on the shop floor.'

'Shame,' Billie couldn't help answering, suddenly seeing a picture in her mind's eye of Graham Harper's teenage daughter being happily pawed by Johnny Briggs at Ellis's home the night before and his treatment of Safia earlier in the day. The girl would need to have all of her wits about her to stop the sharks who would be circling, knowing that she was the sole heir to such a successful business.

'On the subject of my private life. Let me make clear that my wife and I had an understanding, Ms Wilde. She also indulged in casual liaisons–'

'Anyone who may have expected to benefit from her will?' Billie asked, cutting through his explanation. She wasn't interested in making moral judgements about his family's less than careful vetting of friends. She wasn't exactly innocent of falling foul of that oversight herself in the past. But she did need Graham Harper to come completely clean about anyone at all that he might be able to think of, who may bear him or the company, a grudge.

The door suddenly swung open without a knock. Tina walked in, smiling. Graham Harper sent Billie a warning glance as he quickly locked away the photo.

'Did you see the paper this morning, Dad?' Tina asked, nodding to Billie in greeting. 'Did you, Billie?'

Billie was trying to stop her eyes from flicking to the newspaper headline on the front page. 'Um, yeees,' Billie answered, wondering why Tina was looking so happy if she had seen it too.

'Disgraceful. I'll see that employee doesn't work again in this town and we will be pressing charges–' said Graham.

'For stealing four pies?' Billie was aghast, having dealt mostly with banging up serial killers in her previous job.

'We have to set an example. If one does it, without punishment, they will all start–'

'No, not *that*.' Tina headed across the room, picking up the paper from the desktop, ignoring the headline page totally as she flicked through. 'Here, on the arts page.' She held the double-page spread up for her dad and Billie to see the report and feature about her exhibition, including photographs of her alongside her admittedly impressive mixed-media work. 'The reviews are great, people saying that I could have an amazing future.'

'Well done. Your photos on the wall of Freedom Angels are certainly brilliant.' Billie had to agree that the girl had talent.

'Wonderful, darling, but you already have a magnificent future in the bag. I can't help thinking that all of this arty stuff is a distraction from your business studies. Don't forget our meeting at eleven with accounts to discuss the financial review of the national launch.' There was a loud knock, before Graham Harper's PA popped her head around the door.

'The photographer and model have arrived, for the vegetable products campaign,' she advised.

'A photographer? But I could have done that, Dad.' Tina looked from the PA to her father. 'Why didn't you give the campaign to me? You've just seen my work last night; I mean, actual *experts* are giving me rave reviews—'

'You've got better things to do with your time, that's why, and so do I. The finance meeting. We're running late. Polly, please show Ms Wilde to the exit.'

At that moment Johnny Briggs stepped past the PA, into the room. A serious business type of camera hung around his neck. Tina's face showed that she was as shocked as Billie. The odious man was already like dog dirt on a ribbed soled shoe lately, in Billie's opinion. Johnny Briggs held out his hand to Graham Harper, as though he was a long-lost friend.

'Hi, mate.' His manner was overly friendly for a freelance employee.

'You *will* remember to send me that updated list of your special contacts.' Billie turned to Graham Harper pointedly, wondering if Johnny Briggs was one of them. He certainly seemed to be free and easy with his favours, so it was a possibility. Billie didn't trust him as far as she could throw the man. She'd already had a glimpse of his dark side and she could tell that he was the sort to cultivate influential friends. As she was about to walk out Johnny Briggs winked at her pointedly.

'Well, if it isn't the crack investigator Billie Wilde, again. We do keep bumping into one another, don't we, honey? This one just can't keep away from me, Graham, matey.' He grinned at Graham Harper.

Billie was about to set him straight on that score before the sight of Maya in the doorway stopped her in her tracks. 'I could use a second model on this shoot. Mistress Wilde is practically Maya's stepmum already, isn't that right, kid?' Billie felt bile immediately rise in her throat, as Johnny Briggs's cloying perfume headed her way. Or maybe it was just the sight of the odious man stroking his finger down Maya's arm when she came to a halt beside him. Too close for Billie's liking. She didn't want to get into an argument here, but she had expected Maya to be driving Boo to the morgue to formally identify the children at any minute now.

It was Tina who broke the stony silence.

'What's going on? Johnny, you never mentioned anything to *me* about this.' Tina had a petulant and tearful look on her face. Billie noticed that Johnny didn't reach out and stroke her arm in response. Not in front of her father. He was too clever for that.

'Oh, sorry, lovey. Your dad and I were just chewing the fat last night at your exhibition. Bumped right into him in the dark when I crept in whilst you were doing your welcome speech. I offered to step in quickly today and do him a favour. I said to my friend here, "Big up the veggie products". That will calm down the earache from the activists on the street right now, though as I pointed out, didn't I, Graham, the kids shaking those banners mean well. Your dad's agreed that if he reaches out, shows he's heard them, by bigging up his veggie product campaign, they might chill out a bit.'

'I still could have done it.' Tina folded her arms, her mouth set in a grim line.

'Yeah, you're doing great as one of my students, but you've still got a lot to learn, sweetie. I practically started all this photo digitisation stuff and I've got a partner in one of my businesses who's in town. Absolutely ace at these things. We can have the whole thing turned around, posters up on digital boards on high streets, across the world even, by tonight. Easy.'

'Thank goodness someone is doing something positive in that respect.' Graham Harper shot a look at Billie.

'Coming up with solutions has always been meat and drink

to me, my friend.' Graham smiled at Johnny. However, Tina was looking daggers at Maya.

'But you said you respected the protesters, Maya. You're always going on about the business selling meat products. I can't believe that you want to advertise Porkie's, and that no one even told me about this. I mean, at the very least, it should have been *my* shoot.'

'I...' Maya looked sheepish. 'I do agree about not selling meat pies, Mr Harper. But Johnny has made me see that the best thing I can do is promote the vegetable ones. I mean, maybe they'll become so popular that everyone will want to buy those inste—'

'Let's face it, who could resist such a beautiful thing as Maya here, lips parted around a juicy Porkie's vegetable roll.' Johnny slimed up to Graham Harper, running his tongue over his upper lip. Billie wondered if he was doing it on purpose to rile her. It had worked.

'A beautiful *thing*?' Billie retorted, looking aghast at Maya. 'I hope you aren't doing this against your will, Maya?' Billie tried to brush aside the memory of Johnny Briggs propelling Safia up the alleyway. Maya usually knew her own mind, but—

'The *thing* is,' Tina interjected, 'that *I* didn't know a *thing* about it all. I thought you were my best friends, when all of the time last night, you were plotting against me!' Tina pushed past the group and tearfully stormed out of the room. Graham Harper sighed as he started to shepherd Billie, Johnny and Maya out. 'I told you she's highly sensitive,' he whispered to Billie before striding off along the corridor that Tina was now running along, heading for the ladies, Billie guessed.

'That's how you make friends and influence people,' Billie said with irony. 'Maya, aren't you meant to be helping Boo this morning?' Billie was trying to contain her anger as she was technically in a business meeting, however, she simply couldn't help smacking Johnny Briggs's ever-stroking hand off Maya's arm. The girl looked sheepishly down the corridor. Johnny Briggs shrugged as he stuffed his hands in his pockets in a show of nonchalance.

'I've told Maya that with her looks she could be a top fashion model. I think her dad would agree that Freedom Angels isn't the final staging point for a girl with such outstanding potential. She's too young to be pinned down.' Johnny Briggs wasn't smiling now that Graham Harper wasn't watching.

'This is a private conversation, between me and Maya,' Billie snapped back. She caught hold of Maya's arm and led her a few steps away, but it seemed that the man was determined to be in control. He continued talking.

'I'm only stopping by Freedom Angels myself to offer my consultancy talents... pass on my knowledge, dig out new genius. Giving back.' Johnny had taken a few steps after them. Billie held up her hand to stop him approaching any further.

'Or more likely to manipulate those gifted young people for your own benefit, whilst pocketing a big whacking consultancy fee. I think you'll find that gig is now history. Did you know that I sit on the board there?' Billie had donated a large sum of money to help set up Freedom Angels and she was damned if any more of it was going to go into his manky pockets.

'I don't think there's any need to be so rude to Johnny,' Maya whispered to Billie. 'Boo said that she didn't need me to go with her. I was a bit scared to be honest. I mean, I'm sorry about what I said last night about you and Dad, but I just wanted Dad to get off my back. I know I let him down by dropping out of the police training, but I desperately want to try out new things. Find out who I *really* am. Johnny persuaded me to do this. He said I need some fun in my life, rather than trying to save everything all of the time. Who knows, maybe he's right?

If I try out lots of different stuff, I might find out where my passions truly lie.'

'Not in his direction, if you take my advice.' Billie flicked her head towards Johnny, where he appeared to be now fiddling with his camera. She silently swore to God that if he pointed it towards her, she would respond in such a way that he wouldn't be capable of doing it again for a very long time. Maya squeezed Billie's hand.

'Please don't let us fall out, Billie. I don't know what I would have done without your help in the past couple of years. You know that.'

Billie decided to let the matter drop for the moment. She'd landed up with her fair share of creeps in her life. Maybe that was making her overreact in Maya's case. She couldn't stand the sight or smell of Johnny Briggs, but it was true that Maya was indeed a beauty who wouldn't look out of place under the bright lights on a red carpet. Billie had no right to stand in her way, if that was a dream that she currently wished to explore. In fact, Maya's need to find out where her passions honestly lay, were striking a chord with Billie in relation to her own life right now, too.

'Just don't be bullied into doing anything that you don't want to do, promise me that.' Maya nodded with a small smile. 'Oh, and as you are now turning into a supermodel, maybe you can identify this fashion emblem. It's off an item of clothing. Bit like Cinderella's glass slipper. I'm trying to pinpoint the owner.' Billie pulled a little clear packet out of her pocket, holding the silver charm logo that she had ripped off the glove of the animal activist during their tussle. Unfortunately that had tested negative for DNA traces too.

'Oh, look, Johnny, isn't that the same emblem that's on your new gloves and stuff?'

Johnny frowned as he sauntered across and took the bag

from Billie's hands, slipping the silver logo out into his palm before she could stop him. He made a show of rubbing his thumb over it. 'I'm not sure...'

'Yeah, I think it is.'

Maya seemed pretty certain, Billie noted.

'Who knows?' Johnny sounded like he was thinking hard before he looked up. 'Let's face it, babe, you wear my stuff more than I do.' He glanced at Billie as he casually dropped the silver charm logo back into her bag. 'Every time I get out of bed, I come back to find you wearing one of my shirts and absolutely *nothing* else.' Billie noted that infuriating slow smile again, as though it had been practised in a mirror for effect. It was working on Maya. She nudged him playfully, a blush spreading across her face.

'Why do you want to know?' Maya glanced back at Johnny playfully as he mouthed a kiss in her direction.

'Just part of an investigation I'm currently involved in.' Billie was staring hard at Johnny Briggs now, noticed his eyes blink once or twice. Come to think of it, Billie realised, he was around the same height as the animal rights activist she had chased and tussled with the night before. Johnny suddenly gave a wide smile that didn't reach his eyes.

'Whoops, shame you didn't mention that earlier, before I'd handled it. Aren't you great detectives meant to protect the integrity of your DNA samples?'

Quite the clever clogs, Billie had been tempted to reply.

'Still, I've got yours right here now for the future,' she answered instead, giving a cold smile in return. 'Had those gloves on last night, did you? Think hard because I'd definitely like to reunite this charm with the lucky owner.'

'Well, I might be mistaken...' Maya trailed off, seeing Johnny's smile drop. 'I'd better go and see if Tina's okay.' She glanced at Johnny again. Billie hoped that she hadn't seen fear in Maya's eyes, before she hurried off along the corridor.

'I do hope that you aren't pressurising Maya into doing this.' Billie dropped any pretence at affability now that Maya was out of hearing range. 'She's been through a lot recently. I'd hate to think anyone was playing on her vulnerability.' To her fury, Johnny Briggs moved towards her as though to whisper in her ear.

'Takes one to know one,' he said softly.

'You what?' Billie snapped back, unable to stop her hand moving to waft the strange perfume away from her.

'A woman under pressure, being bullied into a situation, sweetheart. Scared of saying no to lover boy Ellis Darque, are you? Because I hear that he can be rather domineering. Like that, do you?' Johnny frowned, looking Billie up and down as he did so in an insincere look of concern.

'Are you out of your tiny mind?' Billie was astonished at the anger that enveloped her. She wanted to punch the guy's smarmy lights out, but Graham Harper's PA was making her way back across the room towards them.

'Because from where I'm standing, you've got the look of a chick who's just taken a sidestep into a life that's going to be the death of you. Next thing you'll be walking up the aisle taking pride of place in a shotgun wedding. You mark my words. Break away whilst the going's still good, sweetie-pie. Don't do anything you don't want to do and if you need a knight in white shining armour to come along and save you, then I'm your man.'

'The room is ready for you,' the PA trilled, all eyes and teeth and batting eyelashes as Johnny tuned his gaze to her and gave that practised smile of his.

'Ace, darling, just ace. I bet you're the best at making coffee too?' The PA readily agreed. 'No sugar, baby, I'm sweet enough,' he said, lazily walking across the floor alongside the PA, who was laughing way too loudly. Billie's mobile started ringing. To her fury as she pressed the button to answer and then looked up, Johnny Briggs had turned his head back in her direction and was blowing her a kiss.

'Billie Wilde,' Billie snapped perhaps a bit too angrily.

'Keep your hair on.' Ellis sounded equally annoyed. 'Just wondering where you've got to. I dropped Connie at her school on time by the skin of my teeth, thanks to bleeding Ethel Rutherford, giving me earache about women's rights, then I get here to the main Porkie's outlet and the security guy who's meant to be donning the Porkie costume has taken the day off sick. I've still got to do that insurance client job up in town, so the outfit is all yours, last wearer's sweat and all. Get yourself here pronto.'

'Oh bugger off,' Billie answered, not sure if her response was aimed at Ellis for his words or Johnny for making her wonder for a moment if the creep had been more astute about her state of mind than she was ever going to give him credit for.

'What?' Ellis sounded shocked. 'I can't let the insurance client down, he wants this interim meeting, like I told you this morning and you sound like you're done there with Harper.'

'I'm done with a lot of things right now.' Billie knew where she had to be pronto, and it wasn't donning a damn Porkie's pig outfit in some shop which the owner, by rights, should be closing down and bringing in a whole crime-fighting team to investigate. After all, there was still a big chance that the threats were being sent by some sad sack filling in the time of day. Her mind was on a much more serious issue.

'So where are you going instead?' Ellis sounded suitably huffed.

'To hell,' Billie answered, cutting the call dead. It wasn't a lie. Boo was seemingly all alone at Beech & King Forensics, where the buried children had been taken, their premises and experts being much more able than the old police morgue to accommodate the deceased. Their identification wouldn't be a job for the faint-hearted. Boo was one of the strongest women that Billie had met, but she wouldn't let her friend face that situation alone.

As she headed fast for the exit and on towards her car, she did feel a stab of guilt. Was she letting Ellis down? He had once complained that she was more interested in the dead, than the living. Her desperation to head to the morgue right now seemed to be proving him right.

As Billie started the engine and sped out onto the road, overtaking a lorry with a Porkie's Big Eats pie advert across the side, cutting in to avoid an oncoming car, she tried to sweep away Johnny Briggs's smarmy appraisal, but was he right? Had she really sidestepped into a world that didn't fit a former head of a highly successful murder investigation team?

It wasn't that Ellis had pressurised her into anything. She had taken the jump from her high-ranking job as a police detective to becoming one half of Wilde & Darque completely of her own volition and it had been the right thing to do at the time. She was sure of that. But was the same true now? Would the day-to-day reality of her new world of wayward partners, insurance scams and corporate conundrums, resulting today in her being expected to dress up as an undercover giant cartoon pig, eventually be the death of her?

EIGHTEEN
WET AS FRESH BLOOD

W hen Tanko awoke, in a deep ditch, muddy walls rising up either side of him, he at first thought that he was dead and about to be buried, just like the girl with the tattooed arm. That's what the man with the machete and the others had been busy doing when Tanko and some of the others had made their escape.

Tanko blinked. The sun seemed to be shining down on him, unless this was what hell was like and at any minute the bright-yellow fireball above was about to rapidly descend and burn his soul for all eternity. Perhaps he hadn't escaped at all, but had dreamed the past few days? His mind might be playing tricks, as part of his transition from life to death.

Or maybe the Devil himself had created the scene of his small fellow prisoner crushed under the wheels of a huge lorry. Or Tanko's journey away from that terrible place, clinging on to the cold hard metal of a different lorry, the icy wind trying to tear his grip away, making him terrified that his fingers would freeze and that he too would drop under the wheels.

Had he imagined too, the rubbish skip, swinging dangerously through the air, the shouts of angry men accusing him of stealing, or seeing the skeleton face of death itself only inches away, as a rat had tried to nibble his leg?

The worst thing had been the attack by the boys that he had mistaken for friends, however. In his own country, only Boko Haram were the clear enemy of his people and had tried to kill them all, because the feared terrorist group were against any teaching of western culture, and in Tanko's old school they had been taught about being welcoming to all men and learned other languages in order to share their thoughts widely. But here, in a country that he had been brought up to think of as fair and just to all people around the world, it seemed that *everyone* was against him.

Tanko braced himself, closing his eyes tightly, fists clenched. Surely this was the end. The hot sun was going to bear down and scorch his body until it was only ashes, like a flame-breathing dragon. He could only hope that he would see his mother and father and all of his family very soon now, rather than have the Devil drag him down to his lair.

Tanko stayed in the pose for a minute or two, tension stiffening his body against the coming onslaught, until he felt a gentle breeze graze his face and a strange sound as though a rope was being swung around and around. He opened one eye, realising that the sound was coming from birds' wings. They were pale grey and sweeping close above the ground in circles which were becoming lower and lower. The movement entranced Tanko for a moment, taking his mind from death and destruction as with each graceful wide circle above his body, he watched as a pigeon broke free from the flock.

Twisting around to gingerly peek over the edge of the muddy trench, he noticed now that the birds were breaking away to enter their loft, an open hatch in a long wooden building which was across the patch of land behind him. Sitting up cautiously, he realised that he was in a vegetable patch rather than a graveyard. He had arrived at the spot the night before, exhausted and terrified and dropped into the trench neither knowing or caring if he was entering his own grave, but simply grateful for the feeling of peace and silence, save for a bird that he had recognised as an owl making its unmistakable call from the darkness of a clump of trees, which he now realised carried apples.

The view calmed his terror for a moment. Though the crops being grown here were different, his father had been a farmer, of yams and Guinea corn mostly, so arriving in cultivated land felt like something of a homecoming. Looking around, still crouched low, Tanko recognised from his school lessons, leeks and English potato leaves, swaying in the breeze and a patch of something known as rhubarb, the watermelon-pink stalks that he had tried with a crunchy topping called crumble, in the café at Freedom Angels. Finding it so delicious, he had then eaten the same dish every day for a week afterwards.

As the last three birds circled, Tanko was aware of a low whistling. He quickly squatted down again, his face in the dirt, holding his breath as he tried to listen out for someone approaching. Could he have been followed by the boys with sticks, creeping up right now on his hiding place?

'Here, birdie, here, birdie.' It was a man's voice and that same repeated whistle. Two of the birds broke free and headed towards the long low building with the open hatch and disappeared inside. The third pigeon, which Tanko now realised had a ring around one ankle, was perched on the side of the ditch, looking at him, its head on one side.

'Here, birdie. Here, Queenie.' The man gave a low whistle once more. The bird looked up as though listening before turning back to Tanko, its head on one side again, as though questioning what on earth he was doing hiding in the ditch.

The man whistled again, but the sound was more distant

now, as though he was moving away. Tanko couldn't actually see the figure due to the long grass and vegetables around him, but as he heard the call, 'Here, Queenie' once again, definitely fainter than before, he kneeled up. The bird fluttered back a little but then held its ground, observing him. Tanko gave a low whistle. He liked the fact that he could actually do that. At Freedom Angels his therapist had explained that in some places, like the island of La Gomera in the Canary Islands, which had high hills and valleys, people spoke in a whistling language, just like birds. So the fact that Tanko could whistle was a good sign and they had already practised whistling yes and no answers. The pigeon gave a low cooing sound, still staring at Tanko, who smiled, despite his nerves. It seemed as though he had made a small friend at last.

Gingerly, Tanko pulled himself to his feet, breathing in the smells of the foliage all around and the fresh clean air. He had been locked up inside before his recent escape, thinking that he might never breathe fresh air again. But this scenery was totally different to that which he had run away from, and he felt a small measure of safety surrounded by vegetables, growing tall and full of life. He gave another low whistle as he climbed out of the ditch. The man was nowhere to be seen and he wanted the pigeon named Queenie, it appeared, to get to the safety of its own home. Who knew what predators might be waiting to pounce if the man returned and locked the hatch closed, leaving it to fend for itself?

The pigeon hopped after Tanko, as he carefully manoeuvred around the plants, being careful not to damage them, whilst trying to lead the bird in the direction of the pigeon loft. Queenie dutifully hopped behind, until Tanko was only a few feet away from the loft, giving soft short whistles in the hope that the small creature realised that he was doing his best to protect, rather than harm it. Suddenly, as Tanko gave one last whistle, the pigeon took to the air and flew inside the open hatch, home at last.

Tanko sighed, relieved and yet also enveloped in a sudden crushing sadness at the shortness of his new friendship. As he turned, wondering in which direction to head next, he noticed a clear tunnel to his right. Inside, were pots full of strawberry plants. It was like a sign from the other side. Tanko's eyes filled with tears. His father, always keen to extend his knowledge about other countries and the crops grown around the world, had decided that strawberry plants could be grown on their family ground. No one else in the village had ever seen the plant before, but his father had always encouraged Tanko to try new things, to learn from others and so the original strawberry plants were finally sourced and were clearly happy with their new home alongside Tanko's family, as they grew like wildfire.

It was the strawberry plants, once sold, that had paid for Tanko's education. Regular donations by his father from every sale, had helped the upkeep of the local school. Tanko was attracted to the scene like a moth to a flame. Could it have been the innocent strawberries, non-native plants, however well they thrived in Nigeria, that had so incensed Boko Haram, causing them to raze both the school and village to the ground?

As he crept nearer, looking around to check that the man was nowhere in sight, Tanko could smell the sweet scent of the red strawberry fruits. Before he could stop himself he was inside the greenhouse, lifting a plant to his face. There seemed to be dozens of the bright-red jewels all around him, so many that he almost hoped to see his father standing behind him as he threw caution to the wind, grabbing a huge strawberry and holding it to his lips like a starving animal. In truth, that is exactly how he felt. The sweetness hit his tongue like a soothing balm, as though his father had his arm around him.

'Aye, aye. What's all this then?' A firm and loud voice had

Tanko spinning around in fright, caught in the act he realised, of stealing. He couldn't deny it. The juice of the fruit was as wet as fresh blood on his gloves and lips. The man looked stern, broad-shouldered and tall. A large hammer held in his hand. Tanko dropped to his knees; his hands held together in prayer, body trembling. He wished he could say something, though he could feel the familiar tightness in his throat, his heart hammering in his chest like someone banging a drum, knowing no words would come out. Could the man understand that he desperately wanted to beg for forgiveness?

NINETEEN
A DATE WITH HER DESTINY?

'I'm so sorry.' Billie raced into King & Beech Forensics, realising immediately that she had been too late to support Boo during the identification process of the three missing child asylum seekers. Her friend had seen a lot in her time, but her face was streaked with tears and etched with distress, having experienced this latest blow. 'Had I known earlier that Maya couldn't make it—'

Boo held out her hand to grasp Billie's. 'I wouldn't let her come and I'm glad I didn't. Those poor kids...' Boo took a deep sigh to steady her emotions. 'Maya's already experienced so much trauma at too young an age... the kids, they all had bruises around one ankle as though they had been shackled, Billie, and that was just for starters...' Boo's words trailed off as she shook her head.

'Billie, this is Matteo Scalera.' Josta had been walking a few steps behind with a tall, dark-haired man. Billie glanced up distractedly from Boo, before she did a double take. Josta's companion had the most striking hazel-coloured eyes framed by thick black lashes. He smiled and held out his hand to shake

Billie's own, those captivating eyes crinkling at the corners as he did so.

'Matt's just fine,' the man answered in perfect English, though his olive skin and easy charm, together with his name, denoted an Italian influence somewhere in his life. 'Billie Wilde, we meet at last...' He trailed off, biting his lower lip for a moment as he stared at Billie in a slightly unnerving way... a good way. Billie pushed that thought aside. 'I've been hoping to make your acquaintance for a very long time.'

'Matt's from the National Crime Agency.' Boo had cheered up for a moment. 'We go way back. We trained there together. He was with me when the old legs got flattened. It was him who got me to hospital in time and it was his bad taste in get well soon cards and cheer me up gifts, that finally got me out of bed and into a chair to escape his bedside manner,' Boo joked.

'So you know Ellis then too?' Billie smiled, as she took Matt's hand. It was smooth and warm. He shrugged. 'Long time ago. He was a good agent; I'll give him that.'

'Ha, no love lost between those two. A couple of alpha males together. You can imagine, Billie.' Boo rolled her eyes in amusement.

'But very different in our approaches.' Matt left his hand in Billie's for a beat longer than necessary for a first meeting, but Billie registered that she had been in no hurry to break the moment herself. 'I like to think I take a little bit of a more considered approach to each investigation.'

'I have coffees waiting in my room,' Josta boomed in her usual jolly manner, despite the seriousness of the occasion. 'Rest assured that I will take the very best care of my young charges and do my utmost to assist them to divulge their stories.' She sighed. 'Alas, so much sadness in the world these days.' Billie knew that Josta had faced down more than her fair share of it herself in recent years and had even disappeared for a while to deal with a murderous situation that had been too close to home – for Billie, as well as the eminent forensic pathologist.

'Matt was the NCA point of contact in Italy when Liz and I were working on the boat victims there.' Josta was referring to Lizbeth Beech, her new partner in the business as well as at home. 'So we couldn't have a greater expert with us, trying to track down the perpetrator of these latest atrocities.' Billie glanced at Matt again, realising that his gaze was still on her.

'So someone *is* actually dealing with this madness of kids being dumped in hotels around the UK, then being kidnapped to God knows where?' Billie was relieved. She had begun to think that there was some high-level cover-up. The situation hadn't even popped up in newspapers or on TV, which would have been utterly unimaginable if a pile of British kids had first been left in a strange country to fend for themselves and then secondly been spirited away en masse. The fact that it was happening right here in the UK, without anyone outside of the charities dealing with asylum-seeking youngsters seeming to care, had been eating away at her. Matt nodded.

'Of course, but it isn't a job that the local police force are able to handle alone, or at all... not since you left your former employment.' Billie suddenly realised that Matt already knew about her. She imagined she had come up in conversation as the reason Boo herself had left the force soon after. Billie's team had been a tight-knit group, apart from one or two jokers hiding in the pack. Ash was the only one of Billie's former MIT team left working for the police nowadays.

'Stop beating about the bush, Matt.' Boo nudged him, before turning to Billie. 'Every time we have a catch-up call, Matt's been champing at the bit to get you to join them over at the National Crime Agency. He was straight on the blower the minute news reached the NCA that you had ditched the force, but I told him then that Ellis had already got you in his clutches.'

'Quite.' Matt shrugged with a look of regret on his face. 'He even put your name first in the joint enterprise, which shows the man's admiration for you. Believe me, when Ellis Darque is the man in question, that sort of gesture, means a lot.' Billie guessed that he was referring to more than just an appreciation of her investigative talents, on Ellis's part. Deep down, she knew that to be true, but until now she had stubbornly refused to acknowledge the fact.

'But who can blame him? Even when you're not on a case that is within NCA territory, you are there, right in the middle.' Matt was addressing Billie in admiration rather than rebuking her for overstepping the mark. 'Billie, the work that you did on the Columbian drugs syndicate and then the major trafficking ring, was astonishing.'

Matt was referring to the last case that Billie had been involved in as head of the MIT team and then a situation that she had inadvertently become involved in when a Wilde & Darque small-scale investigation had gotten entangled with the plans of a major international criminal gang.

Ellis, for one, had made it clear, thanks to the personal consequences for him, that he didn't want to have the company involved in such situations again. If it hadn't been for the high income offered by Porkie's Big Eats, Billie was well aware that Ellis was determined to steer their PI business into much calmer waters, snooping on small-scale scammers in love or finance. Billie tried to brush aside the fact that, during the long nights in her car, staking out the love nest of a wayward spouse, her soul was screaming out to run for the hills. It was at that moment that both Matt and Josta's mobiles rang together. Both stepped back, listened, spoke a few words and then ended the call exchanging glances.

'I'm afraid I must leave you lovely people. Put please avail yourself of the coffee and biscuits in my room. I'll get my kit, then follow me, Matt. I know the location,' Josta advised. Billie felt a pull to follow them both. If Matt was involved, then Josta's call-out must be to another suspicious death related to the missing children. Boo had clearly been thinking the same.

'Not another one of the kids?' she asked in horror.

'I'm afraid it could be very likely, my dear.' Josta patted Boo's shoulder. 'A farmer has just rang in to say that his tractor has had a run-in with a child, non-Caucasian appearance, who for some reason was in his field. It's a bit of a conundrum as to why the child was in situ. Clearly the farmer's praying that the boy was already deceased when his body came into contact with his vehicle.' Boo slapped her hand to her mouth as though she might be sick.

'I'll have to get back to Freedom Angels. This is unbearable.'

'I'll drive you.' Billie could see that Boo was in no fit state to do so.

'Thanks, I'll just go get my stuff...' Boo turned her power chair and headed off to the waiting-room area, where Billie presumed she had left her coat and bag. Her mobile buzzed at that moment. It was a text message from Ellis. *Got someone to cover the Porkie costume but it'll be free again in twenty minutes, if you can drag yourself away from whatever is more important than Wilde & Darque biz.*

Billie knew Ellis was being terse due to the stressful situation regarding Connie, as well as for her own less than polite refusal to do the job earlier. She guessed that she would have been equally annoyed. She had been out of order. Wilde & Darque was her PI company not just Ellis's, after all. But she always did her fair share where work was concerned and it wasn't her fault that Ellis flatly refused to engage in any conversation about Freedom Angels, so that she couldn't tell him why she had better things to do than arse around a shop floor wearing the bloody big pig suit.

'Bad news for you too, huh?' Matt had his car keys at the ready as he waited for Josta to collect her crew and equipment. Billie imagined actually telling him the ridiculous job that she was about to head off to do, whilst he was going to the tragic scene of another dead young person. She simply shrugged instead, suddenly feeling that her issues were so trivial, that it would be disrespectful to the newly deceased child to even mention Porkie's Big Eats in the same conversation.

'I'd really like to talk to you some more, Billie. I'm sure it's already clear that I really admire your work. I'd certainly value your insight into this latest case. Ears on the ground are everything and I know I shouldn't really say this, but the current law enforcement team I visited today are so out of their depth, that they're clearly more than happy to leave it all to the agency. But I'm only in town for one night...' Matt trailed off for a moment, thoughtfully. Billie didn't know if she wanted to be with him or wanted his job. Maybe both.

'We've been investigating a similar situation involving hostels for child asylum seekers, over the border in Scotland, so not under English jurisdiction, but this is the first case in the north-east of England. We could do with a good contact here. We desperately need new information that might just help us catch the people involved with this. Look, there's a lovely Italian restaurant in town, Cucina's. Do you know it? Arancini to die for. I visit every time I'm in this area as my cousin owns it. Will you meet me there at seven?'

Billie did know the restaurant. She loved it, but even if she had detested the place, she simply couldn't refuse. She immediately swept away the thought that had just seconds before passed through her mind, that she would offer to swap with Ellis tonight, infiltrating the animal rights group once again, to make up for refusing to play the pig earlier.

'You'll share confidential details about the case with me? Is that allowed in the NCA?' Billie raised an eyebrow.

'I think I can make an exception for you, Billie Wilde. In fact, I should actually be moving on this evening. But for you, I'll gladly delay.' Matt smiled as he walked away to assist Josta, now emerging back into the hallway, loaded down with kit.

Billie felt her heart do a little flip, despite her attempt at a businesslike attitude. She desperately wished that she was going the same way as Matteo Scalera and it wasn't just in order to solve this spate of heinous crimes, no matter how much she tried to argue with her inner voice. The truth was a whole lot more overwhelming than even that, and right now, she couldn't exactly make sense of the overwhelming feeling that she was about to have a date with her destiny.

TWENTY

BACK FROM THE DEAD

'You're not one of those fellas that've been stealing my leeks, are you?' Tanko was huddling in fear behind a bunch of tall tomato plants now, at the back of the greenhouse, where he had skittered on hands and knees, worried about the heavy hammer in the man's hand.

'I can see you back there. Come on out. Has the cat got your tongue?'

Tanko stared wide-eyed at the man as he stepped nearer. He was old, so at a push Tanko felt that he might be able to jump up and shove past him without being hit by the hammer, but what if the man fell and hit his head? A sudden vision cut across Tanko's mind's eye of an old man lying dead on the ground, back home in Nigeria after one Boko Haram incursion, blood pooling out underneath his body. Tanko felt his entire body shudder at the memory. He simply wanted to get out of here alive, but the man, he was wearing a beret similar to Nigerian troops. Was he in the army, also carrying a gun maybe?

The old man frowned, bending forward to peer through the tomato plants, placing his hammer down on a table in the middle of the room, scattered with plant pots and soil. 'It's all right, son. You don't look like a leek-show type. Been some skulduggery I can tell you, with the vegetable competition next week. Sabotage. I was just worried that you were one of those lot...' The man bent nearer. 'Is that blood on your face? Have you cut yourself, son?'

Tanko swallowed hard, sensing that the man was kind and meant no real harm but had mistaken the strawberry juice on his face for something more sinister. The picture of the old man lying in a lake of blood shot through Tanko's mind again, as he wiped his hand over his face. Then he had an idea. He quickly pulled off his new leather gloves and carefully moved out from behind the tomato plants, placing the gloves together on the ground. Trembling, he held out his hand, hoping the old man would realise that he was offering a gift rather than only wanting to steal.

'I can't take those, son. By the look of you and the footprints in my potato ditch there, you've been sleeping here all night. Must have been nippy.'

Tanko nodded, his head down, large brown eyes gazing up. He was sorry for his theft of the man's produce. He remembered when Boko Haram had first arrived in his village, torn up his father's strawberries and then burned them. He knew how bad he had felt on that day. He reached for the gloves, stretched out his arm and tried his peace offering again. It was all he had. It was all that he could give. The man clearly realised how important the gesture was to Tanko, as he finally took the dark leather gloves with the one charm missing, from the boy's hands.

'Well, if you insist. Thanks, son. A dapper pair of mitts these are. Are you sure you want to part with them?' Tanko nodded again. He needed the man to know that he had come in peace. 'My name's Jimmy. What's yours?' He held out his thin gnarled fingers to grasp Tanko's hand and shook it. Tanko felt as though he was going to cry. It was as though he was holding the hand of his father, who had also been lost in that first massacre back in his home village. He couldn't say his name.

'Still a bit shy, son? Here, see if you can write it down. I've got a scrap of paper somewhere here and a pencil for marking up my plants.' The man was holding on to Tanko's hand, pulling him upright. 'Once we've been properly introduced, then we can have a bit of breakfast together whilst I wait for my other group of birds to come back. They were competing yesterday, flying all the way to France...'

Tanko knew the place; he had not long ago come from there. He had wanted to tell the man that he wished that he too could just take flight like a bird and cross over country borders without fear. He wished that he and all of his family could have done exactly that on the day that Boko Haram first came to his village, then everything would have been different today.

Tanko took the stump of a pencil from Jimmy's bony hand and wrote his name on the paper, realising that it was the first time he had actually written since his school had been burned down. *Tanko Abubakar*, he wrote, which was the name given to him at birth, though circumstances had forced him to take other names since that day of the village massacre.

'Ah, Nigerian lad, are you? My father fought in Burma with the Nigerian Forces. 81st West Africa Division. He said they were the best lads he ever teamed up with. Battled like lions and they could march carrying all of their stuff on their heads. They were tough, he said.'

Tanko felt his heart leap. His own great-grandfather had fought in the Second World War with British troops in Burma. His tales of bravery had been legendary, stories passed down through the generations. Tanko shoved his hand inside his shirt, bringing out a wodge of photos that had been secured in the waistband of his tracksuit bottoms, as the man called Jimmy looked on patiently. Rifling through, Tanko proudly brought out a photo of his great-grandfather in uniform. Tanko held his hand to his breast as he handed it to Jimmy.

'Aye! That's the West African Division uniform. Part of the Royal West Africa Frontier Force they were. Not that they got any thanks for it afterwards mind you. I was out in Nigeria myself on secondment, during the disbanding in 1960 leading to independence. Had some good times in your country, son.' Jimmy nudged Tanko playfully and winked as he handed the photo back to the boy.

'I hear the British lads are back out there on the quiet even now, helping to train your boys to fight Boko Haram, though I believe that there's been argy-bargy on both sides. The word is that government forces are as much of a headache as the rebels. They are never straightforward, these wars, my son. Never a simple case of good men against evil ones, like you see in the old films. Personal agendas on both sides and it's the poor people in the middle who have to suffer.'

As Tanko tried to push his photo collection securely back in place in the elastic of his waistband, two photos fell out onto the floor. One showed Tanko, his sisters, father and mother. The other, his grandparents and the great-grandfather who had just been seen in the army photo. He had still been alive aged a hundred that last time that Tanko had seen him. Tanko reached down to sweep up his precious photos from the soil-strewn floor, pulling his finger across his neck in a slicing action, before pointing to first one photo then the other. Jimmy nodded in a show of understanding, his face grim as he held his own hand to his heart.

'All gone, son, eh? I'm sorry to hear that. It sounds like you've had one hell of a journey to get this far. Come on over to the bench next to the loft. I've got a nice hot flask of tea there and some corned beef sandwiches. Got a couple of egg ones too, if by chance you're a bit picky that way.'

Jimmy put his arm around Tanko. It felt like a friendly embrace, though Tanko hadn't experienced many of those recently. He reckoned the old man was also partly balancing himself on Tanko's young but strong shoulders, in case he fell over on the uneven ground, given his age and bearing.

In some ways this elderly man reminded Tanko of his great-grandfather. He too had been proud yet kind. He certainly hadn't deserved an end to his life in the manner it had come, or so painfully. Tanko could still see quite clearly in his mind's eye, that look of terror and complete disbelief in the ancient man's eyes, when the machete had sliced across his skinny throat. His great-grandfather's eyes had stayed open and staring as Boko Haram had swept out again, leaving utter devastation behind.

Tanko wiped a tear away from his face as this old man who felt like his great-grandfather coming back from the dead, settled him down kindly, rug tucked across his knees against the morning chill, offering him food and drink, whistling softly for his winged travellers to fly back to him. Perhaps, Tanko hoped, his luck had finally changed. Could he have found a true friend at long last?

TWENTY-ONE
TRUE TO HERSELF

'It's as though some people have their lives mapped out to be a disaster.' Boo was checking her face in the passenger mirror of Billie's car, as they neared Freedom Angels.

'I mean, it doesn't seem to matter what these poor kids do, sometimes almost superhuman acts of bravery to get to safety and freedom and then something even worse is waiting to knock them back. Even in places like England, where everyone seems to think they are just on a jolly jaunt to live an easy life.'

'It's a good job they've got charities like Freedom Angels to support them,' Billie pointed out. Where's the Home Office whilst all this is going on, I want to know?' Billie turned the corner at speed, anger surging in her body once again.

'The truth is no one cares if they go missing or end up in a grave somewhere. One less mouth to feed,' Boo answered through a sigh. 'It makes me so mad, Billie, but it's also made me understand clearly that this is my mission in life, to do my best for kids in these circumstances. I mean, I've been a bit lost over the past few years, what with my accident and having to work in the office most of the time, rather than out there in the middle of all of the action–'

'But you were the best MIT office manager in the business,' Billie argued. 'God knows how many extra lives have been saved by you kicking butt and making sure that interviews were completed and filed correctly, and that the team delivered on time. In fact, sometimes I reckoned that it was you keeping the whole show on the road. I can't think of anyone better to be running Freedom Angels.'

'Thanks for the vote of confidence, it means a lot, and of course for the massive donation to Freedom Angels. But what about you? I'm sensing that Wilde & Darque isn't turning out to be the great saving grace that you felt it would be when you jumped ship from the MIT.'

'Maybe you're right,' Billie replied. 'But I can't let Ellis down.'

'You can't live Ellis's life for him either, Billie. I saw that look in your eyes when Matteo was talking... envy, it was.' Boo suddenly grinned. 'With maybe a dollop of lust thrown in, am I right?' She nudged Billie, chuckling now. 'You can't hide it from me, girl. Women have always lusted after Matt, but he's very discerning, I'll give him that. He was a good friend at a time when I was desperately in need of one, that's for sure and he rates you highly. I mean for your work as well.' Boo chuckled again as Billie rolled her eyes.

'Fair enough that Ellis feels the need to slow down, now he's got the girls to look out for, but Maya needs space to find her own direction and maybe you do too. Remember, I know Ellis from old. He's got a forceful personality, but don't let it overshadow your own shining light, Billie.' It wasn't the first time Billie had been given words of wisdom on the subject today, albeit she was much more likely to take note of her dear friend Boo's advice than Johnny Briggs's, but the feeling of being unwittingly drawn into a mummy and daddy scenario with Connie had been getting to her lately. As her mind turned to children once again, she thought of the hotel for the unaccompanied child asylum seekers and decided to have a look at the place for herself.

'Just down here is it, the hotel that the kids stay in?' she asked, turning the car to the right as she slowed down along a street of ramshackle mid-Victorian terraces.

'Yeah, down here. Next turn on the left.' Boo gazed out of the window. 'Hang on. What now?' She frowned as Billie turned the car into a similarly run-down street, in which young people were scattering, alarm etched on their faces as a large black van, passenger door still partly open, sped out of the other side of the road. Billie immediately clocked that it had no number plate on the back. One of the teenagers ran towards Billie's car, flagging it down. She clearly recognised Boo.

'You must help us, you must help us.' The teenager was of Middle Eastern appearance, wearing a dark headscarf, as she earnestly leant forward, as soon as Billie wound down her window. 'She's gone, please help us.' The girl held her hands together in a praying motion.

'Who's gone?' Boo leaned forward in her seat.

'It's Safia. When she left, to go to Freedom Angels, the men wearing dark masks were waiting in that van. They jumped out and dragged her inside.' The girl looked towards the end of the street.

'And now they have gone and so has Safia.'

'Looks like they're going round the block, I'll try and head them off.' Billie was out of the car and halfway back up the street, even as she finished her sentence. Veering sideways into a garden attached to a side terrace, she raced across the lawn, over the low brick wall at the back and almost landed in front of the black van, the driver of which slammed on his brakes, momentarily. It was enough for Billie to grab hold of the passenger door, which was still partly open. Not any longer, as she pulled it wide and made a grab for the dark puffer jacket of a youngish white man, just lifting up his balaclava. Billie could see the muscular driver was still wearing his, such was the hurry to get away.

'Drop her!' the driver shouted, as they approached the end of the back lane and the start of the busy main road, but Billie was hanging on for dear life, even though the driver had put his foot down on the accelerator now. Billie could hear banging and screaming from the sealed container at the back. It was Safia's panicked voice.

Billie lunged across to the handbrake and tried to pull it on. The van jerked and spun, lifting her off her feet at the same moment that the driver reached with one hand behind his seat, bringing out a baseball bat. The passenger grabbed it from his hand, smacking Billie across the head with it, in exactly the same spot that she had been hit with the dustbin lid only the night before. She finally lost her grip, rolling over to avoid being hit by the back wheels of the van as it righted its course before careering out onto the main road. Then it was gone.

Billie sat up, winded, dabbing her hand on her bleeding wound. It hurt, but not as much as the loss of the children and now rising star Safia. Her heart almost broke at the realisation. The girl had so much to look forward to. Billie brushed herself down, annoyed that she'd just lost out on saving her, from... what? Safia would fight against any incarceration like a demon, Billie knew that. She was feisty, just like the girl with the tattooed arm who had as a result, no doubt, been murdered and dumped in a ditch. The same fate might now face Safia. Billie could hardly bear to think of it.

She made the decision then and there, that she couldn't go on being a bystander in life when acts of such outright evil were taking place right under her nose. She knew that her decision was going to put her at loggerheads with Ellis, but if she didn't stop reacting instead of taking action at injustice and cruelty, then she knew that her own life would shape up to be one long disaster. At the end of the day, she could only be true to herself. Now was the time to set out on the path that was right for her, not anybody else.

TWENTY-TWO

TELLING PORKIES

E llis was sweating like a hog in the damn Porkie's pig mascot suit. He could have done without it, but Wilde & Darque already had all of their casual operatives in place at every other outlet in the area. Undercover bakers in the twenty-four-hour back-of-shop bakery spaces, undercover giant Porkie's pig mascots on the other shop floors. If everyone was on their mettle, then nothing sinister could creep through without them either eyeballing the suspect pie or the dicey person. The whole shebang was costing an arm and a leg which is why Ellis had originally agreed to leave Porkie's Big Eats's usual security guy in place here, at their flagship shop. Now see where it had gotten him, wearing the damn suit himself, when the security guy had pulled a sickie and Billie had pulled a strop.

Luckily he had at least squared things up with Billie and had insisted on stepping into the sweat-suit himself. He'd apologised for being a bit antsy after the run-in with the bleeding social worker from the funny acronym division, CAFCASS or whatever it was, but he could see that Billie must have been under pressure herself to have been so stroppy earlier. He'd seen her giving short shrift in her time, to the odd rabble-rouser, and then some – he chuckled to himself as he mentally pictured some of those scenes – but never him.

No question about the fact she'd been stressed, when he had spotted her running up the street for their rendezvous in the café, to sort out their beef and then spotted another whopping big wound on her head. God, how he had wanted to take her in his arms, brush away that amazing red hair flying behind her in the wind, and kiss her beautiful face better. Of course, he couldn't do that. Not right now, when she had already told him to bugger off once that day. He smiled at the thought. But maybe one day. Well, at least he could hope.

He'd let her tell the whole sorry story about the kids and the clash with the lowlifes who had taken the older girl. Of course, she'd had to go and report it to the cop shop. Teenager gone AWOL. He told Billie not to worry about not having gone straight over to Porkie's to step into the suit, when she had finally stopped talking, that was, and let him get a word in. She'd refused his offer to run her to A and E, to check out her head. He didn't know why he'd even asked. No question she would agree to go that way.

Sickened him to the core that did, the kiddie hotel business, especially after what Maya had been through with a trafficking gang less than a year before. *That's* why he didn't want Maya mixed up with the Freedom Angels place. That whole experience last year had changed her, Ellis was sure of it, though his girl had tried to keep up a brave face and had insisted on helping Boo set up the refugee centre.

His heart broke for the kids caught up in the whole asylum-seeking deal, but he'd been in the undercover game half of his life and was well aware that amongst those genuinely desperate people, there were truly evil bastards lurking under the cover of innocence. He didn't want his Maya anywhere near that. He didn't want Boo or Billie involved either, truth be known. That's why he gave the whole place a wide berth.

Billie might look as hard as steel, Ellis reflected, but she was as soft as butter inside. He'd seen it often enough when she had been tucking Connie into bed, reading her a story, kissing her goodnight. She had her wild side though, that was for sure, and he'd already made clear at the start, *that* would get her into trouble, if she didn't think hard about getting so involved with this Freedom Angels malarkey.

The whole business got him riled up inside. If Billie hadn't had the hots for the guy who had offered the other donation of dosh needed to set up the place, then she wouldn't be in this situation. Freedom bloody Angels wouldn't have existed at all without his input, playing the big guy, trying to impress Billie. But Ellis tried not to dwell on that.

He had put his foot down on one point though. Insisted that Billie head back to the office to sort out the work rota for the coming week. God knows that would give her a headache too, but she had been looking as white as a sheet and he didn't want her keeling over on this shop floor. Not after what had happened yesterday with the old woman on the very same spot.

They needed to keep this whole shebang low-key from now on, until the week was up and they had worked out if what they had on their hands was just a crazy joker, or a serious threat. Word from the head office at Porkie's Big Eats was that they'd checked out the staff on the admin side of things, and hadn't found anyone suspect, so if the danger was in-house generated, then the bakery or shop floor would have to be where any incriminating business happened.

Ellis had been standing here for an hour now, watching people coming and going, trying to not run over the conversation that he'd had with the formidable Ethel Rutherford. He couldn't believe these people were even *thinking* of allowing his little Connie anywhere near his crazy ex-wife, Storm Benbow, especially as no one had heard a squeak out of her for nearly a year.

She could have been dead and buried, for all anyone had known until now, having been in bed with a major criminal. A criminal who had tried to take Ellis's head off. He absent-mindedly rubbed his ear, half of it now missing due to that run-in. The fact that Storm wasn't six feet under or fish food, said a lot to Ellis, because in his experience true innocents didn't survive long in such circles. No sign of her giving a toss about Connie in all that time. He'd made that fact loud and clear to Mrs Do-gooder, who rambled on about Storm having been ensconced in a women's refuge, because of abusive treatment from a *number of men.*

Ellis had recounted that bit to Billie. In his opinion, Storm was every bit as abusive as her ugly boyfriend and both of them had been hellbent on taking Connie away from him, just for spite. Well, it wasn't going to happen.

Ellis remembered his current role as Porkie the pig and started waving cheerily whilst bobbing up and down on his trotters, when a little girl came into the shop with her mum. The kid reminded him of his little one. Looked like it was her first day at school too. Same uniform as Connie. He watched the two like hawks as the Porkie's Chocolate Pie was purchased for the small girl. If he caught anyone trying to slip anything in a kids' product he would be taking no prisoners. End of.

As he exchanged another wave with the little girl, now heading towards the exit with her mum, he breathed an inwards sigh of relief that Maya had made contact by text, telling Ellis that she would pick Connie up from school today. It wasn't exactly full of flowery language or kisses, nor Maya's *Love you Dad x* signature, that his eldest daughter usually sent him. The one that always made his heart flip as he responded in kind. But she was a good kid really and they would get over the little bump that they were currently experiencing.

If she dropped that oik that she was hanging around with pronto, Ellis reckoned, that would help matters. Bit of a shock when he had come face to face with the two of them having been doing God knows what upstairs in his place, but he knew that if he pushed her on the subject she would only become more stubborn. She'd learned a lot from Billie Wilde when she had been training with her for that short time in MIT, Ellis thought, smiling to himself. Maybe picked up some of Billie's feisty characteristics which was no bad thing, when push came to shove.

It was as Ellis was thinking about Maya that he caught sight of a child running past the window of Porkie's Big Eats. A couple of fairground-type rides had been constructed that morning in the public square immediately in front of the window and as he moved nearer, Ellis realised that it was indeed his young daughter Connie, heading for a horse-ride carousel. He smiled when he spotted Maya walking behind, waving at her little sister. Keeping an eye on her, Ellis was pleased to see.

The carousel moved again, blocking Ellis's view, as people milled in front and around at this busy time of day. He could still see Maya standing but now the roundabout was moving faster. Ellis frowned, unable to see Connie at all. He hoped that Maya would catch her little sister and move her back to a safe distance. He remembered well getting hit on the head when someone's boot flew off an identical ride when he was a little kid.

Suddenly, as the man pushed a lever forward the colourful horses rose into the air, as though galloping up and down above the heads of the crowd as the roundabout started to spin faster. Surely Connie wasn't on there *alone*? Ellis felt his heart beating fast as he headed for the door. He pushed past two disgruntled workmen tucking into their Porkie's pies, stepping onto the outside pavement. He suddenly spotted Connie at last, following the direction of Maya's waving hand. His heart leapt into his throat before the roundabout came back full circle now and he realised that a woman was sitting on a horse next to Connie. For a split second, Ellis felt relief wash over him. He knew that he was overprotective, particularly at the moment. Clearly a friend of Maya's was ensuring that Connie was safe.

'Hey, Mister Porkie, can we have our picture taken with ya?' A group of young scallywags, fresh out of school and full of energy, made silly poses around him as Ellis lifted his hand to wave, in a rather comical attempt to attract Connie's attention. As the carousel came back around again, the dark-haired woman, who until now, had her head bent down against Connie's fair hair, suddenly looked straight towards Ellis in Porkie character and pointed, mouthing the words, 'Look! Wave to Porkie Pig!' To Ellis's absolute shock, the woman pointing straight at him, her arm around his precious Connie, was her dangerous blood mother, Storm Benbow.

Ellis set off in a race across the square, impeded by the huge heavy suit he was wearing, pushing people out of the way who were either disgruntled or amused by the sight of a giant pig legging it across the pavement on less than stable trotters. The boys chased after him taking photos on their mobiles, full of laughter as Ellis poked the carousel operator in the back. The man spun around, rather startled to be faced by a giant pig.

'Stop it!' Ellis shouted, his voice a loud muffle through the heavy fabric.

'Wha...?' The man frowned.

'I said stop that bloody carousel right now.' Ellis probably missed the whole kit and caboodle of having a police identity card on him less than Billie did, but he desperately wanted to pull one out of his pocket at this moment. Instead, he tried to yank the lever himself, unable to get a proper grip in his suit, as the operator tried to wrestle the control from his hand.

'Stop it. Someone is going to get hurt!' the carousel operator shouted back. 'Hey, police!' The man beckoned desperately in the direction of two police officers, holding Porkie's pies in their hands, as though they had been planning on heading for a rest stop. 'Help, police!' the man shouted louder. Ellis yanked his Porkie's pig head off, starting to unzip the suit as the police officers marched over.

'What's going on here?' The female officer tried to look stern.

'I want my daughter off this thing. It's dangerous!' Ellis shouted. He could see Maya staring at him in horror. It was nothing to the red mist that was descending upon him right now. How long had his daughter been in some sort of cahoots with his ex, taking Connie to meet her, God knows where or when?

'No, it isn't,' the carousel operator protested, taking a certificate out of a little door next to the control lever. 'I just had the safety inspection check this morning. It's as sound as a pound.' The man held his certificate for the police officers and members of the public, mobiles out, now filming the spat.

'I think this man wants me to charge you with telling porkies, sir...' The policewoman put the emphasis on the word *porkies*, trying to mask a grin, as she addressed Ellis. The surrounding crowd, gathering now, cheered at the small joke. Ellis pushed past them, as the carousel slowed down to a stop. Maya was fast approaching one of the painted horses to help Connie off.

'Leave her!' Ellis marched over to the ride, lifting Connie off in one sweep, holding her close to him. 'What the hell do you think you are playing at, Maya?' Ellis snapped at his oldest daughter.

'Just letting her see her own mum,' Maya answered sullenly. 'I mean, I know what it's like to not have a mum. I don't think it's fair to–'

'Yeah, well let me tell you that *you,* young lady, didn't have a mother like this piece of work.' Ellis was standing across from Storm Benbow now, who was about to alight from the carousel.

'How would you know? Maya tells me that you never hung around long enough to find out. Funny how you want to play the devoted father now.' Storm sneered at Ellis. The two police officers had started dispersing the crowd. One of them looked across, the one who actually thought that they were funny.

'Hey, you lot. You've had your rasher of fun. If you want to have a domestic, take it back to your pigsty right now, or we'll be marching you all down to the cop shop,' the officer bellowed loudly, amused with herself.

'In my opinion you should be marching *her* down to the cop shop.' Ellis was staring Storm out now. 'Don't give me that innocent lover crap, Storm. You forget I *know* you.'

'Yep, and I know your secrets too, Mr Darque. I know you're not Mr Clean-Cut, much as you want to play that part these days. I know where the bodies are buried, remember that.' Storm kept his gaze, with a smirk on her lips.

'Here, take Connie home, Maya,' Ellis ordered, tight-lipped.

Maya shook her head. 'No. I'm not coming near you. Look at everyone filming, you look ridiculous. You'll be all over the web by now. You're an embarrassment.' Maya's eyes were smarting with tears. 'In fact, I'm ashamed of you.' Maya turned and pushed her way out of the crowd.

'Maya?' Ellis shouted after her. Maya broke into a jog.

'She doesn't want anything to do with you, can't you see that?' Storm goaded. 'Dressed in a bloody pig suit, trying to drag your little daughter off a fairground ride, for God's sake, Ellis. The sooner the kid is back with me the better.'

'Okay, let's break it up, the show is definitely over.' The female police officer was still herding the crowd away, whilst the other was gently moving Ellis back, Connie still in his arms.

'She's never coming back to you. So get that idea out of your evil little brain,' Ellis shouted over the head of the police officer, as he moved back a few steps.

'I want my mummy!' Connie started to wail tearfully, wrapping her arms tightly around Ellis's shoulders.

'Don't worry, she doesn't mean *you*.' Ellis angrily pointed his finger in Storm's direction, not resisting being propelled slowly further back by the officer. He was in no mood to get closer. Not knowing what he might feel like doing, he inwardly decided. Storm gave a disparaging smirk in response, suddenly holding her mobile in the air for him to see.

'That's what my little girl's telling me loud and clear on camera. I've caught your whole crazy outburst here, when all I was doing was giving my daughter a lovely time. I'll be sending the evidence of your abusive behaviour over to Ethel Rutherford pronto, so kiss goodbye to custody, loser.'

TWENTY-THREE
KILL OR BE KILLED

'You win again, clever lad!' Jimmy sat opposite Tanko at a low coffee table in his neat but sparsely furnished living room in his bungalow. 'It's an age, mind you, since I've played mancala chess. You tidy the stuff up now, while I get us a cuppa and some sandwiches for our tea. If I'm not mistaken, I've still got a few slices of cake in the tin, that my good friend Billie brought to bingo last week.'

The old man's smile was wide as he heaved his body upright, still wearing his army-style beret and steadying himself on the walls of the room, as he hobbled towards the kitchen at the back of the small low house. Tanko held his hands together in thanks. He was feeling much better now, having helped Jimmy to whistle his birds back home. Tanko liked the high notes that he could still create and hoped that the more he practised whistling, the more he would be able to open his throat and make a proper sound, then perhaps even whole words once more.

Jimmy had rummaged in an understairs cupboard for what must have been hours, Tanko reflected. It seemed to have been so, as he had fallen asleep on the old man's sofa, late in the morning after having been invited to his home and Jimmy had still been rummaging when Tanko had awoken again to a darkening sky outside and a warm fire burning in the grate.

A grey blanket had been laid over his body, which made Tanko feel safe and grateful for such kindness. He'd been startled awake by the clatter of more belongings being dragged out of storage until Jimmy had triumphantly held up the box holding the mancala game. 'I got this when I was stationed in Nigeria in the forces, all those years back. Now I've got someone who actually knows how to play it with me, I'm not giving up that chance.'

To Tanko, that showed a man with grit and determination, even at his advanced age and compassion too, because of course he would have been well aware that Tanko would feel at home playing mancala, the ancient game of North Africa, in which wooden balls are 'sown' around a game board with long rows of carved-out pits sunken within it.

Tanko had started playing this game when he had been a baby. Then, he and his friends had made the pits with their fingers in the dirt outside of his house and used seeds, or small stones rather than these rather smart carved balls. In fact, Tanko had been the local champion in this game of cleverness and complex strategy, not unlike chess in the guile needed to win. After all, the sport was bred into him. He had lots of experience of sowing crops right there on his father's land. As he had grown older, he had actually owned a beautifully carved mancala set that had been his pride and joy, gifted to him by his great-grandfather, but alas, as with so many other things precious to him, he had to leave that behind in the race to leave his homeland.

One of the things that Tanko had been most grateful for was

that after exhausting all attempts to get him to speak, to tell Jimmy where exactly he had come from today and what horrors might have caused him to stay so tight-lipped, the old man had accepted that for now at least, Tanko simply could not tell him everything. Yet, instead of telephoning the authorities to take him away, he had invited him to stay anyway. He could only hope that the man didn't change his mind. Tanko knew that he could never totally relax wherever he was. Maybe never again.

'You know, son, I had the same thing as you myself a few years back. That's why I got discharged from the army. Got struck dumb for a good while. Shock trauma. Used to call it shell-shock back in the Second World War. Hit me after the Falklands fiasco. I was a forward observer, responsible for directing artillery fire into enemy positions. Front line it was. Hand to hand combat to claim Mount Longdon, I'm talking about fists and bayonets.

'Most of our lads had never even known where the Falklands were before that, but in the dead of night, even now, over forty years later, when I wake up in a hot sweat, I'm back on Mount Longdon, looking into a young lad's eyes as I stick a bayonet right through his stomach. Shame it's a real memory, rather than a nightmare. He'd been a conscript no doubt, like most of them. Just a kid. He called out for his mama.'

Tanko had watched tears fill up in Jimmy's eyes. 'He called out for his mama, and I was the one who stopped him ever seeing her again. I'd like to say he was the only one, but he was just the first. Plenty of our lads bit the dust the same way, mind you.'

Tanko held his hand to his heart, to show sympathy for his new old friend's grief. Jimmy patted Tanko's shoulder in thanks, as he tried to gather himself, before continuing to speak.

'They love to make a song and dance of it back in Blighty,

the nuts and bolts of who did what in the middle of wars and suchlike. Whether this killing or that one, was technically legal or not, but out there in the bloody middle of it, the madness, the screaming, the guts and the shit, the plain fact is you have to kill or be killed.'

Tanko had reached out and put his hand over the old man's then, because he realised that someone else understood what it felt like to be in the middle of a version of hell whilst the rest of the world went about their business as though it was nothing to do with them. The picture in his mind's eye of his one-hundred-year-old great-grandfather lying on the ground after he had been kicked over, Tanko cradling his skull like a broken bag of pottery in a thin leather bag, before the slash across his throat, his blood spattering up onto Tanko's face, still tormented him every single day. But he could have done nothing to stop that. Boko Haram could not be reasoned with.

'People say today, "You were a hero, Jimmy. You still keep a stiff upper lip about it all now. Never brag about your exploits, despite your medals." But I'm not proud of what I did, son, I stay schtum about it all because I can hardly live with the shame of the things I've done. My voice came back in the end, when I'd dossed down on the streets for long enough, not caring where I was heading.

'It was my dear departed wife who made me get a grip of myself, made me see that I would be doing a disservice to the dead by not speaking out when I still had the ability and others didn't. I thought of that lad when she said that. I thought I at least owed him that. He was the one who made me find my voice again in the end, even though I took away his. But him shouting for his mama in the mud and guts of Mount Longdon still comes back to haunt me every single night and I reckon it will do until the day I die.'

Tanko couldn't help but shiver at the thought. The man had just admitted to being a killer. He hoped that he didn't walk in his sleep and then imagine in his delirium that Tanko was the boy who had cried out for his mama, the boy that the man had felt the desperate need to murder.

TWENTY-FOUR
A SUCKER

'Yeah, well, as I keep on telling you, when Connie says "Mummy" she sure as hell isn't referring to Storm Benbow.' Ellis was pacing the floor at Wilde & Darque, on his mobile, having a heated difference of opinion with Ethel Rutherford, the social worker from the Children and Family Court Advisory and Support Service.

Billie had just had an ear-bashing herself from Graham Harper, demanding to know why his loveable brand mascot Porkie the pig had not only been photographed but videoed outside of Porkie's Big Eats flagship store, dragging a child from a fairground ride and refusing to hand her back to her mother. The resulting evidence was all over the web, apparently, and trending on X. Luckily the mascot suit was in a steaming heap on the office floor right now. Billie didn't really think she could cope with the visuals otherwise, not as Ellis had just kicked a wastepaper bin across the room in temper and had almost tripped over in the process.

Billie had an even worse thumping headache than when she had been smacked with the baseball bat. She rifled through the top drawer of her desk, hunting for any rogue headache pills that might be lurking in amongst the detritus. She reckoned the pain in her brain was more to do with the stress of getting absolutely no joy at her old police headquarters on rushing there to report Safia's kidnap, than the run-in with yesterday's dustbin lid or today's baseball bat.

Yes, the young officer had taken all of the details, albeit with a slightly detached air, asking for contact numbers for Safia's family, which was a joke as Billie had just explained the young girl's situation. Then she had asked if Safia had any friends, or boyfriends that she might have just run off with – despite Billie herself giving a witness account of the kidnap and having the scars to prove it. The young officer had simply droned on with the usual, bog-standard practised response, before saying that she would pass the report on to someone higher up. If they caught anyone in connection with Billie's attack, someone would be in touch. It wouldn't be her, as she was going on maternity leave the next day, baby shower tonight as soon as this goddamn endless shift finished. Blah de blah de blah. Billie had known that she was on a hiding to nothing.

Hardly anyone in a high-ranking post, whom Billie might have gone straight to with her urgent request to get onto the case and fast, was still around today. She sometimes felt like kicking herself for instigating such a big clear-out. Those of her close colleagues who hadn't been pushed out of the local force by the incompetent hit squad that had come in, had largely jumped anyway, not wanting to hang around with the new regime. Since then, there had been a regular turnover of staff who were in Billie's view, woefully incapable.

She had been certain that leaving the local police force was the right thing to do at the time. She had believed that historic cases of police corruption could be investigated independently without her having any influence on the outcome, seeing as she had been associated with some of those being investigated on a very personal level. But in truth, those probes had petered off to nothing very much, quickly swept under the carpet to allow the force to move on. Billie often felt when she lay awake in the dead of night, that nothing positive had ensued from her move into civvy street, at all.

Ellis had slammed his mobile down. 'She wants another bleeding meeting with Connie, straight after school tomorrow. Of course, Storm was on the blower pronto to her. I kept saying, when Connie says Mummy she means–'

'Yes, listen, Ellis, we've really got to put a stop to that. It's not fair on Connie–'

'What? It's not fair that she thinks someone like *you* is her mum, rather than that lowlife scumbag?'

'But Storm *is* her actual mum. I'm not. That's simply a fact.' Billie tried to keep her voice even, though she had been feeling more and more uptight about the situation, on behalf of Connie as well as herself. She hadn't heard Ellis put the child right, not in her hearing anyway, so far.

'You don't have to sound so pleased about it.' Ellis harrumphed. Billie hoped the ancient headache tablet that she had just sourced jammed in the back of the drawer would take effect soon. Boo had been able to get hold of Matt, at least, and his team were on the case. She couldn't wait to meet up with him later to find out what was happening, if she could find a way to wheedle it out of him, not being naturally privy to such details nowadays.

She could maybe give Matt a few ideas of her own. Billie gave a little inner smile at the thought; despite the level of stress she was experiencing about Safia. She could feel her headache lifting already. It had been a very long time since she'd had a date with a man and this wasn't your average bloke, she had been able to tell *that* for sure, even during their one, all too brief meeting.

'And Maya's taken the humph again. Stomped off, so she won't be babysitting tonight. I was lucky that I managed to get Connie back into after-school club, which is where I had arranged for her to be in the first place if people hadn't been going behind my back. Turns out this isn't the first time Maya's taken Connie to meet Storm either, not if what Mrs Busybody on the blower has just told me is right. Been on a couple of jolly jaunts behind my back...' Ellis rubbed his face in stress before suddenly checking his watch. 'That reminds me, I've got to go and pick her up any minute.'

Billie wondered if she could change the dinner date with Matt to earlier, like in an hour. That way she could quickly grab a bite, though in truth she wasn't feeling too hungry right now, get any useful intel out of him and then step in tonight, undercover with the animal rights activists again. This shift was Ellis's shout, by rights, but she'd now studied several online pics taken of the protest the night before, some featuring the main activist that she had chased. If they were there tonight, then Billie was determined to nab them. Either they had printed the banner that they had unfurled themselves, the one that had an identical phrase to that of one of Graham Harper's threats, or they would know who had. She wouldn't let go of them this time until they spilled.

Billie quickly texted Matt to make the request. She'd had it with this investigation and between Ellis's unexpected custody battle and her determination to track down the people blatantly kidnapping and murdering children who no one else seemed to care about, the two of them had enough on their plates, without Porkie's Big Eats. Frankly, Billie was sick to the back teeth of the damn pies.

To her relief, as well as secret delight, Matt responded immediately to confirm the time. Billie checked the clock. She had time to try and tidy up the congealed blood still on her face and at least change her top, thanks to the various undercover garments that they had stuffed in one of the cupboards. Ellis looked all in, the least that she could do was step in for him later.

'It's okay. I'll take the activists again tonight. You pick up Connie and get yourself home. She'll want to tell you all about her first day at school.' Billie headed for the cupboard. There were actually one or two nice tops in there, considering Cucina's, the Italian that Matt's relative owned, was considered a bit smarter than the average trattoria. She could always stick a wig, hoodie and mask on in the restaurant bathroom before slipping out. The square where the activists would be gathering again, outside of Porkie's Big Eats was just around the corner from Cucina's.

'No way,' Ellis protested. 'Not after the knock you've had. You know what they say about things coming in threes and that guy seems to know how to handle a bin lid. Absolutely no way.'

'Done deal, mate. No stopping me. They just caught me by surprise yesterday,' Billie tried to argue.

'Yeah, well I'll be giving him the big surprise today, you mark my words.' Ellis looked at Billie, his tense face showing a momentary look of tenderness. 'Could have finished you off if that old ginger nut of yours wasn't so hard.' He gave a cheeky grin. Billie was pleased to see him cheering up a little.

'Anyway, with all this Storm business I can't face just sitting still at home.' That was true, Billie noted, he had started pacing again, full of pent-up energy, his mind no doubt reflecting the various thoughts hurtling around his brain. 'In fact, I'll head back over to the square now, see if I can spot any of them getting set up before they stick their stupid masks on. You don't mind picking Connie up from after school club and taking her home, do you? Give her a bit of tea. With a bit of luck I'll be back before her bedtime, and you've got a much higher tolerance level for all those kiddie cartoons. I think you might even be hooked on them.'

'Er, no...' Billie started to argue and not only about her viewing choices. But Ellis was already out of the room and heading up the corridor as Billie left her seat.

'Get a takeaway pizza in,' Ellis shouted. 'Don't forget, ham and pineapple is Connie's favourite, though she's a sucker for any weird shit. Takes after her birth mother for that.'

TWENTY-FIVE
HOT ON HIS TAIL

The smell of Italian cooking enveloped Billie as she sat looking across a table, which was draped with a crisp white cloth, expensive china and sparkling glass, caught in the light of a single white candle. The sun was just starting to go down over the busy city street outside. Matt smiled as he finally picked up the menu.

'Is that my interrogation finished for the time being? You really should think about joining us in the National Crime Agency if your present business interest starts to lack lustre.'

'The glamour of it all you mean?' Billie waved her hand ironically in the direction of the double set of cuts and bruises, mostly hidden, thankfully, under her wild red hair hanging loose beyond her shoulders.

'Well, in the NCA we certainly do our fair share of crossing the globe visiting exotic locations. Many of them can also be deadly of course, but I see the fire in your eyes, Billie, for far-reaching projects rather than small-scale hurts and disputes. We believe the kidnapping gang here is part of a syndicate spreading across Europe and beyond. Our guess is that the sadly deceased children connected to Freedom Angels have been taken to a location somewhere in Scotland. It makes sense from a criminal perspective, muddying the waters of normal police investigations because of slightly different systems between the two nations.

'It's also less than two hours' drive north and though the bodies discovered so far have been located this side of the border, Josta has found certain stomach contents which correlate with plant life in particular locations in which we've been interested in the past. One of the many leads we're following is that a forgery network that we managed to smash up last year in another UK region may have reformed on Scottish soil. The street that we closed down was nicknamed Counterfeit Alley, in a location on the border of northern and southern Ireland in that case, selling high-end fakes—'

'I think I read about that.' Billie was in fact sure that she had seen the raid footage via video broadcasts, whilst scrolling through her mobile news feed during another seemingly endless night of hanging around outside of a suburban house waiting for a wayward spouse to emerge. She could still recall the almost overwhelming feeling that she had experienced watching it, that she was in the wrong place, staring enviously at the officers doing something truly important with their talents. Little had she known then that before too long she would be sitting facing one of the crack team that she had so admired on that night.

'I tell you; this job never fails to surprise. When we did the raid, we found an Aladdin's cave of goodies. Chanel handbags going for thirty quid, Apple AirPods for twenty. It wasn't just designer goods though, it was fake guns, drugs, fake prescription medicine, you name it. The frauds had all sorts of knock-on damages to the economy, driving out jobs and businesses for local people. The counterfeit goods in that one location were funding more than thirty organised criminal gangs worldwide.

'But the worst thing was the number of trafficked people we

found there, many in spin-off operations. Women sex workers controlled by the gangs, smuggled refugees having to work in cannabis farms above the shops to pay back the cost of their transport here, kids sent across the country on county lines drugs deliveries, turning up during police raids all over the place.

'I know that you are an expert on much of this, Billie. You did an amazing job with your own investigations into county lines drugs. Let me tell you, we all gave a big cheer in our base when we heard what you had achieved when that evil crime model came knocking at your door. Not to mention your last investigation, taking out people traffickers, I mean, *come on*, you weren't even a serving police officer then.'

'Thanks, but I wasn't celebrating either of those situations. Maybe I helped smoke out a few true monsters, but I'm not kidding myself that others haven't already taken up the spaces that they vacated.'

'Exactly. So we can't give up the fight, or other good people will die.' Matt touched Billie's hand, left his over hers for only a moment, but Billie didn't try to pull away. 'Like that poor child who fell under the tractor wheels whilst hoping to reach freedom, that Josta and I were called out to earlier today...' Matt's eyes darkened for a split second, showing his pain at the memory. 'Hopefully the girl that you tried to save today won't face a similar fate.'

'Boo did tell you that Safia is a very talented fashion design student? She would be invaluable in a place making counterfeit clothing,' Billie offered. Her mind was racing. Matt's eyes lit up at the news.

'Boo gave lots of information of course, but mostly on Safia's past in Afghanistan. She was extremely upset, naturally, having just identified the other children and also with having been unable to help you when you were assaulted. She would have been right there behind you, the old Boo I knew. She told me how keenly she felt about being helpless to come to your aid this afternoon.'

'Yeah, well, Boo was always a brilliant copper and I have never known her with working legs.' Billie took a sip of her wine. She also knew that Boo was great at putting on a brave face, but she had once been in the NCA herself, so Billie could imagine how heartbreaking it must be for her friend not being able to use all of her talents in situations such as this, whilst Billie felt more keenly than ever that she was squandering hers.

'But I think you might be onto something.' Matt broke through Billie's thoughts. 'I've just had the earlier autopsy reports from Josta. There were unusual fibres on the three buried bodies, which seem to match those found on the young lad killed under a lorry the other day. As you already know, it looks like the kids were chained and that's often the case with illegal sweatshops the world over.'

'Well, hopefully Safia is too valuable to kill... at least if she toes the line. Though Safia isn't the type to be pinned down.' Billie was thinking of the young woman's daring escape from Afghanistan.

'So we have to get to her before she decides to try and check out.'

'We?' Billie bit her bottom lip, knowing that she wanted to dump everything and race off right now, concentrating only on finding Safia and the rest of the still-missing children.

'Think about it, Billie. Maybe you're ready for a new adventure? If people like you and me give up, then who is left to care about the children?' Billie was distracted by a small voice calling her name. The problem was, once again, that it wasn't really *her* name, but she was beginning to answer to it, nevertheless.

'Mummy! Mummy, look!' Connie was bouncing up and

177

down, waving at Billie. Along with some other children of fellow diners, she had a small apron over her school uniform and was making pizza, watched by one of the cheery waitresses. Billie smiled and waved back. She could hardly take the kid to task about her manner of address, not in a room full of people. Matt was staring hard at her, a smile now playing on his lips.

'You seem to have won the heart of at least one child yourself.' He nodded towards Connie, giving a wave of his own as her beaming smile was directed their way.

'Sorry about this,' Billie said through a sigh. 'Childcare glitch. Ellis asked me to pick her up from after-school club after we'd already made arrangements. He's out on a job.' She adored Connie but she wasn't quite sure how on earth she had become so entangled in her young life.

'No problem. I have nephews and nieces of my own. I love spending downtime with them.'

'Do you get much of that?' Billie raised an eyebrow.

'Of course not, but when you love your job as much as I do, it's no great sacrifice.' Matt smiled at the waitress as she topped up the expensive wine into their glasses. 'And I get to go to such interesting places and meet *amazing* people.' He held Billie's gaze for a split second, before thanking the waitress.

'So no children of your own then?' Billie wondered how Matt juggled his seemingly hard-hitting jet-setting lifestyle, when she had felt the same way about her police work and had hardly ever taken a day off unless she had been forced to, even whilst operating here in the UK.

'Nope. Of course, I adore my nieces and nephews. There are a lot of them, and we have great fun together during holidays. But they have their parents and grandmas and grandpas and other uncles and aunts to keep them happy. Much of my work involves children across the world who have no safety net. I like to think that in some small way, every one of those I have been able to save is one of my own family. But I would be deluding myself if I thought that I could give up this work that I am so passionate about, settle down with a wife and two kids and expect to live happily ever after. I would be restless then and no doubt start to feel resentful despite any good intentions. That wouldn't be great for anyone.'

Billie looked across at sweet Connie, delighted with her cookery skills, all loveable giggles and prettiness. Billie did love the child, as a niece figure perhaps, similar to Ash's girls. But was she already starting to feel stirrings of resentment at being forced into a mothering role that she simply wasn't able to fill? As she turned back, she realised that Matt had been following her gaze. Could he see inside of her mind? It felt like it with his next words.

'Life is for living, Billie, but we have to live our own life, even if regrettably, it doesn't fit into the mould others would like to shape for us.' Matt chinked his glass with Billie's. His words reminded Billie of Safia's similar reflection on the night of her show. They had hit a nerve, definitely resonating with Billie's own feelings right at that very moment.

Ellis entered the square for the second time today, relieved to be wearing a nondescript hoodie, jeans and face mask, rather than a stupid giant pig outfit. The look of utter embarrassment on Maya's face, as she had backed away from him that afternoon, still stung like hell, as did the realisation that she had taken Connie, her precious half-sister, whom Ellis had entrusted to her care, to meet Storm – more than once at that. It was like taking a Dalmatian puppy to visit Cruella de Vil.

It wasn't like Maya and Connie shared the same mum. Yeah, it was true that Maya hadn't actually ever met Storm before, so was falling for some innocent line the evil witch was giving her about missing Connie, but surely she'd earwigged him voicing his opinion of his former wife often enough. He hadn't pulled any punches about his certainty that she'd been a player rather than an innocent onlooker when her sleazy thug of a boyfriend had been running his various criminal exploits, so how would she think he wanted Connie within a thousand miles of her?

The truth was Maya was still an innocent kid in many ways. The fact that she seemed to be giving it the sheep's eyes with that sleazy piece of nothing Johnny Briggs, said it all. She was beautiful, his Maya. Inside and out, but too trusting. Her mother had been the same, a kind woman as well as a stunner, taken in by Ellis's undercover story that he was a fellow environmental activist.

Of course he'd taken the whole thing too far, gone the whole kit and caboodle into a full-on relationship and not just because the top brass turned a blind eye in those days and his cover demanded it. He'd regret that until the day that he died, not telling Maya's mother the truth, face to face, that he had been a liar all along, working on the investigation. Letting her find out much later. But he'd had a big shock too, leaving that undercover post without ever knowing that Maya had existed. Not until two years ago. They'd made up for lost time though, him and his girl, they'd had a great relationship until recently.

Ellis looked around the angry chanting faces. He wished to God they could get this poisoned pie investigation over and done with quickly. He'd only taken it on because he had thought Billie was desperate to get her teeth into something a bit spicy, rather than insurance scams and benefit frauds and away from home-hanky-panky snooping. In truth, those sorts of jobs were the meat and drink of any PI investigative company, no matter what sort of high drama they liked to portray on the telly.

The thing was, Billie seemed to sniff out serious crime like a dog with a bone and she couldn't mask her restlessness at the tedium of their day-to-day stuff, not from him. He knew her too well.

He, on the other hand, was looking at life differently these days. He'd had a close shave himself when they had got mixed up with Storm's other half a few months back. He'd been lucky to lose the top of his ear. Had it not been for Billie it would likely have been the top of his head. Not that it was the first time Ellis had faced down death, but now he had to think of more than just his own welfare. He had sole care for two daughters these days.

Maya would come home after this latest argy-bargy, he was sure of that. He'd given her a penthouse flat at the top of his place that girls her age could only dream of, for starters. Looked like it had dropped off the front cover of one of those swanky magazines. She looked the part of a top model too, sitting in it. Ellis couldn't help smiling to himself. That was his girl.

He was certain that she would kiss and make up with her old dad and once he'd laid down the law once and for all, as far as going anywhere near his former crazy wife was concerned, he'd book up that swanky new Italian restaurant around the corner, Cucina's it was called. Take Maya and Connie there along with Billie and Boo and Ash and his kids, like one big happy family. It's what they were, as far as Ellis was concerned. He thought of Connie calling Billie 'Mummy' again and chuckled to himself. His little one knew where her bread was buttered no matter what Storm Benbow and the stupid social worker chose to believe. Connie was going nowhere.

Enveloped in the smell of olives and wine, basil and oregano and to background 1950's Italian jazz, currently a track, titled

'Via Con Me', Billie and Matt were sharing a huge salad full of fresh lollo rosso leaves, olives and parmesan along with an equally huge bowl of delicious arancini. Billie could finally feel herself relaxing as Connie came triumphantly to the table alongside a waitress, carrying her handmade recipe.

'Quite the little chef,' the waitress addressed Billie and Matt. 'She insisted on adding some additions herself, a little snack from her schoolbag. I think it was lemon flavoured.'

'Bellissima,' Matt replied. The waitress fluttered in response, but he was looking at Billie, whose attention had been drawn suddenly to an advertising screen up high on the wall across the road, running a video advert.

'Look, there's me!' Connie shouted, pointing at the screen, causing everyone else in the restaurant to stare in the same direction. 'Me and Maya!' Connie jumped up and down in excitement. Billie's heart, however, immediately sank, as though a needle had scratched right across the chill-out music. She felt sure that Ellis would never have agreed to his youngest daughter being shown on a video screen, several feet high, eating a Porkie's Big Eats Vegetable Pie. Not for security purposes for starters and definitely not when Ethel Rutherford, let alone Storm Benbow seemed to be on the hunt for anything to prove that Ellis was a less than perfect guardian for his daughter.

'Quite the supermodel.' Matt patted Connie on the shoulder as other people commented in recognition, to Connie's delight.

'But I'm pretty certain that Ellis wouldn't sign off on this. Maya must have taken Connie out of school... on her first day...' Billie's voice trailed off quizzically as she recalled who had been booked as the cameraman for the day's shoot only that morning. The odious Johnny Briggs. Ellis would go absolutely ballistic – again.

'Connie, did Maya film that video with you today?' Billie

frowned, something wasn't quite right in the footage, but she couldn't put her finger on what. Connie shook her head, reaching for a slice of pizza.

'Not necessarily.' Matt leaned over towards Billie, so close that she caught the faintest hint of his tantalisingly elegant scent. 'It looks like a deepfake to me. We've had to get savvy about them at the NCA. Some deepfakes are really difficult to spot. Looks like Connie's photo has been superimposed on a moving figure template. Pretty easy to do nowadays, people can even have apps on their phones superimposing anyone's head on say, a famous actor or footballer's body. Of course, it can be used in crime too. Online fraud and job interviews mostly. Going forward it's going to make identification really difficult in court cases–'

A sudden high-pitched scream from Connie cut across their conversation. Billie spun around to see a look of pain and horror on the little girl's face as blood streamed from her mouth.

'What's wrong, Connie? What have you eaten?' Connie dropped the slice of pizza that she had just tucked into. A glint of glass caught Billie's eye. 'Oh my goodness.'

'There's something in this. What is this?' Matt was standing up now, calling to the waitress as Billie tried to open Connie's mouth, dabbing it with a white serviette now splattered with blood as the child screamed and squirmed, horror in her eyes. The waitress hurtled across.

'The children all wanted to add their own ingredients. Like I said, Connie had brought something in her food bag. It was a pie. One of those types of pies up there!' The waitress waved her hand at Connie tucking into the Porkie's Pie on the big screen.

'The hospital's just up the road. Let's go.' Billie lifted Connie onto her hip and started to stride for the door, damming the fact that she'd swapped her usual hefty boots for a pair with a heel that she'd found in her work cupboard.

'And keep that pizza and the pie wrapping. We'll need it,' Matt instructed the shocked waitress as the other guests looked on in horror. He took Connie from her arms as she wrenched the door open with one hand and then he took off at speed, racing flat out along the street carrying the child, with Billie hot on his tail.

———

Ellis looked at the clock in the town square. No sign of the key animal rights activist who had been so aggressive towards Billie. Ellis was determined to nab him tonight, should he make an appearance, make sure he didn't try that move ever again. He'd studied the photos online, together with Billie's description and now scoured the crowd for someone wearing a hooded puffer boiler-suit ensemble and a skeleton mask.

Ellis recalled that he'd caught plenty of guys in the past when he worked for the NCA, drugs dealers and the like, who fancied themselves as Billy Big Bollocks, but once they were stripped of their kit and muscle-head mates, they turned out to be nothing more than just evil little runts begging for mercy in a dark corner when he got them alone, face to face. Yeah, he'd had some hairy moments back in the day, but he'd had his fill of all that. It had got to the point sometimes when he had worked on so many undercover jobs, that he didn't know who he was himself. That had definitely been the case when he'd had the whirlwind fling and then stupidly signed on the dotted line with Storm.

Now though, since his girls were both on the scene and he'd sorted out his own gaff and had Cousin Teddy as his partner in crime at all the local footie matches, a couple of pints in the pub afterwards with their mates, he knew that he'd finally found his happy place. All he needed now was a gorgeous woman to share it with – long-term friend as well as a red-hot lover. He'd learned that lesson good and proper. He just had to take it slowly, convince Billie that he wasn't too ugly to share a bed with for the rest of her life. Ellis gave a silent chuckle. His little Connie was doing a good job of bringing her around to the idea after all, though she pretended to protest. Ellis had never heard Connie utter the word *mummy* in relation to the bitch who popped her out, that was for sure. Not even once.

Now that he looked around the crowd, Ellis relaxed a little. Most of them seemed harmless enough. Some of the young girls reminded him of his Maya, trying to find their feet, deciding what was important to them in life. In fact, many of the protesters appeared to be students. Ellis had to give credit to youngsters so keen to stand up for what they believed in.

Chances were, as with most of these things, one or two rogue chancers with no real ideals at all in their tiny brains, had infiltrated this largely innocent-looking group, trying to cause big trouble. If they were found to be the ones threatening Graham Harvey, they would go down for it, so end of that story. He was a meat and two veg man himself, but now as he watched the crowd parading with gruesome pictures of some of the stuff done to animals, allegedly to put cheap food into the system, he decided that maybe he was willing to give this veggie thing a go. Two pretty girls parading around with a slaughtered lamb in their neatly manicured mitts were putting him off his Sunday roast, truth be told.

Maybe he'd have a go at veggie Mondays? Ellis considered. That would get him on the right side of his Maya. She never touched meat. Neither had her mother come to think of it and that was in the days when being a veggie was all pulses and muesli and rampant wind issues. He'd remembered joking with

Maya's mum about that. Yeah, she'd been a good sort. Maybe he would talk to Maya about getting some sort of memorial stone made for her mum, go with her a few times a year to her mother's grave, take flowers, just Maya and him. Make it into special dad and daughter time together. He'd ask Billie what she thought of the idea.

At that moment a dark figure wearing a skeleton mask jumped up onto a stone plinth outside of Porkie's Big Eats, taking the slaughtered lamb from the two pretty girls and holding the half-skinned, bloody corpse above their heads. The girls took a banner and held it up below the figure.

Pies to die for, the message read. The crowd broke into loud booing.

Ellis, who had been leaning against the structure of the thankfully covered roundabout, that had given him so much grief earlier, had already snapped to attention. There was no doubt that this was the target. Hadn't Billie mentioned a similar line being used on Harpers latest threatening letter received only that morning? Lots of cheering and clapping ensued as the figure handed the lamb carefully down to the girls and then took another banner, unfurling it and then holding it wide above their heads. **Kill Porkie's Big Eats**. It read. The same banner Ellis had viewed via the online footage from the day before, the same phrase as one of Graham Harper's threatening missives. Billie's hunch was right.

As the crowd started chanting the phrase loudly a police car slowly pulled into the square. Ellis reckoned the officers were just making themselves visible, to ensure that another beef didn't kick off again tonight, but as the two officers alighted from the car, an egg struck one of them on the head and then another. Suddenly they were engulfed in angry protesters.

By nature, Ellis wanted to dive right in and help out the two officers who had clearly not expected such an onslaught, but he could already see the skeleton-masked ringleader jumping from the plinth, just as Billie had described the night before. But what Ellis's target didn't realise was that unlike Billie, he had prior knowledge of his likely escape route. As the black-boiler-suited figure ran along the wall, about to jump into the back alleyway, Ellis was already almost neck and neck with them.

'Not so fast,' he shouted. The figure seemed startled, hovered on the wall for a moment before trying to jump over Ellis's head onto the cobblestones. Ellis swung his arm up, managing to catch a wodge of boiler suit. The figure lashed out as they toppled to the ground, catching Ellis on the head with their boot, momentarily dazing him and allowing his grip to loosen. The masked figure seemed to stop for a moment and then scrambled upright and start running fast along the alleyway. Ellis shook his head, understanding the meaning of the phrase 'seeing stars', but was already rolling up onto his feet and giving chase.

The masked figure grabbed a dustbin and hurled it behind them, scattering rubbish. Ellis jumped over it and reached out as the figure tripped over one of the rolling cans, losing balance. Ellis's fingers managed to grab the suit again and this time he wasn't going to let go, despite the fight that the figure was putting up. Now on the ground, Ellis knew that he had won. He'd had years of training and experience in bringing down enemies, after all, often with his life depending on his successful techniques.

'Let's have a look at you.' Ellis pinned the still squirming body on the hard ground scattered with foul-smelling rubbish, tearing the skeleton mask down. The eyes that were now staring into his were wild and angry. They were the striking amber-coloured eyes of his precious older daughter, Maya.

TWENTY-SIX

FINALLY MET HER MATCH?

M att and Billie burst into the hospital A and E department, swerving around the people waiting with worried faces, being ignored by the receptionist. She did flick her head around at the noise of banging doors and screaming child, however. This was no small result, as she had until that moment, been studiously avoiding the group of injured, irritated or simply deranged individuals waiting by her glass-fronted desk, desperate to get her attention.

The high-pitched screams and coughs coming from Connie even drowned out a particularly volatile woman, marinaded in alcohol and the cloying smell of dope, complaining about the length of her wait. Billie's main concern of the many hurtling through her head, was whether Connie's anguished gasps were caused by a blocked airway, glass injuries or simply shock at the amount of blood spilling out of her rosebud lips. Luckily a young woman doctor, at that moment crossing the waiting room, recognised a serious emergency when she spotted one and beckoned a nurse across to take Connie from Matt's arms.

'She's swallowed some glass,' Billie explained as she and Matt followed the nurse and doctor through the doors marked

STRICTLY NO ENTRY to the examination section of A and E. The doctor immediately shouted instructions to various team members as they laid Connie on the one free bed.

'Can you take the mum and dad across to the waiting room, please?' the doctor directed a young medical student, as the team started their examination on a borderline hysterical Connie who between coughs and splutters, was crying 'Mummy' whilst holding out her small arm in Billie's direction, kicking out at those attempting to check the extent of the damage. Billie headed for the bed, but Matt pulled her back, holding her shoulders as he firmly turned her around, leading her towards a side door, which the intern was holding open.

'Best if we just let them do their job, Billie.' His voice was soothing, his head close to hers as he propelled her into the small waiting room.

'What the fu...' Billie gasped, running her hand through her hair as Matt sat her down on one of the hard chairs and headed over to a coffee machine, pouring them each a plastic cupful. Billie was trying to think quickly, wondering how on earth Connie had gotten hold of a Porkie's Big Eats Pie in the first place. The waitress had mentioned the addition having been in Connie's schoolbag. Had Maya given it to her?

'She dropped the slice of ham pizza with the lemon pie segment on it.' Matt slid his jacket off. His shirt was sticking to him. Billie shook her head in disbelief at what had happened.

'I should have seen it. If I had known she had a Porkie's pie, then I would never have let her–'

'You mean you were expecting to find glass shards in a mass-produced pie sitting atop a pizza?' Matt said, looking astonished.

'It's part of a malicious food threat that Wilde & Darque are investigating. We've been hoping it was just a joker messing around... Billie trailed off, patting down her pockets in search of her mobile phone. 'Needless to say, no one is going to be laughing now, thanks to my useless childcare abilities. Give me a minute and I'll fill you in. First, I've got to give Ellis the news about his precious daughter.'

'Get the fuck off me!' Maya was kicking out now. She caught Ellis with her knee in the groin, momentarily winding him. Maya rolled over, attempting to squirm free as he gasped in pain as well as shock, but despite her police training Maya wasn't a match for her dad with a lifetime's experience of fighting crime. 'My dad is a crack cop. Lay one finger on me and you are dead!' Maya screamed, as Ellis straddled her, pinning her wrists over her head with one hand. He couldn't help feeling flattered for a split second at her threat, even though this wasn't the time or place to take compliments. He pulled down his mask. The look on Maya's face showed he might be a long time waiting for another one.

'Have you been the one sending all of these threats to Graham Harper?'

'What are you doing? I don't know what you're talking about.' Maya finally pulled her wrists free. 'Get off me!' She pushed Ellis backwards. He acquiesced, feeling a bit uneasy at the position he was in at that moment himself, but he pointed his finger in warning.

'One move to leg it before you spill the beans, my girl, and you'll be sorry, I'm warning you.' Ellis's face was stern. Maya's eyes filled up with tears.

'I can't believe you've been stalking me. Now I know how Mum must have felt.'

'What?' Ellis sat back on his knees, frowning.

'Skulking around undercover, pretending to be a fellow protestor. It's just history repeating itself. Good people like

Mum and me, simply lawfully protesting about something disgusting that's going on, trying to make the world a better place and people like *you* getting paid to snoop around, trying to wreck their lives.'

Ellis felt like he had been kicked in his groin all over again. 'I don't think that's fair,' he said through a sigh.

'No, it isn't fair.' Maya was sitting upright now, pointing her finger at Ellis furiously, her eyes flashing. 'Look at poor Mum, all she was protesting about was the environment. She'd get a medal for it now and all I'm saying is that there's no reason for anyone these days to kill innocent animals to stay alive. Maybe everyone will see the truth of *that* a few years along the line too, so this snooping business is a waste of your life all around, *big daddy*.'

'That's enough.' Ellis was hurt but he wasn't going to show her how much. As an undercover operative, he'd spent a lifetime it seemed, having to mask his true feelings. He had bigger worries than his own pride right now.

'You do know that malicious food threats will get you banged up inside? If Graham Harper presses charges against you over this–'

'So you're going to grass me up. On what charges? Lawfully protesting, just like Mum was lawfully protesting all those years ago? Maybe she just escaped jumped-up charges because you were shagging her. Plenty of her mates got dragged away on your tip-offs. It would be *you* who would be getting banged up for your behaviour today.'

Ellis knew Maya was going for his Achilles heel and she was right, that was the awful thing. But he couldn't let her continue with this. He at least owed her dead mum *that* much. She could hate him forever. By the looks of it, that was the truth of the matter, but he wasn't going to let her smash her young life to smithereens, not when she held so much promise.

'The poster you've been parading around with. Same wording that's on threats sent to Porkie's Big Eats head office, threatening to spike their stuff with poison. Confirmation of that is spread all across social media sites worldwide. Were you *actually* going to doctor any pies, then give yourself a big slap on the back when some kid chokes to death, mark it down as a good PR campaign?'

'What are you on about?' Maya blinked in shock. 'I don't know anything about threats to products. You're crazy. Do you really think that *I* would do *that*?'

'Like I said, same phrasing was used in one of the threats as in that banner you're giving it large with and you were making no bones back there about wanting the shops shut, just the same as the demands being made in the warnings.'

'So? I didn't print the banner; I was just holding it.' Maya tried to look defiant, but Ellis could recognise the look in her eyes when she was scared. He rubbed his head in despair. This was an absolute nightmare. He hoped that he could somehow talk Graham Harper out of reporting his precious girl to the police.

'Fella recently got fourteen years for spiking baby food, so I hope to God you haven't actually gone and done it.' Ellis reached for his mobile which had started reverberating the annoying emergency ringtone that he and Billie had agreed upon, otherwise he would have ignored it. Luckily Maya looked shocked now. A bit less lively.

'Yeah?' Ellis answered, hoping Billie wasn't going to tell him the security guard at the flagship store had bailed out again tonight. He couldn't face that stinking pig costume twice in one day, especially now it looked like he'd nabbed the culprit. However, the words he heard were a million times worse. The blood drained from his face.

'Right, on my way.' Ellis jumped upright.

'What's wrong, Dad?' Maya pulled herself to her feet.

'Got to get to the hospital...' Ellis felt as though he was in a daze as he started to head off, almost turning in the wrong direction. Suddenly all of his focus had moved from one daughter to the other.

'Who's in hospital? Dad!' Maya was running behind him now, an alarmed look on her face as Ellis started to stride back along the alleyway.

'Dad!' Maya grabbed Ellis's arm. He shrugged her away and kept on moving, gathering pace.

'Your little sister has just gone and eaten a Porkie's Pie spiked with glass. Happy now, are you, with your plan to make the world a better place?'

'But I've never put anything in one, or given a pie to her. Dad, you've got to believe me.' Maya was racing alongside Ellis as they emerged into the busy main street. There in front of them on the huge screen that Billie had been watching earlier was the same advert appearing to show Maya and Connie happily tucking into a Porkie's Big Eats veggie pie. Ellis stopped still in horror at the view, before holding his arm up to prevent Maya from approaching him again.

'Well, there's the evidence for all to see. Right now, I want you to back off and get right out of my sight.' Ellis's mind was in a whirl as he sprinted off in the direction of the hospital. Was one of his children about to be charged with trying to kill the other? Even worse. Had she actually succeeded?

Billie had been unable to sit still. She paced the waiting room, filling Matt in on the threats so far sent to Graham Harper.

'It's a big job for a PI firm to take on. Sort of thing that the

National Food Crime Unit handle, normally.' Matt raised his eyebrows as Billie paused for breath.

'Tell me about it. I did make the same point, but the client is at pains to keep it all under the radar,' Billie answered sheepishly. The truth was she should have stood her ground and insisted to both Ellis and Graham Harper that the outlets were immediately closed, and the relevant authorities informed. Somehow she was starting to doubt her own judgement, happier to keep the peace than stand up for what she truly believed. It suddenly reminded her of her relationship with her former fiancé. Both he, along with his and her own parents, had tried to mould her into a role that didn't fit her true personality. It hadn't fitted her fiancé's either, as it had turned out. At that moment, the door opened. The young medical intern who had led them into the room, popped his head around the door.

'How is she?' Billie asked, half afraid of the reply.

'She's been sedated and is having scans right now, but I'm just checking – you are...' He looked down at his clipboard. 'Connie Darque's parents, right?' He looked from Matt to Billie.

'No, we brought her in,' Matt answered.

'She was with us in the restaurant when it happened.'

'Oh, right.' The intern nodded his head. 'It's just that there's a man kicking off out there in the main waiting room, claiming to be her dad and really we can't allow a crowd–' At that moment, following a commotion in the main A and E examination area, Ellis loomed into view.

'Try and stop me coming in. I'm here to see my daughter, she's only five years old! Connie Darque. Where is she?' Ellis suddenly spotted Billie and raced towards her, pushing the young intern aside. 'Where's my little angel?'

Billie quickly approached Ellis. 'She's getting the best treatment. Come and have a coffee–'

'Em, sorry, but we really can't allow more than two people

in here at one time,' the intern politely interjected as Matt stood up.

'It's okay. I'll go.' Matt touched Billie's arm. 'I'll give you a call later.' Ellis focused on Matt, as if for the first time. He frowned.

'Matt Scalera? But... I don't understand...' Ellis looked dazed. 'What are you doing here?'

Billie ran her fingers through her hair. 'Matt was with me when Connie ate, well, whatever she ate.'

'I'm not following...' Ellis looked suspiciously from Billie to Matt.

'We were having dinner – my uncle has Cucina's restaurant in town.' Matt attempted to explain, but Ellis had turned to Billie now and she didn't like the look in his eyes.

'What, so you had a hot date lined up when you offered to look after my little one? Sorry if she was cramping your style. You should have said that you didn't want her around, if you knew that you would be too distracted to look after her properly.'

'That's not fair, Ellis,' Matt interjected, but Ellis spun around, a look of fury on his face.

'No, I'll tell *you* what's not fair. You and her getting it on together probably like love's young dream while my kid is eating fucking glass for all the notice you take. *That's* what's not fair, mate!' Ellis was shouting full blast now and poking Matt in the chest, as two security guards burst through the door. The intern felt emboldened enough to intervene.

'I'm sorry, but you'll all have to leave if you don't behave. This is very upsetting for the other patients–'

'It's okay. We are leaving.' Billie had finally had enough. She could see other patients and their worried families looking their way.

'Take a honeymoon. I've had words with the culprit. Job's

done, while you were canoodling with lover boy here. So the Porkie's contract is finished.'

'You did? You caught the main activist?' Billie did a double take.

'Shame you didn't manage that last night, or Connie wouldn't be here now. Guess your mind was on other things.'

Billie smarted at Ellis's words. She had already been kicking herself for not hanging on to the animal rights activist, but even so, his criticism in the circumstances was particularly harsh.

'Let's go, Billie.' Matt touched Billie's arm.

'Come on, move along here.' One of the huge security guards opened another door leading out into a corridor.

'Yeah, bog off the two of you,' Ellis sneered. 'I'm Connie Darque's dad. Those two have no right to be in here. It's their fault my little girl's in this mess in the first place.'

Ellis spat the words out. Billie knew he was hurt and afraid and had a right to feel concerned about how well she had cared for Connie. But she also saw something else at that moment, that Ellis was furious that she had been spending time with another man. She'd tried to put her head in the sand about the situation, refused to accept that he was looking for more than just a business partnership, despite Maya's words about the two of them playing happy families earlier in the week. They couldn't go on like this.

'Are you okay?' Matt touched Billie lightly on the shoulder as they left the hospital, the cool air on Billie's face a welcome relief after the heat of the hospital interior. 'I see Ellis Darque hasn't mellowed much in the past few years. Great if he's on your side but–'

'Ellis's bark is worse than his bite,' Billie couldn't help coming to Ellis's defence, despite his harsh words towards her. 'He saved my life,' Billie added. It was true. There might have been a lot of water under the bridge since, but she would never forget that.

Matt's mobile suddenly rang. 'Sorry, I have to take this.' Matt stepped to one side of the main door as people milled around. Billie checked her watch. It wasn't too late to make a house call.

'Sorry, I've got to run,' both Matt and Billie said in unison, as he finished his call. They stopped mid-sentence and grinned. Billie broke the moment.

'I know this hasn't actually been a dinner date worth staying an extra night for.'

'On the contrary,' Matt replied. 'I kind of like my life to be full of surprises and I also kind of like the fact that you consider this to have been a date.'

'No, I mean, meeting. Of course...' Billie felt like an idiot. Christ, was she actually blushing? 'I really appreciate you sharing your intel on the missing kids.'

'Some more intel coming in, hence having to go back to my hotel to update.'

'And I've got to go get these pie outlets closed down immediately, whilst I work out whether Ellis really has nabbed the culprit and ensured that there aren't hundreds of other glass pies out there just waiting for opening time.'

Matt frowned in response. 'Strange don't you think, that he seems to be convinced that after him having had words with the perpetrator they'll just stop? Doesn't sound like the Ellis Darque that I used to know.'

Billie had been thinking the same thing, hence her decision to take action, whatever Ellis was claiming. She hadn't exactly been in a position to have a rational conversation with him, taking into account the circumstances. But one thing was for sure, she wasn't willing to take any more chances of another child been rushed to A and E due to crossed communication wires.

'Yeah, well I'm going to put this thing to bed right now,' Billie replied. If Ellis wasn't in the mood to spill the whole story, then he could hardly blame her for taking further action.

'Talking of which.' A mischievous smile played on Matt's lips. 'I tend to stay up late, so if your business is done and you are in the mood for a midnight snack and a debrief–'

'Is that the best chat-up line you can come up with?' Billie laughed, backing away.

Matt shook his head in dismay. 'Honestly, I meant the missing kids case. You've got me blushing now.'

'Might take you up on it. See how my next date goes first.' Billie bit her bottom lip, deciding she really might do just that.

Matt smiled. 'And if not, well, I hope to see you again very soon, Billie Wilde. It's been a long time coming and an absolute pleasure.'

Billie couldn't help glancing back, as Matt crossed the street, looking striking in perfectly cut, expensive black suit and crisp white shirt open at the throat. Daring, devilishly good-looking and clearly dedicated to his job. Had Billie Wilde finally met her match?

TWENTY-SEVEN
OTHER PEOPLE'S DREAMS

B illie had parked her car out on the street rather than driven right up to the front door. Years of training meant that she was always alert to the need to plan a quick means of escape even in the most pedestrian of settings, such as this leafy lane housing Graham Harper's borderline mansion, set back behind tall trees and a curving drive.

Billie's plan was to tell Graham Harper that Wilde & Darque were done with this investigation, that according to Ellis the culprit had been caught, but that either way, it was now a job for the authorities to prosecute. They could come in mob-handed and investigate further, with legal backing, rather than skating over the surface, whereas Wilde & Darque had their wrists tied by the CEO, on account of being hired investigative hands, with a confidentiality agreement signed and sealed.

Once again, the feeling washed over Billie that maybe she had been in too much of a hurry to jump ship from her senior police role. The situation with Ellis was beginning to take its toll. The issues had become crystal clear that evening, though Billie never for even one moment doubted Ellis's abilities as an investigative officer.

The problem that she had been trying to ignore was that they were way too close in their personal lives, sharing friends and now even childcare, though Billie had tried to make it clear over and again that she didn't feel able to take on the role of substitute mummy for Connie. Jeez, she'd made her lack of credentials for that role clear enough tonight, that was for sure.

Billie ran her fingers through her hair, feeling tension in her neck. She had rung the hospital before alighting from her car, in search of an update on Connie and had simply been told that she was on a ward and comfortable. Billie felt sure that Ellis would be bedding down with Connie there, so the least that she could do was go straight to Graham Harper to update him. Though it was dark now and the moon fully out, it wasn't yet too late, Billie felt, to come cold-calling. If he'd gone to bed early, then he would be the first CEO of a big company in history not to be burning the candle, in order to keep all of the balls in his empire up in the air.

As Billie walked up the drive, which was shaded by the tall trees, the cool breeze lifting her hair, it was the smell that caught her attention at first, odd and cloying, the unmistakable smell of a snake in the grass. She spotted Johnny Briggs standing by a lorry parked outside of Graham Harper's grand front door. The vehicle looked rather incongruous next to his Jag. The branding across it was for Porkie's Big Eats pies. Right now, Billie felt sure she would never eat one again. Suddenly Graham Harper came into view, under a security light which had flashed on as he had walked down the stone steps from the entrance. He grabbed Johnny Briggs in a clinch and kissed him like a love-stricken teenager.

Billie stood still for a moment, caught off guard. It seemed that Johnny Briggs held some sort of attraction that had completely passed Billie by. It was pretty clear the other day at

Ellis's place, that he was romantically entangled with Tina as well as Maya. The girl had seemed miffed to have been uninformed about the photo shoot that morning. Billie could only guess how thrilled she would be to discover that her lover appeared also to be romantically entangled with her dad.

Billie realised that decorum should have ruled, that she should hang back and let the loving duo have this moment alone together, but she had no truck with decorum. She wanted this issue pinned down and the safety of the public ensured. Then she could give more thought to the missing asylum-seeking children, whom were never far from her mind.

She wondered what the latest intel had been that had caused Matt to hurry back to his hotel, trying to push that rather striking image from her mind, as well as the memory of the touch of his hand on hers in the restaurant and on her shoulder as they had left the hospital. His scent was subtle and sensual as well. Johnny Briggs's stuff was making Billie want to gag as she moved closer, unseen by either of the men who were both more interested in exploring tongues down throats. Billie coughed. Loudly. It was either that or upchuck, she reasoned. The two men sprang apart.

'What on earth?' Graham Harper stammered. Billie could see his shirt was open. Clearly this wasn't a kiss of greeting she was witnessing.

'Sorry if I gave you a shock, Mr Harper, but the gates back there are open. Did you not take our chat about security seriously? I mean, at this time of night you can't underestimate how many lowlifes might be lurking in the undergrowth.' Billie looked Johnny Briggs up and down, noticed him react with anger for a split second before catching himself.

'Ah, if it isn't our most delicious Billie Wilde. I really don't think you can leave me alone, can you, pretty one? Graham, I do believe your little Sherlock Holmes is still searching for her perfect Watson, despite her sidekick Ellis Darque being after her like a dog in heat.'

'I guess you would know all about that,' Billie answered, as Graham Darque hastily buttoned up his shirt.

'Thanks for the loan of the wheels, Graham. Maybe ask the hired staff to make an appointment to visit in future.' Johnny jumped up into the cab of the lorry before starting the engine.

'You really can't be too careful about who you befriend in your position, Mr Harper.' Billie was watching the lorry disappear from view down the drive, thinking how little time it had taken Johnny Briggs to get into Graham Harper's pants. It had sounded this morning as though they had met for the first time just the night before.

Was Graham Harper aware of the odious man's relationship with his own daughter, or had he experienced the threatening side to his personality? Billie imagined not. If one thing was clear it was the CEO's desperation to do the best for his girl, with so much pressure on her to continue the family business.

'Ours isn't a new relationship, Ms Wilde.' Graham Harper finished off fastening his top button, seeming to gain control again. 'We first met some time ago at my summer property in Spain. Though for reasons I stated previously we can't express our love as we wish. The board wouldn't approve and as I've said, with my dear wife out of the picture, my focus must remain on ensuring that Tina is brought up to speed on running the business without any other distractions. I gave my wife my absolute word that I wouldn't let her down on that.'

'But Tina seems pretty fond of Johnny Briggs.' Billie frowned. Fonder than Graham Harper could ever imagine, she guessed. 'I think it would be wise to tell her of the situation,' Billie advised, though decided against revealing the reason why it might be an idea to share his choice of lover with Tina.

For all she knew, Johnny and Graham favoured an open relationship. After all, Ellis had caught Graham Harper with his pants down only a few days earlier. It was a stretch however, to think that Graham would play along with his daughter being in a three-way scenario. Being open would at least clarify the situation. Billy had to admit to herself that years of being a detective had made her perhaps more suspicious than most. However, she would put money on Johnny Briggs having just been caught out, playing some sort of unscrupulous game with both father and daughter.

'Truth be told, Ms Wilde, I am not a natural entrepreneur. The marriage between my wife and I was orchestrated by our parents. We were considered to be a good match. I'm sure that sounds odd to a young woman in this day and age,' he added. In fact, Billie knew exactly what he meant, she'd very nearly played the same game, worn the T-shirt, before hidden skeletons had come out from dark places and changed the course of her own life. In fact, she was still caught in the tailwind of that unbelievable journey.

'Had I been able to make my own choices as a young man, then I would have created a different life for myself. I actually loathe the damn pies that my wife's great-grandfather rustled up so long ago. My true love is fine wines. I like to consider myself something of a connoisseur. I have land in Spain where I met dear Johnny. A beautiful villa and acres of rolling countryside. Once I have ensured that everything is in place for Tina to take over the reins of the company then my dream is to live there permanently, with Johnny by my side.' Billie could appreciate the attractions of one half of that dream at least, but she was perturbed by the nightmarish Johnny-shaped wedge of that sunny ambition.

'Haven't you ever considered that he might be behind the threats you have been receiving?' Billie wished to God that Ellis had filled her in with the details of the animal rights activist he had collared, but Maya had alluded that morning to the silver logo that Billie had ripped off the activist's glove being similar to that on an identical pair belonging to the creep. He seemed to love to cause a disruption, so *dear Johnny*, as Graham Harper referred to him, was the man she would put money on being a likely culprit.

However, Ellis had said on arrival at the hospital that he'd caught the perpetrator and put a stop to the situation, so that didn't make sense. Billie could see that there was no way Johnny Briggs would go quietly into any dark night, not if he had a chance to wind up Ellis by staying around.

'Johnny?' Graham Harper was visibly shocked. 'Absolutely not. In fact, the dear boy is well aware of the situation that I've been facing. We share absolutely everything.'

'Even the company vehicles,' Billie observed.

'He's helping the students at Freedom Angels ferry some props around for a show. We sponsor a café in that venue, Tina helps out the young people with events. As a company we like to give back to the community.'

'But might Johnny simply be trying to get into your good books, Mr Harper? Might it be to his benefit to have Porkie's Big Eats closed down?'

'Really. What an outrageous claim! Johnny has Porkie's Big Eats's best interests at heart at all times. He certainly has nothing to gain from any closure. In fact, he wants this threat concern sorted out as quickly as I do. He needs the business to stay thriving and for Tina to be up to speed ASAP because–' Graham Harper suddenly stopped mid-sentence. '...because of a separate commercial issue.'

'Which is?' Billie persisted. 'I really can't help you if you don't come clean with me.'

Graham Harper was silent for a moment before he sighed loudly, then began to spill. 'We are going to create a hotel and vineyard on my land in Spain, just as soon as we are able. As soon as I am free of the day-to-day running of the company and have sold my shares, Johnny and I will be married. The new business will be a joint enterprise. It will give me a new lease of life. But Johnny is as much at pains as I am to protect Tina, as she takes on such an enormous role.'

Or at pains to protect himself from having his father and daughter affairs out in the open, and to stuff his hands into Graham Harper's ever deepening pockets, Billie thought, but didn't voice.

Graham Harper looked wistful for a moment. 'I am already past retirement age now, Ms Wilde. I'm sure that you are very happy in your own choice of career, but imagine for a moment that you are me, having lived all of your life as a round peg in a square hole, as it were. My marriage was in truth a lie, though my wife and I were friends and neither of us for a moment regretted Tina.

'But I simply couldn't have imagined that at this late stage, I might find a man who loves me as I am, warts and all. Someone who has encouraged my dreams, rather than knocked them down as the silly ramblings of an old man. So I'm going to grab this last chance of happiness with both hands. As dear Johnny said to me when he encouraged me to follow this vision, "at the end of the day you die alone, darling, so don't spend all of your life trying to live someone else's dream".'

Graham Harper's words had hit a vulnerable spot in Billie's own soul. But she still was less than convinced of Johnny Briggs's intentions, other than having a gut feeling that they weren't good.

'I'm glad that you mentioned being true to your own

instincts in life because it has been my strong compulsion from the start to urge you to shut your outlets whilst this investigation continues and to inform the local authorities of the situation. You now need to call in the National Crime Unit as a matter of urgency. A small girl is tonight in hospital having eaten one of your products which contained broken glass.'

'Oh my goodness.' Graham Harper appeared visibly shocked.

'The child is the daughter of my partner, Ellis Darque.'

'Oh dear, oh dear. But in that case, there's no reason to bring other people in. We can pay compensation... I mean, the shares would plummet if such an incident were to be made public. I'll have to speak with Johnny about this first. He's away now for a few days.'

'It doesn't take Johnny Briggs to tell you that more people are now at risk–'

'But our dream is a risk, don't you see, and my daughter's future–'

Billie cut Graham Harper's protest off in mid-sentence. 'Much as I applaud your concern for your daughter's welfare, I'm more concerned about the health of Joe Public out there, including the bog-standard kids who eat Porkie's Pies. I'll be at your office at 9am tomorrow morning, when I hope to have your confirmation that all of the outlets will have by then been closed. Then we will make the call to the National Crime Unit. I also think now is the time for Tina to step up and put on her big girl boots. If she really is keen to take over the business, then this might be just the challenge she needs to make her dream into a reality.'

Billie marched down the drive glancing at her mobile as it lit up in response to a call. It was from Maya. She sighed, hoping that she wasn't going to be stuck piggy in the middle between another domestic between Ellis and the girl. She was done trying to pussyfoot around playing happy families. She never thought that she would be quoting Johnny Briggs's words, but it was true that she couldn't spend all of her life living other people's dreams. All she was dreaming of right now, was finding Safia and the remaining missing asylum-seeking kids alive.

TWENTY-EIGHT
NOWHERE LEFT TO RUN

Tanko watched the old man nodding in and out of sleep on his old threadbare winged chair, as the flames of the fire turned into a low glow and the music on the gramophone filled the small room. He remembered an old Nigerian saying that his great-grandfather had taught him. *Pretend you are dead, and you will see who loves you.*

Well, Tanko's great-grandfather was dead, as were his whole family and he definitely still loved them. His mother used to say, 'Love is like seaweed; even if you push it away, you will not prevent it from returning.' She had been right. Waves of love for his family still washed over him now that he had sailed far away across the world. It was those feelings that had saved him when otherwise he felt that his mind would leave his body due to one deadly scare after another.

Tanko wondered who was left to love this kind man called Jimmy. He had mentioned a friend called Billie. Maybe he was an old man too? Tanko thought that if he liked this man so much in only one day, he could soon love him too, like a grandson would love a grandfather. He was strong, he could stay and help Jimmy grow his vegetables and look after his birds. Perhaps one day he might even feel safe enough to pick up his studies again and make his dream come true to be a great teacher.

Tanko remembered another old Nigerian saying that his father often repeated. *A fowl remembers who trims his feathers during the rainy season.* He meant that a person will never forget the help given to him by another person when times were hard. At his home in the rainy season it was difficult for birds to seek food as their feathers grew. Tanko knew that he would never forget the kindness of this man Jimmy who was so gentle with his birds. Perhaps his father had foreseen the future when he had taught Tanko this proverb and was even now guiding him to safety? He suddenly wondered if Jimmy had sensed him staring, as the old man slowly opened his eyes and smiled.

'This music is a bit fuddy-duddy for a young lad. Frank Sinatra this fella is called. This song's called "My Way". My wife said it was made for me.' Tanko listened to Jimmy singing along with a few words about having his fill, his share of losing. Tanko knew just how he felt. He almost felt like singing along, he could feel a humming noise rising in his throat. Maybe if he could stay with this man, he would feel calm enough to sing these very words one day?

'Here, I'll put something on you might like.' Jimmy hauled himself up and headed over to the table where he turned off the ancient-looking gramophone with a turntable and needle. 'One of the things I missed most, when I was homeless, living on the streets, was having a record player and records. So this was the first thing my Hilda got for me from the local charity shop, when we moved in here. She got me this disc I'm about to play because I'd told her so many tales about my time serving in your neck of the woods, that she said she felt like she'd been to Nigeria herself.'

Jimmy carefully slid his Frank Sinatra record back into its sleeve and fumbled amongst his collection, finally lifting an old, dog-eared album cover up. He slid the black plastic LP out of its case, whilst Tanko watched transfixed as Jimmy carefully placed the needle on the revolving turntable. Tanko's grandfather had talked about having one of these contraptions, but it looked like some ancient antique to Tanko.

All of a sudden, as if by magic, the room was filled with the sound of his home village on the outskirts of Baga town, as a folk song rang out in Tanko's own Eastern Kanuri dialect. The song was accompanied by the percussion sound of the huge half calabashes so familiar to Tanko, being played along with a goje fiddle, like the one his own great-grandfather had been able to play so well. He had been playing it outside of his home in his village, which had lain only a mile from where Tanko's parents were slain, when Tanko had been a witness to Boko Haram marching in and wiping out the residents, having had suspicions of them conspiring with the state authorities against the rebels.

The music had transported Tanko to the scene in an instant. The modus operandi of Boko Haram had been to march in formation into locations which might have harboured armed government forces. At the front, small boys strode, kidnapped from villages on earlier raids. These were followed by cattle. The reason for this was to see how many armed men might be hiding, waiting for the attack. The number of children and animals felled in the initial spate of defensive fire, would give a good indication of the armed strength of the forces waiting.

Only after this estimation had been made, would the true Boko Haram fighters swoop in from behind, heads and faces swathed in dark scarves and heavily armed, to conduct the swift and brutal massacre. When it was over and they had swept out once more, without a sound to be heard, save for the odd moan of someone unlucky enough to be suffering a slow and painful death, having half-escaped into the bush, Tanko had hung back and picked up his great-grandfather's goje as a keepsake, reminding him of his rapidly depleted family.

Of course, they, like everything else that Tanko had once held so precious to him, had been lost in his flight from Nigeria, but here in a small bungalow in a cold part of the earth seemingly a million miles away, Tanko's past life danced inside of his head to the beat of his breaking heart. Tears started to run down his face as though a dam had burst. It was the first time that Tanko had been able to cry in all of the time since the Boko Haram attacks had started to shatter the peaceful law-abiding life of his family.

Jimmy hobbled over to Tanko and patted him on the shoulder. 'Reckon a good old cry will do you the world of good, son.' Tanko gripped the kind man's bony hand in thanks. 'I'll put the kettle on,' Jimmy added, heading slowly towards his kitchen.

Tanko had learned already that in this country, people looked for solace in tea to soothe all of their woes. Little did they know how lucky they were to have such a simple solution to their problems. Tanko could hear noises coming from his throat now, a whispering sound that turned into a name. 'Mama,' he heard himself saying quietly.

It had not escaped his notice, despite the shock at finally finding his voice, that his very first word spoken since leaving Africa, was oddly identical to the last word that Jimmy's war victim had keened.

TWENTY-NINE
A NEW PATH FORWARD

'I'm sorry to be such a nuisance, but I didn't know where else to go.' Maya was sobbing into a handkerchief, wringing it between her fingers, as Billie entered Boo's house.

'It's okay, honey, you can stay here anytime,' Boo soothed. 'And I'm sure Billie is happy to have you stay at her place too, if you're ever stuck.' Boo glanced up at Billie like someone relieved to see the cavalry on the horizon. Her friend had, after all, Billie considered, already been through a harrowing day.

'But until you made me ring, I wasn't sure if Dad was at *hers*.' Maya glanced up sheepishly towards Billie, who mentally rolled her eyes at the comment.

'Can I make this clear once and for all, your dad and I aren't in any special relationship, other than a business one.' Billie said the words through a sigh, wondering what had got the normally level-headed girl so worked up.

'Well, it won't be for the want of Dad trying.' Maya wiped her face. 'It's like that thing he does, you know, singing a song or humming along to it, when something's on his mind. If he's been ranting on about Connie's mum, for example, he'll start singing "Devil Woman" and then

212

when he says something about you it's followed by him humming "Love to Love You Baby", without even realising.'

Boo burst out laughing as Maya wiped her nose.

'He does not.' Billie couldn't help shaking her head with a smile at the vision that came into her mind.

'You know that he *does* do that singing thing, Billie,' Boo answered through a chuckle. Billie did, she'd mentioned that habit of Ellis's herself more than once. It was a big giveaway on what he was thinking at any given moment.

'Well, it's just a coincidence because there is nothing between me and your dad except a simple friendship and our business affairs. Ask him yourself.'

'Well, he won't talk to me, will he?' Tears started to trickle down Maya's face again. Billie realised that she and Maya were in the same boat. Ellis wasn't in the mood to talk to her right now either.

'His phone's probably just off. You've heard about Connie. He's at the hospital,' Billie said, trying to reason.

'Yeah, it's horrible. But he wouldn't let me go to the hospital to see her. I kept telling him it wasn't *me* who spiked her pie with glass!' Maya started crying again. Billie flopped down in one of Boo's chairs.

'Right, can we go back to the start here. I'm not following...' Billie looked from Maya, blowing her nose into a handkerchief, to Boo, who finally came to her assistance.

'That's why I got Maya to call you over tonight.'

'Yeah, because my dad was stalking me, just like he used to do with Mum all those years back–'

Billie shook her head in order to clear it. The story of Boo and Ellis working together way back in an investigation for the NCA, in which Ellis had a relationship with Maya's mother whilst using an undercover persona, had been dissected so many times that Billie couldn't understand why it was being brought up again.

'Why do you think he was stalking you, Maya?' Billie tried to concentrate on getting to the bottom of this distressed daughter scenario. Suddenly her night of adult conversation with just a hint of romance, in the company of Matteo Scalera seemed an awfully long way off. Boo answered.

'Because he knocked her to the ground and unmasked her when she was working undercover with the animal activists. He probably didn't realise who he was chasing. She was wearing that...' Boo waved her hand towards the black boiler suit that Maya had been wearing, almost identical to the one Billie remembered from the night before.

'Were you also wearing a skeleton mask?' Billie asked, unconsciously rubbing the wound on her own head partly caused by the injury of the night before.

'Yeah, but only because people start to jump to all sorts of conclusions once you show your face. Good citizens end up in secret dossiers, just look at Mum–'

'So you were the one who binned me on the head last night?' Billie demanded.

A look of shock crossed Maya's face.

'No. I was not! You see? This is what happens. Suddenly I'm being blamed for *everything* when all I was involved in was a lawful protest! Suddenly I'm what, hitting you with a bin or something and poisoning kids with glass pies? What is wrong with you people?'

Billie sat back in her chair and surveyed the very agitated girl. At one time Maya had wanted to join the police force and had assisted Billie in the MIT as part of her uni course. She had shown great promise, working undercover on a murder enquiry. But more than anything, Billie had been impressed by the young woman's honesty. If Maya claimed that she didn't bin her or spike Connie's pie, she absolutely believed her. She also now totally understood Ellis's reticence on the subject.

'You might want to be aware that your dad didn't tell me it was you who he caught tonight. So he's been pretty loyal in that respect, I think.'

'Really?' Maya looked sheepish. Billie shook her head slowly and mimed a lip-zipping movement.

'Not a word,' she answered, her heart going out to poor Ellis. He must have already been bricking it, having caught Maya at the Porkie's protest, so thinking she had issued the threats and spiked the pies, even before he discovered that Connie had eaten one. No wonder he had been in such a bolshie mood at the hospital. 'Right then. Can I look at the gloves you were wearing tonight?' Billie asked.

Maya nodded. 'They'll be in the pocket of that boiler suit.'

Billie headed over to the suit which was lying on the seat almost like a faceless body. She pulled out a pair of navy knitted gloves.

'So just like Cinderella's Prince Charming, I am looking for the person who was wearing that suit and the same mask last night, and who ran off leaving me the charm logo that I ripped off their black leather gloves. Do you know who was up there on the podium last night if it wasn't you?'

Maya shook her head. 'I have absolutely no idea. We all just take turns to put on one of those big suits and masks so that exactly this sort of thing doesn't happen. There's another couple of those outfits at the activist base. It could have been anyone. But if I did know who it was, then I couldn't grass them up.' Maya folded her arms stubbornly. Like father, like daughter, Billie mused. 'Next thing you'll be dragging me along to the cop shop holding cells.' Billie couldn't help admiring Maya's feistiness, but all the same, she wasn't in the mood for giving up that easily.

'Didn't you have a discussion with the delightful Johnny Briggs about him having a pair of gloves with a charm logo just like that, only this morning?' Billie raised an eyebrow in question.

Maya responded with indignation. 'I wondered when you would try and put Johnny in the picture. I said that I was probably mistaken about the glove thing. Since Johnny's gotten me a couple of modelling contacts I've been wearing loads of different clothes for test shots. I probably saw the logo on one of those outfits.'

'Johnny hasn't ever tried to make you do anything you don't want to do, has he, Maya?' Billie watched as the girl fell silent for a minute. She'd never seen Maya look so stressed. 'Because you well know that I've had some experience of con men myself.' She wiped away one or two horror-filled memories as she spoke. 'In fact, I reckon I could just about run courses on sussing them out now.' One thing she had learned was that clever con men swiftly discovered what people were desperately yearning for and pretended to fill that space.

With Maya it was a sense of direction. Boo needed a talented person devoted to helping out at Freedom Angels, whereas Graham Harper was on a last-ditch search for someone to truly love him and make his secret dreams come true. Truth was, Billie guessed, that Johnny Brigg's only real devotion was to the advancement of Johnny Briggs. She just didn't have any hard evidence to prove that yet.

'I agreed to do some special pictures...' Maya trailed off looking uneasy. Billie's heart sank. 'I really didn't want to do those, but Johnny said that they were just for the two of us. You know, private stuff...' Billie's stomach turned at the thought.

'But then he said that a friend had gotten hold of them and was threatening to share online, if we didn't pay them not to...

that if the photos got out, then it would put an end to any idea of me doing high fashion and catwalk modelling.'

Billie wanted to beat Johnny Briggs to a pulp right at that moment just as much as she wanted to take Maya in her arms and give her a tight hug. She had learned that heartbreak, unfortunately, felt just as painful whether it was in connection with a good guy or in reaction to getting too close to the scum of the earth.

'How much?' Boo asked, glancing at Billie.

'Three thousand...' Maya swallowed hard, more tears now trickling down her cheeks. 'But Johnny said if I got the money to him, he would pay it back as soon as he could. He's blaming himself for the whole thing... It wiped out my savings, but as we're in a long-term relationship, I know that he *really will* repay...' Maya was clearly battling to convince herself, the actual truth finally dawning on her, but just in case it wasn't, Billie decided to speak up.

'I'm so sorry but, Maya, I feel I should let you know for a fact that Johnny has asked someone else to marry him.' Billie had learned herself the hard way that the quicker these things were out in the open the soonest mended. A look of shock swept over Maya's pretty features for just a split second before she put on a brave face, answering in a whisper.

'So, we're not exclusive. Johnny says that's such an outmoded concept. But we'll always be in a forever relationship. He came back with me last night and he was at Tina's exhibition earlier so he couldn't have been the activist on the podium yesterday evening.'

'I think I recall him saying that he slunk in after the exhibition had started. Don't even try to keep on defending him, Maya. He's a fucking evil abuser, who's been using you. Face up to that. So, that bastard aside and regardless of who was on the podium protesting yesterday, I absolutely need to know who printed the banner that the protester was holding. Your dad and I are involved in a food fraud investigation involving threats to spike products. No prizes for guessing which business is involved or why activists holding banners which might be seen as inciting by a blind man on a galloping horse, right outside their door, might be considered suspects.'

'Like I said a moment ago. Even if I knew, I couldn't grass them up,' Maya whispered.

'Time to grow up, lovely.' Billie stroked Maya's hand. 'The spiking of a product with broken glass has just resulted in your little sister being rushed to hospital. Both the threats received to poison products and some of the animal activist's banners have the same wording. Let me jog your memory on the print.' Maya looked down for a moment sheepishly, whilst Boo craned her head over Billie's shoulder, as she scrolled through her phone for online news photos featuring the protesters that very night. She stopped at one picture.

'Here we are. See the words on the banner? It says "pies to die for." Are we agreed? This was taken from tonight's protest and the person wearing the skull mask is holding it. I think we all accept that was *you*. Now look at this threat received only this morning by Graham Harper...'Billie clicked across to the photo she had taken of the latest threatening letter before leaving it at King & Beech Forensics, after rushing there to try to support Boo. Technically she was breaking a confidence in sharing the posted message, but she was determined to make Maya spill the beans. '"Pies to die for",' Billie said, reading the words out loud once again. 'Identical.'

'No they aren't.' Boo suddenly gasped out loud. 'The big banners aren't printed in capital letters.'

'But the words are the same,' Billie argued. 'It's not the first similar message either–' she started to explain, but Boo cut over her words.

'They sound the same. But they aren't the same when they are written in capital letters. The posted threat in capital letters, has the number one printed out instead of the letter I.'

Billie blinked, realising that Boo was right. How on earth had she not noticed that anomaly when she had first set eyes on it? Billie mentally kicked herself before remembering the arrival of Tina, Maya and Johnny Briggs in Graham Harper's office and then rushing off to King & Beech, telling Ellis to bugger off in the process. The day had progressed even more crazily for all sorts of reasons after that point. The oversight emphasised that she had been right to insist that The NCA should be called in to lead the investigation. Back in the day when she had been heading up the local MIT one of the team would have spotted it if she hadn't. Back then, Boo *had* been one of her team.

'What about the others?' she asked herself out loud, quickly flicking onto the photos that she had taken of the other posted threats. 'They're all in lowercase...' Billie added, checking carefully. The letter i was printed as expected in all of the other threats, as were all of the letters on the banners being used by the animal rights activists. Billie ran her fingers through her hair. It was a lead of sorts, but how on earth would they be able to follow it up quickly? Boo, though looking distraught, offered the answer.

'The printer that's been used, at least for the "pies to die for" threat, in capital letters, I'm sure it's one of ours at Freedom Angels. The letter 'I' when capitalised, always misprints as a figure 1.' Boo sounded distraught. 'It's a problem with the print driver being corrupted. We've been waiting ages for the guy to come in and fix it. It doesn't happen with lowercase letters.'

'Johnny Brigg use it often when he's been entering into the wonderful world of design with the young people there?' Billie questioned, shaking her head in dismay, silently chastising herself for not taking action to get rid of the man after the first time she had set eyes on him. Her instinct hadn't been far wrong after all.

'Oh my God, this will look bad for Freedom Angels, if word gets out in the press that a place that champions the rights of asylum seekers, is found to be involved in food spiking,' Boo announced. 'The press are always eager for a shock horror story like that. This will finish us.' She started circling in her power chair, as she always did when she was stressed.

'Hopefully it won't finish off Connie too, Maya. If you do know who's responsible for all of this, then for goodness' sake just spit it out now. The lives of countless people are in jeopardy in addition to the future of Freedom Angels. Do you really want to wipe out the amazing work that both you and Boo have done in setting the place up? Don't you think that the people coming through those doors have suffered enough?'

Maya nodded, her head bent down, as she finally took out her mobile and scrolled through her photo album, whilst Boo and Billie exchanged tense glances. Finally, with a big sigh, Maya held a photo up to face Billie, who was struck dumb for a moment. The identity of the individual whom she was staring at was a million miles away from the person that Billie had expected.

THIRTY
GONE DEAD

B illie felt absolutely dead beat, having spent the previous
night dossing down on Ellis's sofa, but had refused Boo's
offer to stay at her place. The air there was too fraught with
tension for Billie to think straight and she dearly needed a long
hot shower and a good night's sleep in order to face the meeting
first thing the next morning at Porkie's Big Eats head office. She
thought of texting Ellis one more time, but then decided to leave
it for tonight. Hopefully no news was good news.

Billie checked her watch as she left Boo's house, her
stomach rumbling thanks to a scant supper, simply a mouthful
of delicious Italian food before the pie-spiking drama involving
poor little Connie, had kicked off. There had been some
highlights to the day, though, she reflected, thinking of her
rather delicious dinner companion. The time with him had
been cut short way too soon, unfortunately, for both professional
and personal reasons. They seemed to share a similar mindset
and Matt had access to a world that offered the very best
possibilities to carry out the most in-depth investigations. She
hated being on the sidelines, hands tied by lack of authority to
dig into cases more deeply. Would she ever come across the

seemingly globe-trotting Matteo Scalera again? She had to admit that she hoped so.

It was nearly midnight, with a full moon overhead. The myth was that all sorts of madness became heightened at this exact time, but Billie wasn't sure how much more madness she could take right now. Once again, she thought of the missing asylum-seeking children. Were they looking up at the same full moon tonight hoping for some sort of magic to happen to change the course of their sad young lives?

As Billie climbed back into her car, she heard her mobile ping. She hoped it wasn't more bad news. As she clicked on the message, a photo burst into view. Shockwaves momentarily paralysed her body. She blinked, hoping that she was imagining the vision, but no, the photo was still staring back at her. It was her own image, looking straight at the camera, a coquettish smile playing upon her lips. Behind her was Ellis and sitting beside them smiling at the camera, was Connie. Billie thought she might vomit, for a moment her mind was racing, trying to work out how on earth such a photo could even exist, because all three were perched together on a large bed.

Connie, thank God at least, was fully clothed and holding one of her dolls, but the heads of both Billie and Ellis had been transposed onto naked porn star bodies. Billie clicked on the screen, for she had now realised that what she had been sent was a piece of video footage, in all of its grunting, cavorting porn session glory. The mobile fell from her hand for a moment before she scrabbled on the floor of the car to retrieve it and stop the recording. Below the footage were a few words. *Back off now, or this goes viral.*

Her mobile suddenly rang, the caller ID not flashing up. Could this be the sender, having been waiting to see when she had opened her message? Billie thought of not answering, but only for a split second, coming to her senses, realising that it might be a call made from the hospital.

If, on the other hand, it was from the sick individual who was threatening to upload the footage, then she needed to face it head-on. If the video was spread worldwide, it could not only finish Wilde & Darque PI, but any chance of Ellis retaining custody of Connie in his upcoming battle with Storm Benbow. Especially after the events in the park involving young boys and the police only the night before. Billie needed to put this to bed right now. She damned herself for having conjured up such an unfortunate choice of words.

'Yep,' she answered, deciding not to give anything away regarding her shaken equilibrium, if this was indeed the person threatening her.

'Billie? It's Matt.' Billie felt all of the tension release from her neck and shoulders. She held the phone closer to her ear, switching off the loudspeaker she had clicked on to give some distance between herself and the caller. 'I'm just ringing to see if Connie is okay?'

'I think so. Boo managed to have a word with Ellis earlier. They are keeping her in for observation so...'

'You sound upset. Ellis isn't still blaming you?' Billie pressed the receiver closer to her face. She liked the sound of his voice, it was soothing, sounding in control somehow.

'No, I mean, I don't know.' A thought suddenly ran through Billie's mind. 'Look, you know the deepfake that you pointed out in the advert, featuring Connie. Would you know how to track down the person who posted that, or any other deepfake?' Billie ran her fingers through her hair. This was a nightmare, but if anyone had the necessary contacts then a National Crime Agency operative surely had.

'It depends. If it's a video file then the Cyber Crime Unit can analyse the metadata used to create or edit the video, though a clever creator can alter that, or they can track the IP address. It depends how devious or smart the creator has been. Are you talking about the video with Connie eating the pie on the big screen? Surely the CEO of the company will have details on who made that,' Matt advised.

'No, it's not that one. It's much worse. Is it too late to bring it around to show you exactly what I'm dealing with?' Billie suddenly desperately wanted to see this man even if he didn't have the answer she needed.

'Not at all. It would be a pleasure. I will rustle up some midnight snacks. I have some intel about the missing kids you might be able to help me with, so you show me yours and I'll show you mine,' Matt teased. Billie couldn't help giving a wan smile. 'Mine doesn't make for good viewing, I'm afraid. So brace yourself. I'll be with you in ten.'

Whilst Matt looked at the footage on Billie's mobile, she glanced around the opulent hotel suite. It was clear that the NCA valued this operative of theirs highly. No expense had been spared. Billie could see files piled up beside an open laptop placed on a desk and though Matt was now dressed in a white T-shirt and soft, dark tracksuit bottoms, that appeared to be made from cashmere, it had been clear that he wasn't about to turn in early that night, even if Billie hadn't invited herself over.

'It's not actually my body,' Billie was at pains to point out.

Matt had been biting his bottom lip, concentrating on the footage, but now glanced up with a soft smile. 'I think I had worked that out. I do know that Ellis hasn't got dark chest hair like a shag-pile rug too, having shared digs with him way back on past jobs.'

Billie felt squeamish once more. She hadn't been able to bring herself to view the footage again yet.

'Well, the sort of good news is that young Connie is featured in this. As you know, it's a serious crime to post any visuals of a sexual nature involving a child, even if the child isn't involved in any acts. That means that I can get it over to a friend I know who is the best in the business at pinpointing the source of deepfakes. She's based in our Cyber Crimes Unit.'

'Thank God.' Billie flopped down on a velvet upholstered chair in shades of old gold.

'The quite surprising fact, to most people, is that if Connie hadn't featured in this, if it had simply been you and Ellis, then it isn't currently illegal in much of the world, to create and post such scam porn footage online, even without the consent of the person whose image is being used.'

'You are *joking*.' Billie couldn't believe what she was hearing, bearing in mind the possible consequences for the victims of such abuse.

'A new law has just been passed in the UK, making it illegal, should the creator be caught in this country and charged here and it can be proven that they had the intention to harm or humiliate the victim.'

'Could there be any doubt?' Billie was aghast.

'In certain situations. Lots of loopholes in the law to jump through in order to get a conviction. There is even a popular app that anyone with a smartphone can download, to create these types of things with a few clicks, knowing that there's rarely any comeback. There are loads of online sites where such footage as this can be commissioned, sold or swapped and spread far and wide. It's a money-maker because unfortunately there is a huge market for the stuff and until the law in every corner of the world catches up with technology there is nothing to frighten people off continuing.' Matt was clicking on Billie's mobile as he spoke. He held up his own mobile against hers and then clicked on his own. 'There. I've sent it over to her. Don't worry, it's encrypted.'

'Get you, James Bond.' Billie blew air through her lips as she dragged her fingers through her hair.

'Got all sorts of state-of-the-art gadgets at our fingers tips in the NCA, Billie, if you ever feel like joining us there.' Matt raised an eyebrow in question. Billie couldn't help wondering about the nature of his relationship with the techno wizard of a woman who was waiting somewhere at midnight to do his digital bidding. She suddenly felt scruffy and stupid and decided she had better head home. But she needed still more answers.

'What was the intel about the missing kids you wanted to share?' Billie asked.

'Have you seen this logo anywhere before?' Matt beckoned Billie over to his laptop and brought a photo up. Billie bent forward, her eyes scanning the picture, immediately alert.

'Yes. I ripped a logo exactly like this off a glove of an animal rights activist here in the central square only last night. It was attached to a black leather glove. Where did you find these?'

Matt clicked on his screen once more. It showed a montage of shots that Billie immediately recognised as having been taken in a mortuary. There were shots of the dead children that Boo had identified earlier that day.

'Josta found these in the pockets of the children autopsied today, including the boy found in the field, who fell victim to tractor wheels...' Billie squeezed her eyes shut for a moment to block out the desperately sad view of that small, young broken body. 'I think you've just answered the question as to what they are. If you are correct, then it points to the children being used as slave labour in another clothing counterfeit set-up.'

'But as far as I know, there aren't any designer logos like this.

Not that I know much about these things.' Billie guessed that she hadn't needed to point that out to the very stylish Matteo Scalera. One look at her scuffed boots, threadbare jeans and woolly jumper would have told him all he needed to know about her interest in high fashion.

'It's still a step in the right direction. Just let me get this out to the operatives in the field, Billie. Help yourself to food, wine–' Matt was suddenly deep in concentration on his laptop, a man after her own heart. She had often been criticised for being obsessed with her job above everything else when she had been head of the MIT team. A shiver ran down her spine as she watched him. In a good way. She looked across in the direction that Matt had indicated, where a coffee table was laden with enticing nibbles and wine in an ice bucket. Her tummy suddenly rumbled as her appetite started to come back.

Just then her mobile messaging played out a tune. Billie glanced at the clock on the wall. It was now half past midnight. Not normally the time for good news. She braced herself, clicked on to answer and almost breathed out a squeal of relief as Ash's smiling face loomed into view, framed by a dark sky spangled with stars. Palm trees behind him swayed in the breeze.

'Looks like you're having a good time.' Billie smiled. She was thrilled that this long-planned holiday with Ash's ex and their children seemed to be working out as he had hoped.

'Yeah, great. Sun, sea and sand. The kids are tucked up, Jas is chilled and I'm having a few bevvies. Just calling to say, wish you were here.' Ash looked like he'd had more than a few. Billie couldn't help smiling. She'd had so many good times when Ash had been her wingman, despite the fact that they had been investigating murders.

It was at that moment that Billie noticed the T-shirt that Ash was wearing. It had the same logo design across the front as

227

the charm that Billie had torn from the animal activist's glove and that Matt had just shown on the harrowing mortuary photos. She sat up straight, staring into the phone screen.

'That T-shirt you're wearing, Ash. Where did you get it?' she asked.

'Safia gave it to me. The other night, just before the kids modelled for her at Freedom Angels. Gave me one for each of the girls as well, for helping with her show. Part of a new fashion range apparently. The other people involved want to do a major media launch, so she has to keep it all hush-hush until they tip her the wink.'

'Stay right where you are.' Billie jumped up and marched across to Matt, the phone in her hand. 'Look, Matt. The same logo is on Ash's T-shirt. It's Safia's design.'

'Safia who's gone missing?' Matt spun around in his chair to stare at Ash.

'Oh, hello, now who is *this* gorgeous man that you're in some beautiful bedroom with?' Ash teased tipsily. Billie felt herself flushing.

'This isn't a gorgeous man... this is Matteo Scalera, an NCA operative...' Billie trailed off, glancing at Matt as he raised an eyebrow at her unwitting insult.

'Well, he's looking pretty damn gorgeous from where I'm standing!' Ash announced loudly, before giving a whistle of appreciation. Ash was giddy on drink, but if he'd been standing near her in the flesh, Billie wondered if she might have been tempted to knock him out at that moment.

'Do you know where Safia's new clothing range is being made? Ash, listen, this is important,' Billie begged, but Ash was clearly too drunk to jump to attention.

'Search me. She said the people working with her had all that stuff in hand, but she wanted to start involving local people. I'm just wearing the T-shirt because the kids think I look like an old dinosaur on the beach otherwise. Anyway. I don't want to play gooseberry,' Ash teased mischievously. 'Sadly, one of us is ready to go to bed... alone.' Before Billie could question Ash further, the screen went blank.

'My mum thought I was pretty gorgeous,' Matt said, when Billie glanced across at him, putting her mobile in her pocket, a sheepish look on her face. His was deadpan. Was he joking, or had her budding new friendship just gone dead too?

THIRTY-ONE

HIDE YOUR LOVE AWAY

I t was not quite 7am when Ellis was called to the day room of the children's ward, where Billie was waiting, a bacon sandwich in one hand, a cup of strong coffee in the other. His stomach started to rumble as he approached her, shamefaced. He knew that he'd been out of order to have had her chucked out the night before, but here she was first thing, looking absolutely gorgeous, in what looked like new kit and bearing gifts. He didn't deserve her.

Maybe it had been down to the shock of seeing her with that blast from the past Matteo Scalera, who he had always been pitted against from their very first training days together at the NCA They'd always been equally good at the job, but it had been Matt, not him, who had landed the girl-magnet charm and good lucks. The last thing he had expected was for him to turn up in this neck of the woods and worst of all, in the company of Billie.

But still, the nurses had been chattering about him running in like some sort of Greek god holding his Connie in his arms. They were all wanting to know if Ellis could fix them up on a date. Truth was, he should have been more grateful, rather than blaming him and Billie for getting help pronto for his little one. He'd had time to think about it, as he had lay beside his tiny angel who had finally settled down after all of the scans and poking around and had slept like a log, unlike him. He'd watched her like a hawk all night. Every breath in, every breath out.

'How is she?' Billie asked as she handed over the sandwich. Ellis spotted she'd put extra brown sauce in, just the way he liked it. They were like an old couple these days. 'I've put in three sugars. Good for shock. Upgrade from your usual two spoonfuls,' Billie had quipped as he had sat down next to her and taken the cup of coffee from her hand.

'Yeah, she's not bad, ta. Even knocked back a few cornflakes can you believe, for breakfast, so things are looking up and she's playing with one of her new little mates right now, from the next-door bed, loving all the attention. The nursery nurse is with them. Docs reckoned she'd only copped for a tiny bit of glass that had cut her lip and caused all the blood, but they wanted to keep an eye on her. They'll probably let her out later today.'

'That's good. But I have to say, it did look scary.' Billie dragged her fingers through her hair, her usual stress response to anything that was bothering her, Ellis knew. It was one of her mannerisms that he loved, a giveaway that she wasn't really the tough nut she often portrayed to those who didn't know her the way that he did.

'Look, I owe you an apology. I was out of order last night. I should have been thanking you, rather than giving you a bollocking. It's just that sometimes I get all het up over this fathering thing, floundering around not knowing what I'm doing half the time.' Ellis wanted Billie to be sure that he definitely wasn't laying any blame on her.

'It's okay. Someone once told me that anger is really fear in disguise. Mind you, he was a psychopathic killer so what do I know about these things?' Billie shared a smile with Ellis. Little did she know how much her smiles made his day.

'He might have a point. I'm bricking it that Storm is going to bombard the social worker about my parenting shortcomings. Main thing is though, I want to make it clear that I don't think that it was your fault, any of what happened, Billie. It was Maya's for feeding her the bleeding thing in the first place. I mean, what was going through her mind? That spiked pie could have killed her own sister.'

'Listen. It wasn't Maya who spiked the pie. She's adamant about that and I believe her. She wasn't the activist who binned me the night before last either, or the one who printed the banners.'

'You're sure about that?' Ellis hoped to God that Billie was being straight with him. If she was telling the truth, right now he could hug her. The very thought that his eldest girl who he loved to death, truth be told, could have done such a thing, had been eating away at him all night. Especially after she had shown such promise not so very long ago, as a police trainee. But then another thought made him tense back up immediately.

'So the evil bastard is still out there?' Ellis slammed down his coffee on the table next to his seat. It created a small tidal wave. A passing nurse put her finger to her lips.

'Can you keep it down? Got a pile of sick kids in here,' she admonished.

'Yeah, yeah. Sorry,' Ellis mumbled sheepishly, yanking a crumpled paper tissue out of his pocket and wiping the table.

'But I do now know the person responsible for both.'

'So who is he?' Ellis jumped up now and started pacing. 'I'll kill him!' he bellowed.

The nurse stopped in her tracks and turned back.

'Like I said, shut it. If you want to have a domestic in here,

I'll be calling security right now.' Ellis lifted his hand in apology, before sitting down again. 'Leaflets about domestic abuse up there, love, if you need one.' The nurse nodded to Billie whilst pointing to a rack filled with various pamphlets next to where they were sitting.

'I'll fill you in on all of the details later. You've got enough on your plate here,' Billie argued in a whisper. 'I've got a meeting first thing with Graham Harper. He's agreed to close all of the outlets for the time being. All taken care of.'

'I'll be taking care of the nutter who did this myself regardless. So spill his name,' Ellis hissed in a furious whisper, his head close to Billie's as the nurse sat down at her station, keeping a beady eye on them.

Billie sighed. 'Okay. But only if you don't start kicking off. Your job today is to stay here and concentrate on Connie.'

'I'd be able to do that a lot better if I knew who to watch out for. The crazy might be handing out pies here in the hospital next, for all we know.'

Ellis knew that he was irritating Billie as well as the nurse, but he *had* to know that name. Billie shook her head to indicate that she was beat, before leaning forward conspiratorially. As a curl of her wild red hair brushed against his cheek, Ellis had so wanted to press closer to her, but as she whispered the name of the culprit responsible for the whole pie-spiking scenario in her ear, he sprung back in his chair instead, absolutely stunned.

'I don't effing believe it!' Ellis rubbed his head as though he was in pain.

'Came as a shock to me too, but like I said, it's all under control now and Connie seems to be okay, so try and chill.'

'Chill?' he questioned, still trying to shake off the feeling of incredulity. 'I can't get my head round it. Are you sure?'

'Yep. Look, we can talk more later, yeah?' She patted him on the shoulder. Ellis didn't want her to leave, but he could see now why she had to make that meeting. Maybe tonight when he had Connie safely back home he could treat her to a takeaway pizza, crack open a bottle of wine. Happy days between them again. Ellis wolfed down the last bite of his sandwich before wiping his hands on his jeans, realising he was comfort eating, just like Billie told him he always did.

'You'll say ta to Matt Scalera when you next get together, for me. Tell him I owe him one,' Ellis offered, though he still couldn't bear to think of them hanging out together, despite his show of contrition.

'I don't know when that might be. He's heading off today. He's on the missing asylum kids case. Seems it's linked to some European-wide gang.' Billie ran her fingers through her hair again.

Ellis's spirits rose at that news. 'He's been here helping out Boo then?' he asked hopefully.

'Let's hope he can,' Billie answered.

'Bummer about those kids,' Ellis commiserated. He could see that Billie really had a bee in her bonnet about it. Clearly *that's* the reason they'd been hanging out together. 'One thing I'll say is that if anyone can get to the bottom of it all, Scalera will. He's like a dog with a bone, that one. Left broken hearts all over the place, back in the day, because for him work really does come first,' he added, hoping Billie had gotten that message loud and clear.

It seemed to have hit home, Ellis decided. She'd gone quiet. He loved looking at her when she had her mind on something, that faraway look in those true-blue eyes. He suddenly realised that he'd started humming a tune. 'You've Got to Hide Your Love Away.' It summed it all up for him. He desperately wanted to pull her into his arms. But Billie suddenly stood up.

'Right. That's me off. But there's one broken heart waiting, desperate to be reunited with her little sister and her dad.' Billie nodded to the door leading to the corridor outside. Maya was nervously looking through the glass panel. Ellis immediately sprang up and rushed over, grabbing a tearful Maya in a huge bear hug as Billie swung the door open.

'Thanks, Billie. Thanks, mate... Ellis patted Billie on the shoulder as she edged past him and his girl. Ellis had wanted to yank her into a team hug too, like one big family scrum. But it was enough right now that she had been here for him this morning. It was his desperate hope that she would be alongside him every morning, at some point in the future. Scoffing bacon sandwiches with brown sauce, cornflakes at the breakfast table and a wild time in the bedroom. But softly, softly, caught the monkey. If he bided his time and kept his temper, who knew? Maybe it might just happen.

'Guess it's right what they say. All the nice girls are attracted to bad boys.' The nurse had pushed out of the door past a loved-up Ellis and Maya, following Billie in the direction of the lift. 'But take my advice and get out whilst the going is good. If you ask me you've got yourself mixed up with a right heartbreaker there, love.'

———

Billie checked her watch as she left the hospital. She wanted to make sure that she made this meeting on time. She was also praying that Matt would be able to give her some information on the sender of the sickening video message that she had received the night before. She had steered clear from breaking *that* shocker to Ellis, deciding that he already had enough to deal with right now.

Billie was counting her fingers, toes and everything else that Matt's Cyber Crimes Unit contact would come up with the location of the device from which the deepfake footage originated, that would hopefully, in turn, lead them to the perpetrator and fast. All done and dusted, with a bit of luck, before Ellis even got to hear about it. Billie tried to brush away any musings on what sort of favours Matt might be planning to give in return for the special fast-track service. He had mentioned, after all, that his close contact was female and Ellis had just well and truly rammed home Matt's attractiveness to the opposite sex, not that she needed to have that spelled out.

As Billie climbed behind the wheel of her car, memories of the night that she had just spent with the crack NCA operative filled her thoughts. She'd already experienced that he was exceptionally talented in quite a few areas, that was for sure, she reflected, a smile playing on her lips. The captivating scent that made Billie have Matt so much on her mind right at that moment was also tantalisingly close. She was wearing his pristine white linen shirt, after all, along with his blue jeans, rolled up at the bottoms.

Both she and Matt had both been so consumed with trying to pinpoint where the base of the kidnappers might lie, according to various details in the autopsy reports, that it had been 3am when Billie had looked up and decided that she really had better head home.

'What we need is to find any other kids, who might have managed to escape and survived, to give us a clue to the location where they were taken.' Matt had topped up Billie's glass with the last of the wine as he had finished flipping back and forth through the reports.

'I'd better ring a cab,' Billie had announced. She wasn't a heavy drinker and in fact never drove at all when she had consumed any alcohol. She had seen enough drunk-drive road carnage in her time. Being a former copper, old habits still died hard.

'You're welcome to stay here,' Matt had offered. 'There's a

spare robe behind the door in the bathroom and a free toothbrush and all that gubbins. There's even a sewing kit should you have something to hem. No expense spared with the NCA,' he had joked. 'I'm happy to take this sofa. I've slept on a lot worse,' he said with a smile. Billie had hovered in thought for just a moment.

'No, I'll take the sofa, if you're sure that you don't mind?' She meant it. She had, after all, slept on Ellis's second-hand lumpy three-seater only the night before. That was before she had headed to Matt's luxurious bathroom however, and had stood under the hot shower, washing away the stresses of the long day.

When she had emerged, she'd had a rethink. Maybe she could have argued that it was down to the wine, but she didn't feel like making excuses anymore. She had simply been following her own true feelings when she had rejoined Matt, wrapped in the huge fluffy white robe, and announced quietly that she had changed her mind, she would take the bed, then held out her hand for him to accompany her. He hadn't needed any persuading, his obsession with autopsy reports swept aside with more than just a little haste.

Luckily Ellis had been so tired or stressed at his situation when she had headed to the hospital, or perhaps grateful for his unexpected breakfast and the delivery of his oldest daughter, that he hadn't questioned Billie's new attire, or perfume. It was just as well. Billie didn't want to fall out with him all over again, so soon.

She also didn't want to put a damper on her upbeat mood, despite the seriousness of the looming meeting. She had just enjoyed a night that wouldn't be easy to forget, and she wanted to hang on to that feeling, despite the lack of sleep. Both she and Matt had risen early, hesitant to separate, yet eager to get on with their occupations, sharing a soft and rather long goodbye kiss, rather than empty promises, as they had gone their separate ways.

Would she meet Matt Scalera again, even simply to hand back his borrowed clothing? She actually didn't know, both being happy to enjoy the moment rather than hold one another to a future commitment. It seemed like her new lover didn't ever know far in advance where he would be in the world and Billie rather liked that thought herself. Who knew what her own future might hold, after all?

Billie's thoughts turned to Maya as she edged her car out of the hospital car park into the morning traffic. The young girl had been up, dressed and waiting at Boo's front door, when Billie had texted her asking if she wanted to help Billie deliver her dad's breakfast at the hospital, keen to smooth the way back to the devoted father and daughter relationship that Maya and Ellis had so recently enjoyed.

Only a year before, Maya had fallen victim to a trafficking gang controlled by Storm Benbow's partner, a major criminal. Billie was intrigued to know why, being aware of the woman's connections, which had such an impact on her own life, Maya had taken it upon herself to let Connie have contact with her mum.

'Do you remember what Safia said when she introduced her show at Freedom Angels?' Maya had answered when Billie had broached the subject. 'That no one knew what they were capable of, good or bad, until they found themselves in extreme situations. Good men could do bad things and those with the darkest souls could also show kindness.'

Billie remembered Safia's speech and knew her words to be true through her own experiences as the head of a murder investigation team. She also knew that the social worker was taking the view that Storm Benbow had been coerced into helping her criminal boyfriend. Her story was that she had run in fear for her life, leaving Connie behind for the child's own safety. She'd allegedly been hiding away in a far-flung refuge for all of this time, because of her wholly innocent knowledge of her former lover's lethal business dealings.

Unlike Maya, Billie had actually met Storm. Only once, but it had been enough for her to strongly doubt that the heartstring-pulling tale that Storm was using was true. However, she had been proven wrong about people before, so maybe she was being over-suspicious. Perhaps her mind was being swayed by a life dealing close up with crime, as well as Ellis's fervent opinion on the matter? He'd made his own views crystal clear. Billie knew he would rot in hell before he would willingly let Storm have contact with Connie again.

'My dad was a good man who did something bad, when he got my mum pregnant with me. But when Mum found out that her long-missing lover, the one who had just walked out of the door one day, never to be seen again, was really an undercover officer on a job, whisked away when someone spilled that he'd taken things too far, she didn't try to stop me looking for *him*. Even on her deathbed, she had said something similar to Safia, that good men can sometimes do bad things when they are under pressure and that she knew in her heart that it had happened for a reason – that he was meant to be my dad, so go find him, she said, and I did.'

'And your mum was right, Maya. You know how much your dad loves you, so don't think of him having gotten your mum pregnant as a bad thing.' Billie was at pains to make sure Maya realised how important she was to Ellis, despite their current tensions.

'So I don't want Connie to grow up thinking her mum doesn't love her either. Maybe she did do some bad things, just like Dad, then disappeared, because of the extreme circumstances that she was in. So when she approached me, how could I really refuse? She told me that not having been able to hug Connie had been tearing her apart. If Dad could be given a second chance, when he never even met me until I was eighteen, surely Storm can be given a second chance with Connie when they've only been separated for a year?'

Billie had been approaching the hospital then, didn't want to get into a discussion about the fact that Storm had apparently palmed Connie off with childminders and nannies for her entire life, because in truth she'd only heard the story from Ellis's side. There was no doubt that Connie was desperately in need of a mother figure in her life, so Billie had finally reasoned that Maya might have had a point.

As she turned her car into the head offices of Porkie's Big Eats, she was about to confront someone else who had done a very bad thing. She wondered if they could argue their case as well as Maya had just done.

THIRTY-TWO
GOOD MEN DO BAD THINGS

Tanko carefully opened the bedroom door, holding the small tray in his hands. He had laid it out with some bread on a plate and had made tea the Nigerian way, with cocoa. He had been amazed when he had taken a chair from under the kitchen table and stood upon it to open a cupboard door, finding the dark-brown powder in there. He hoped that it was similar to the tea that his mother had made him for breakfast in Nigeria before all of the troubles had started.

Jimmy was still sleeping, making a loud snoring noise, his mouth wide open. Tanko had heard him cry out many times through the night, without any doubt living his own murderous nightmares. But Tanko had pushed a chair up against the door of his own bedroom as soon as he had bid the old man goodnight and tried to keep awake until dawn, in the hope that Jimmy didn't sleepwalk with an old bayonet in his hand, looking to relive his battles. In the morning light it had seemed such a stupid idea, but Tanko knew all too well that it was easy for the brain to play hideously cruel tricks on frail souls.

On the bedside table lay Jimmy's beret. It was the first time that Tanko had seen him without his hat on. His thin pink skin was stretched over his bald head. Tanko wasn't sure quite how old Jimmy was, but maybe nearly as old as his great-grandfather had been when he had passed. Tanko hoped that his new friend had a lot longer to live. He had already made a big difference to his life. If he stayed long enough, then maybe he could one day remove the chair from behind the bedroom door and sleep deeply like Jimmy seemed to be doing now.

The night before, after the old man had brought Tanko some British tea and Tanko had cried a little more at his memories, Jimmy had stayed beside him and encouraged him to find his voice, to tell his tale all the way through, until finally he had become exhausted as he had started to recount his journey across the sea to England. His voice had been husky and dry at first and then sometimes squeaky, not like his confident voice of old, but as the tea had lubricated his throat, he had slowly been able to speak his story out loud.

Jimmy had listened intently, nodding now and then, filling in the spaces when Tanko had broken down once more, wailing at his memories, with softly spoken tales of his own experiences when serving in the British army in different lands. Most, like Tanko's homeland, had been peaceful places, torn apart by warring factions. Jimmy had understood the things that Tanko had experienced, unlike many of the people in countries where nothing really bad had ever happened to them. Maybe like the people in this country, most of whom seemed to think that people like Tanko had come simply for an easy life.

'Good men sometimes do bad things, son.' Jimmy had patted Tanko's shoulder when he had said the words.

Had he been remembering his own bad things? Tanko didn't know, but Jimmy understood about the situation in Tanko's home area in the north-east of Nigeria, where Boko

Haram had emerged because the people there were so desperately poor, and those who were responsible for reducing poverty were extremely corrupt. The result had been that the money donated from many nations, never seemed to arrive in the outstretched hands of those who urgently needed help.

Instead, the rich people simply became even more wealthy. Boko Haram blamed western influences for the situation, as countries such as Britain had big business interests in the region, particularly gas and oil resources, so never addressed the corruption issues and instead wilfully helped fight any revolution with their own troops quietly on the ground. These countries no doubt had good intentions, but it seemed that the bad things were just getting worse.

Tanko had understood Boko Haram's argument too, for a short while, but when his uncle and great-grandfather had been lying in front of him in pools of blood, the very last of his family slain, the rest of the village's cattle and female children swept away by the convoy, he realised that there was no justice in this group's stance at all. They had become as corrupt as the people that they had claimed to be fighting.

His family had simply been poor farmers, scraping a living, with no links to the security services. Yet they'd had everything, including their very lives stolen. Maybe the Boko Haram fighters *had* been good men at the beginning, but now Tanko had no doubt that they were doing unbelievably bad things and he had to get away, hence him running and running as fast as he could, as though he would never stop.

'Breakfast, Grandfather. Your birds need food,' Tanko had whispered and watched Jimmy stir. He would have been happy to go and feed the pigeons himself. Maybe his new grandfather would show him how to do that today. He would dig his ground for him too and collect vegetables, make himself useful in every way, to thank the old man for his kindness and offer of shelter in his home.

'Aye, morning, son. Pleased to hear you've still got that voice of yours. Hope you managed some kip. Sorry, I'm being a bit of a lazybones today. I'm not used to late nights these days.' The old man pulled himself upright as Tanko plumped up his pillows. 'I'm not used to all this being looked after either. Breakfast in bed? I feel like I've died and gone to heaven, lad.' Jimmy gave a gummy smile. Tanko realised his teeth were soaking in a glass by his bedside.

'I'll just have this and then get myself up. I've got a big event on today. You can come along with me if you like. It's down at the old ex-servicemen's club.' Tanko shook his head, backing out towards the door. It sounded like army business, and he had every reason to be scared of armies, of all types.

'Please, no. I would rather stay with your birds and tend your crops, Grandfather.' Tanko kept his head down, willing Jimmy to agree, rather than send him on his way. His heart had started beating fast again with fearful thoughts. When he glanced up, Jimmy was looking at him.

'That sounds like a better idea, son. Happen I'm trying to make you run before you've properly started walking again.' Jimmy was thoughtful as he sipped his chocolate. Tanko watched his face carefully. The old man hadn't grimaced, so maybe he had made a good job of the drink. 'Tell you what. I need to get smartened up for this "do", so I'll put on those dapper gloves you gave me. Keep my old fingers nice and warm. It looks a bit cold out today. That suit you all right?'

Tanko nodded tentatively at the idea. He hoped he would be walking hand in hand with his kindly new 'grandfather' for a very long time to come. But right now he could feel a tidal wave of fear wash over him once more. If Jimmy met other former soldiers, maybe younger ones today, and told them about him being inside of Jimmy's home, might they be suspicious of his motives and come marching in to take him away? If they were like the troops in his homeland, always on the lookout for trouble, might they even kill him?

THIRTY-THREE
SHE'S GONE

Billie shook hands with Graham Harper who looked at her warily. 'I've taken your advice and invited Tina to the meeting this morning, Ms Wilde. The shareholders will arrive in an hour, so I'm hoping to have a strategy in place by then. But please, can we stick to business matters. Tina is already aware of the situation with the child and the shops being closed and I have to say the signs are that she is already highly stressed about it all.'

'I imagine she is. She actually knows little Connie,' Billie said grimly, as she followed Graham Harper to his office.

'But thank goodness that the child's injuries seem rather trivial.' Billie could practically see Graham Harper's inner calculator working out the appropriate amount of compensation to bribe Ellis with.

'Well, I wouldn't say that. Ellis is still at the hospital where he's been with her all night.'

'Quite. But not so bad as you thought, Ms Wilde.' Graham put on a wide smile as Tina swept into the room, her face ashen, closing the door firmly behind her.

'I've just heard about Connie. Is she going to be okay?' Tina, unlike her father, did appear to be genuinely shocked about the situation, which was odd, Billie mused.

'Hopefully,' Billie replied, as she placed her laptop on Graham Harper's desk, opened it and typed on the keys. 'But I saw the amount of glass in that pie, Tina, so the signs are that she's been very lucky in the circumstances. So how about telling us what you expected the outcome to be for Connie, when you placed the glass inside, had she swallowed it all?'

'What?' Tina gasped, as Billie plugged in the small projector that she had been carrying under her arm and pointed it towards the white wall behind Graham Harper's desk.

'The broken glass pie, Tina. It's the same one that you put in Connie's lunchbox when you were looking after her at Ellis Darque's property. Remember? You and Maya were entertaining everyone's new friend, Johnny Briggs. Maya has confirmed she was present when you gave the pie to Connie and I was present when Connie took it out of her bag the following night, added bits of it to a pizza and ate it.' Billie recalled that it had been impossible to separate Connie from her brand-new school bag when she had picked her up, hence the child having insisted on taking it with her to the restaurant.

'But that is preposterous!' Graham Harper argued. 'Why on earth would Tina want to sabotage *her own* company?' he demanded.

Suddenly, as Billie clicked on the keys, CCTV footage appeared on the wall. Billie adjusted the view, making it larger, so there could be no mistakes. Boo might have given up being a top police officer, but her investigative instincts had never abandoned her. After Billie had left the night before, Boo had headed back into Freedom Angels and together with the security team, had spent the night scrolling through footage from cameras fitted around the location.

'Perhaps you would like to enlighten us, Tina? That is

clearly you here in Freedom Angels, printing out the banners being used by the animal activists for the past few days, right outside of your flagship outlet. You can also be seen, if I run this forward, printing out the individual messages sent to your father, including the latest threat in capital letters. The donated printer driver installed in the art and craft room at Freedom Angels has a slight error, particularly clear on the capitalised letter 'I', printing the figure 1 instead. They are still waiting for someone to come and fix it. But meanwhile printouts in upper case from that machine are quite unique.'

Boo had handed over a memory stick containing this damning footage when Billie had picked up Maya. Despite having had little sleep due to the all-night investigation, Boo was willing to fight to the death to ensure that nothing would stop Freedom Angels and the children who came into her care from thriving. Billie knew that she had finally found *her* true calling in life.

'Tina?' Graham Harper looked aghast, as Tina held her hands to her face tearfully. 'Is this true?' He didn't really need to ask, as Billie was playing the footage again, enlarging the picture even more to show the reality.

'Yes, all right, it *was* me,' Tina sobbed. 'Please, turn it off.' Billie complied. 'I did the banners and the letters sent here and sometimes joined in the protests, but I certainly didn't put any glass in any pies, I swear to God. I would never harm a hair on Connie's head. Oh my goodness, this is dreadful.' Tina started to cry more loudly now.

'You're right. It is. I'm going to have to tell the shareholders in a matter of minutes that you have damn well done this to the company that's in your bloodline!' Graham Harper was clearly mortified at the thought. Tina suddenly spun around angrily.

'But that's just it! I don't want anything to do with the stupid company! I want to make my own way in life, set up my own art and design institute, bringing like-minded creatives together, not get rich on pies!'

'But I promised your mother–' Graham Harper tried to argue, before Tina cut across his words.

'Yes, and she promised *her* father.' Tina struggled to speak through her tears. 'But that day, when I sat alone with her as her life ebbed away and you were stuck at a meeting so couldn't get there before she died, she confessed that *she* hadn't wanted that sort of life either, despite how lucky everyone else thought she must be to have such a successful business just fall in her lap. She told me to follow my own dreams.'

'But you never said anything–' Graham Harper glanced across at Billie who raised an eyebrow. She'd had a similar conversation with him about his own circumstances only the night before.

'I didn't dare!' Tina shouted. 'Everyone just assumed that's what was best for me, but when Johnny came along, he showed me that life could be different, less rigid in every respect. That's why he suggested we do this. Johnny said that we could start building the institute out in Spain, first using my savings, the money that Mum left me. Then once Porkie's had been forced to close down due to publicity about the threats and I'd cashed in my share of the assets, we could already be in a position to–'

'You've given Johnny Briggs money?' Billie couldn't help but cut across Tina's words. Graham Harper looked too crushed to be able to say anything right at that moment. Billie had a horrible feeling that he'd handed over a tidy sum to the odious man himself.

'Yes, of course... well, I might as well tell you now, Daddy. Johnny and I are going to get married and then we're moving to Spain. That's where we're building the art and design institute,' Tina explained. But Graham Harper's knees had already given way. He slumped down onto a chair, his head in his hands.

'Tina, is this your glove charm?' Billie delved in her pocket and lifted out the unusual entwined silver logo, deciding that she might as well find out if the rather frail-looking Tina had been so passionate about closing down her inheritance that she'd had the strength to hit Billie with such force with the bin lid. The girl shook her head, as she lifted both hands to her earlobes. Having brushed her hair aside, Billie now spotted that Tina was wearing earrings with the same logo. Both intact.

'No. Safia gave the gloves to Johnny. After all, he's been so instrumental in creating her new design line, with her own label, Safia Jamal. That's the S & J letters entwined.'

'You do know that Safia's been kidnapped, Tina?' Billie asked. 'Did she or Johnny mention where this new range of clothing was being manufactured?'

'Excuse me.' Graham Harper rushed from the room. Billie wondered if he was about to be sick, but outside in the office, she could see him giving instructions to his PA and her picking up the phone receiver.

'No. Johnny told her it had to remain secret for now. There are so many rip-off merchants around...' Tina trailed off, finally realising the truth of the matter. She gave a little whimper as the reality that Johnny Briggs was one of them, hit home. 'I promise you, Billie, I had no idea that there was glass in the pie. Johnny said that he'd just slipped in one of the messages that he got me to print out. Thought it would be amusing, to wind up Maya's dad and he said it would up the pressure, finding an actual threat inside of a pie... there was never any intention to actually hurt anyone...' Tina's eyes filled up with tears once more. '...and I believed him...'

'Con men can be very convincing, Tina. I've fallen prey to more than one myself. Yours seems to be equally as dangerous.'

The message from Matt had come in just as Billie had arrived at Freedom Angels. His contact had tracked down the device that had created Billie and Ellis's deepfake porn video to the location right where they were standing, Porkie's Big Eats head office. The advice was that the upload must have been done at speed, to avoid the culprit being caught on the job, otherwise the work of art would have been rerouted via the dark web as was the norm for such creations.

'But regardless, you have to live with your own conscience. Did Johnny get you to create and upload this?' Billie clicked on the footage and pointed her mobile in Tina's face. 'Because if so, even ignoring the negative impact on the public perception of your company, Connie is involved yet again.' There was only so far that Billie could go with sympathy this morning.

At that moment Ellis's face appeared at the door. He came bounding in, a little breathless. Billie was surprised to see him.

'Nearly made it on time. Maya's offered to stay with her until I get back.' Billie was pleased that father and daughter had clearly made up their differences. It looked like it might be a while before Graham and Tina Harper did the same. Ellis actually looked relieved to have escaped from the confines of the hospital. But that was because Billie hadn't broken the news to him yet about the video footage. She was right to have waited, because as she had guessed, he went ballistic the moment that she shared it with him.

'I swear to God I didn't do that!' Tina started sobbing again as Graham Harper returned, to a furious Ellis and wailing daughter. He looked like he was going to faint himself when Billie managed to get her mobile back from Ellis and shared the evidence.

Her phone beeped once more, whilst the PA was called in and Graham Harper fired off instructions for the IT department to take down the server, whilst Ellis ranted about Connie facing abuse from so many different directions right when he was embroiled in a custody battle.

Billie blocked out the commotion for a moment as it was Matt's name that flashed up again, now that it was firmly in her mobile address book. She couldn't help but breathe an inner sigh of relief. Here was someone who seemed to smoothly get things done.

The work looks like that of this man. Daniel Brigante. Mother, English, father, Spanish. He's done several stretches in Spanish jails for fraud, money laundering and numerous money-related scams. Dabbled in some trafficking and had a deepfake porn site that had a huge following before he was last locked up. Goes by various names but Briggs usually features. It's his old army nickname.

The photo that Billie scrolled down to look at was without a doubt the man she knew as Johnny Briggs.

'Can you track that vehicle you loaned Johnny Briggs last night?' Billie asked Graham Harper. He shook his head in dismay.

'That's exactly what I rushed out to try to arrange just now, but it appears that he's dismantled the tracking device.'

'I checked with Boo at Freedom Angels,.there is no ongoing project involving anyone there who would need the use of one of your lorries,' Billie advised, undoubtedly making Graham Harper feel even more gullible than ever. Billie's mobile beeped again. It was Matt with a further message.

He's been recently identified with this woman. Identity unknown. A photo of a woman with dark shoulder-length hair now filled the screen. When Billie had last set eyes on Storm Benbow, she had short cropped blonde hair, but that had been a year ago. *P.S. Missing you already x* Matt had signed off. Billie showed the photo to Graham Harper and Tina.

'Have you seen this woman at any time with Johnny Briggs?' she asked.

'Yes, that's his creative partner,' Graham confirmed. 'She

was here yesterday assisting Johnny with the advert he was shooting for the vegetarian range. He said that she is an expert at enhancing his photographic work.'

'Which computer was she using? It might save us some time. No wonder she had the photos of Connie to hand,' Billie said through a sigh. 'I think you'll find that both Johnny and his friend are actual deepfakes. Ellis and I know this woman to be called Storm Benbow.'

'You what?' Ellis yelped. 'This is turning into a fucking nightmare,' he exclaimed, taking Billie's mobile from her hand and scrolling through the messages from Matt. 'That's her all right. But at least this strengthens my case with the courts.'

Billie's mobile suddenly rang. She took it from Ellis. Maya was on the line, sounding agitated. 'Is Dad there? It's just that his phone is turned off and I've been trying to get him. Can you tell him to come back to the hospital, like *right now*.'

'Yes. Is Connie okay?' Billie asked. Ellis was immediately alert and looking worried at Billie's words.

'No, not at all. Billie, she's gone.'

THIRTY-FOUR
DEADLY LITTLE TRICKS

Ellis raced along the hospital corridor, trying to control his spiralling emotions. Maya would be waiting for him at the children's ward, and he was at pains to ensure that she didn't think he blamed her for what had happened.

No, he blamed the damn social worker, Ethel Rutherford, for being so stupidly gullible, bringing Storm in to see Connie on a so-called emergency supervised visit, without informing him first. No doubt Storm was as good as gold when the doddering old idiot had been nearby, but the way that Maya had told it, when she had finally got through to Billie's phone in a blind panic, *she'd* been sent down to the café on Ethel Rutherford's orders while the visit had been ongoing.

'Too many visitors might overstimulate the child,' she had claimed. So, it had been poor Maya who had been chucked out. Maya had headed for the canteen, to get Storm the coffee and croissant that she had ordered, from where she had immediately tried to ring her dad to inform him of the situation. Ellis could see the missed calls on his mobile to prove it. Upshot was that when she got back to the ward everyone had scarpered.

Ellis had given the old bag a flea in her ear good and proper when he'd managed to get her on the blower. She'd threatened him over his language. He'd threatened her with a public outing for incompetence, as he now had the police putting out a missing person's alert for his young, unwell and vulnerable daughter, snatched by his ex the minute the social worker had scarpered to dabble in some other poor family's life. Turns out Storm was already on a bleeding Europol watch list, for Christ's sake!

Ellis ignored the lift, standing with its doors open. Instead, he took the stairs, three at a time. Billie had stayed back at Porkie's because there was little anyone could do here, except glean more information from the staff on how they'd just let Connie go walkabout with that mad bitch.

Billie had been straight on to Matt Scalera though, back at Porkie's, a video call giving him and his team all the gen on Johnny Briggs or whoever that bastard was really called, nicking off with a Porkie's lorry and being in cahoots with Storm doing some dirty dealing with the asylum-seeking kidnap thing. He left her to that, desperately grateful if a whole team of NCAs might catch Storm and her latest fling, into the bargain.

Ellis tried not to dwell on the message that Matt had sent with the photo of Storm, the words *Missing you already* along with a kiss had cut like a knife through his already broken heart. All of his future hopes and dreams were coming crashing down on him. But one thing was for sure, if he managed to get his hands on Storm he would kill her for pulling this little trick. She'd never wanted Connie, always palmed her off to anyone who would take her. She clearly only wanted the kid to have a dig at him. Well, he wouldn't let her get away with her deadly little tricks anymore, not once he caught up with her, that was for sure.

As Ellis slammed the ward doors open, Maya spotted him and came running, flinging herself at him, hugging him tightly.

'Dad, I'm so sorry. You've got to believe me. I did my best to get you on the phone.' Maya's voice was heavy with tears, the skin around her eyes puffed up from crying.

'It's okay, baby. It's okay. You're not to blame here.' Ellis eyed up a nurse who was approaching with a wary look on her face.

'Mr Darque, I'm so sorry. It was one of the student nurses who let her go. The doctor had said Connie was fit to leave and then when the older woman left, Connie's mum said she was taking her home. I mean, she showed her identification to the girl. She's just in training and she's obviously devastated by the mistake, but she assures me that Connie's mum had her passport and everything to prove—'

'Hang on, what?' Ellis frowned. 'I didn't even know that Connie *has* a passport. Jesus, what if Storm headed straight for the airport or the Port of Tyne?' Both were less than twenty minutes from the hospital in Newcastle. Ellis reeled back, his hand clamped over his mouth for a moment, lest he scream out the obscenity whirling around his brain. Both Maya and the nurse were looking at him in trepidation.

'Somebody's head is going to roll for this. If Storm has got Connie and her passport, they could be *anywhere* by now.'

THIRTY-FIVE

THE SYMBOL

In the circumstances, Billie could think of anywhere she should be, other than sitting in an ex-servicemen's club at lunchtime, sipping an orange juice and listening to a man with an odd-coloured comb-over, droning on from a stage draped with red velvet curtains. He was standing next to the bingo ball machine. But this was the highlight of the year for some people. Boo had pointed that out when she had rang Billie, just as she had been winding up the video call meeting with Matt, his team and Graham Harper, along with Tina.

'You haven't forgotten Jimmy the Hat's award thing at the club today?' Boo had said in a tone that told Billie that Boo already knew that it had slipped her mind.

'I'm on my way right now.' Billie had jumped up and headed to the door, checking her watch. Jimmy had been shortlisted for the charity volunteer of the year award within his local community, and today was his big day. He had a good chance of winning, both Billie and Boo had agreed, because even now that he had his own bungalow, life on the streets was hard for Jimmy to shake off.

He still enjoyed sitting on street corners, a forward observer on other people's lives, but nowadays with a charity box in his hand. If he wasn't there, then he could usually be found at the local food bank where he donated much of his allotment produce. On other days he would be ironing clothes in one of the high street aid organisation outlets, claiming that ironing was bred into him in the forces and not being able to do it when he was a street dweller made it even more of a privilege now. His contributions and upbeat demeanour made him a very popular volunteer all round, as well as a true community angel.

'It's important we're here, though,' Boo had whispered as Billie checked her watch when Jimmy had taken yet another trip to the toilet, either with nerves or a dicky prostate, the charity volunteer award being the last honour on the seemingly endless list to be bestowed.

'And we won the raffle,' Boo added, making them both glance at the terrifying stuffed clown sitting in the middle of the table, grinning at them.

'Not long to go.' Billie had also been surreptitiously checking her phone for any updates on the missing people in their lives, but there was nothing new so far, other than the information that a European wide AMBER missing child alert was in place for Connie and Matt had whispered to Billie, when they'd had a moment to chat alone, that the intel was that a transfer of people and goods might be attempted by a gang to Europe via Ireland today, using the port of Cairnryan in western Scotland to move them to Northern Ireland and then onwards. He was currently with his crew in that region watching and waiting.

Finally the community volunteer awards were announced and despite having felt at moments that she was crazy to have been here, when she should have been helping in some way to find Connie or the asylum-seeking kids, Billie had to admit to having a lump in her throat when Jimmy's name was announced. He had creakily pulled himself to attention, best beret perched at a jaunty angle as he made his way, with just a bit of help up the stairs, onto the stage.

Boo handed Billie one of her hankies as Jimmy proudly took his award, giving a little salute before he marched back to their table, triumphantly placing his trophy next to the grinning clown monstrosity. Billie decided that Boo had been spot on. Life was full of precious tiny moments as well as high drama. And they had been absolutely right to have been here to cheer on Jimmy today, after all of the support that he had given to them both over the years.

'Well, I'm glad that palaver's over.' Jimmy knocked back the dregs of the pint he had been sipping throughout. 'I've got to get home to my pigeons now. They're due back from a competition today. Been halfway across the country and back, in the time we've been sitting here. They'll be wanting their tea.'

'I'll give you a lift, Jimmy.' Billie exchanged amused glances with Boo. It was just like Jimmy to be thinking of other creatures even when he should have been basking in his own moment of glory. 'Do you want this clown, missus?' Jimmy offered the hideous clown to a woman who had seemed crestfallen to have lost the prize. 'Give it to the grandkids. Stick that on the end of the bed and it'll frighten off any bogeymen.' Jimmy winked, as he hobbled out after Billie, clutching his trophy.

After they waved Boo off, Billie helped Jimmy into the passenger seat of his car, fastening the seat belt and handing him his trophy to rest on his knees.

'Thanks, pet. It's meant the world to me, you and Boo coming along today when you're both so busy with your own lives.' Jimmy patted Billie on her hand.

Billie stopped and blinked hard, suddenly realising that Jimmy was wearing black leather gloves and only one of them was decorated with a charm identical to the one Billie had ripped off the animal rights activist. She was thoughtful as she walked around to her own side of the car and slid behind the wheel.

'Are those new gloves you are wearing, Jimmy?' she asked, checking out his other hand again. There was a slight hole where the charm on that side had been removed, with some force. Billie remembered the moment.

'Aye, love. A proper dapper pair. Got them off my new friend. He's been staying with me for a day or so.'

Billie was immediately alert. Jimmy had various sheds on his allotment. Could Johnny Briggs be hiding out around there? It wouldn't be the first time that she had unexpectedly found a major criminal hidden amongst an innocent-looking vegetable plot. If so, she reckoned that Jimmy was in real danger. If Johnny Briggs was aware that people were out looking for him, then anyone who could identify his whereabouts would be surplus to requirements the moment that he decided to move on.

'Really? I'd love to meet this friend. What did you say his name was?' Billie started the car and turned it in the direction of Jimmy's home.

'I don't think I did, love. Thing is, he's a bit shy right now. Doesn't say much to strangers.'

'Well, the thing from my side, Jimmy, is that I think that those gloves of yours link to a serious investigation I'm working on. It really is a life-or-death situation. The person who gave you those might just be able to provide me with a vital clue.'

'Straight up, love?' Jimmy looked shocked. 'Well, I expect he'll be only too keen to help.' Billie wasn't quite so sure that would be the case, if it was indeed Johnny Briggs hiding out with the frail old man. 'He's at my allotment right now, digging up dirt.'

Billie rubbed the wound on her head. She hoped that if it

was Johnny, then he wouldn't be as nifty with a spade as he had been with the bin lid.

———

Tanko had done the weeding and had just finished digging up a row of potatoes for tea, when he heard the car turning into the lane by the allotment. He instinctively crouched down, all of his senses on high alert, listening for any sign as to whether the driver might be friend or foe. It seemed like he'd been doing this for half of his life now. The carefree days of playing with his friends without any thoughts of imminent danger seemed a million years away.

He heard voices and reacted by quickly scuttling towards the corner of the allotment, before hiding behind a high and wide plum tree, feeling the familiar thump of heart beating fast against chest. Earlier, he had planned to suggest that he might plant yams in the patch of untended land lying behind where he was squatting. His father had grown them. Tanko had hoped that if Jimmy had agreed, he might feel at last as though he had brought his precious family with him to this new place. But now he had a sudden flash across his mind's eye of the young boy who had fallen from the oak tree to his death under the lorry. Tanko held his breath to stifle the whimper that had stammered from his lips. Perhaps Jimmy had told his old soldier friends his story, then led them here with the police to deport him. Could there be no safe hiding place for him?

He heard Jimmy's voice, cheerily chatting to the driver, as the car door slammed. As Tanko stood up to peer through the branches, Jimmy spotted him and waved. Tanko bobbed back behind the tree, swallowing hard. There was one other person behind the old man. He immediately crouched down low again, skirting on all fours around to the back of the shed. Jimmy had mentioned a friend called Billie, but he had never mentioned a woman. This one was tall and beautiful with hair as red as a lion's mane. Perhaps it was his daughter, Tanko wondered, here to tell him to move on, to keep well away from her father. His mouth became dry. He was in no doubt by now, that women had strength and power in this part of the world. Would she report him to the authorities? Would they send him back home to a certain death in Boko Haram-held territory, or to another faraway land in which yet more people would eye him with suspicion?

'Tanko, son. Where have you gone? I've got a young lady who wants to meet you.' Tanko watched Jimmy push the heavy wooden gate to the allotment open. The young woman followed behind. Her eyes were clear and blue, alert. It hadn't escaped Tanko's attention that immediately on entering, she had reached for a spade that he had left by the fence. His muscles tensed even more. Should he expect trouble?

'Tanko?' Jimmy sounded breathless from the effort of manoeuvring around the piles of netting and chunks of wood and discarded pots and pails on the uneven and partially overgrown land. Tanko had a sudden vision of his poor departed great-grandfather, the feel of his head, the bones of his skull jangling inside due to his fall, as Tanko had cradled him when his life had ebbed away. He tried to shake the thought off.

Suddenly Jimmy overbalanced. Despite his fear, Tanko jumped up like a shot and hurtled towards him, catching him in his arms at the same time as the tall lioness of a woman dropped the spade and caught him in hers. Their arms entwined for a split second, before Jimmy made a grab for the greenhouse door and they broke apart, both staring at one another with wide eyes.

'I'm all right. Just a bit wobbly on my pins these days.' Jimmy struggled to catch his breath. 'Tanko, this is my friend,

Billie, come to see you. I told her you'll be a great helper if you decide to stick around with a doddery old geezer like me.' Tanko blinked. Jimmy had just made it clear that he wanted him to stay, which was the best news, but the young woman was staring at him like she had seen a ghost.

'Tanko, did you say?' The woman was gazing at him even harder. 'Tanko Abubakar, from Freedom Angels?' Tanko swallowed hard and started backing away. Maybe she was part of the gang who had stolen him from the streets and now she had come to capture him again?

'It's all right, son. Billie used to be a top-notch police officer.' Jimmy smiled as though in reassurance, but where Tanko came from, police officers were often in the pay of bad people. He looked around in panic. The only way out would be to push between Jimmy and the woman and race for the gate, but he was worried that if he took that route Jimmy might topple over again and this time smash his head on the ground.

'I'm a friend, Tanko.' The woman was giving a kind smile now, but that had happened before too. Tanko remembered the tale he had been told at school about the wolf in sheep's clothing. He wondered why he hadn't taken heed of that great fable in which the wolf had dressed in a sheep's skin, blended in with the flock and every day killed one of the sheep. Tanko could have applied it to so much of his life since that first massacre in his home village, when his parents had been killed. One of the leaders of Boko Haram, the feared rebel force that had wiped out his village, had once been a teacher at his school, before showing his true colours.

'Look, I can prove it.' The lioness took out her mobile phone and punched in some numbers, whilst Tanko felt so nauseous that he feared he would throw up. 'I think I've just met someone you need to see.' She spoke into the phone before turning it to face Tanko. His heart suddenly soared as he dropped to his knees.

'Mother.' He gasped the word. Of course, she was not his own mother but all of the young people at Freedom Angels called the woman now staring at him by that name. After all, most of them had lost their own mothers and she had been so kind to everyone. Tanko had remembered her fighting with the authorities on his behalf when the people from the government had insisted that Tanko be moved to a hotel with the other children and had turned back and noticed her sobbing when they had left.

'Tanko?' Boo yelped. 'He's speaking...' She appeared to be astonished at the sight. 'Where is he? Are the others...?'

'He's been staying the night with me, love. I had no idea he was one of your lads. No bother, in fact he's welcome to stay with me as long as he likes,' Jimmy announced, nodding at Tanko who held his hand to his heart, his eyes now filling with tears.

'I'll get back to you.' Billie had turned the mobile back to her face to speak with Boo, before clicking it off. 'Right, well, you don't know how nice it is to meet you, young man. What I need to know is how you got your hands on those gloves you gave to Jimmy.'

'I didn't steal them,' Tanko whispered, shaking his head.

'No, I'm not suggesting that you did. But you weren't the one wearing them a couple of nights ago at the animal activists march. You're not as tall as the man who gave me this smacker.' She pointed to a bruise near to her left eye, in shades of purple and yellow.

'I know nothing of this!' Tanko started to back away once more, wondering if he should run for it after all. If she thought he had beaten her and she had been in the police force, perhaps she had come to put him away in jail?

'You're not in any trouble, lad. Billie just wants some help on an investigation she's doing. Been telling me all about it on the way here. She's trying to catch some very dangerous people, fraudsters, maybe worse.' Tanko calmed a little. If Jimmy was telling him it was all right then he believed it.

'If I can have confirmation of the man who was wearing this glove the other night then I can link him to a missing girl who was also at Freedom Angels.' Tanko suddenly wanted to tell Jimmy and the lioness all about the others missing, the ones who had been slaughtered right in front of him and those who were running in search of safety even now.

'Someone dropped them by the dustbin behind the high street where I was resting. They took off a black suit with a zip at the front as well. I think they were being chased. I hid behind a big bin. They were wearing the mask of a skull. I thought they had come to kill me for running away.'

'That must have been tough.' Billie's heart went out to Tanko. She could see pure terror crossing his face at the memory. A picture flashed across Billie's mind of the movement in the shadows when she was chasing the person in the suit and mask. Had she really only been a few steps away from Tanko then? She tried to wipe away further thoughts of how much time had been lost by not discovering his whereabouts earlier.

'Before the police came to the end of the alleyway I picked up the gloves as I was so cold, and they were so warm.' Tanko was shaking now, remembering the cold that had seeped right into his bones, but he was also feeling a new fear in addition, for what might happen to him now that he had admitted that he was a thief in this country.

'Would you recognise the man if you saw a photo of him?' Billie was asking him now. Tanko realised that she knew very little. She did need his help. He nodded in agreement as she reached for her phone once more.

'But it was not a man who was wearing this suit and gloves. The one who was wearing the skull mask. It was a woman.' He noticed her look quizzically at him, already showing him a picture of the person she expected him to identify.

'A woman?' She frowned, yet still she looked beautiful, Tanko noticed. Like an angel coming to save him. He felt a little more confident now.

'I thought she had come to take me back to that terrible place. She *is* the Devil, you can be sure of it, even without the mask she was wearing. He works with her. His name is Johnny.' Tanko stepped forward now and jabbed his finger in the face of Johnny Briggs's photo. 'He kills with a machete. I saw him at Freedom Angels before this happened and thought that he was a good man. But he is a wolf in sheep's clothing. Another two men also do their dirty work, forcing young people from the hotel housing children, into a big van. Me to repay my debt. Others, for who knows what? All we had to eat there was a little bread and water. This is what this symbol on the clothing and the gloves means. The symbol was used everywhere in the place where we were trapped.'

'Safia Jamal,' Billie answered. 'It represents the two letters of her name entwined. She is missing. She designed the clothing at Freedom Angels and just like you were, she has been taken, I'm guessing because they want her unique design talents. Do you know where?'

Tanko shrugged, then slowly nodded. He had always had a good sense of direction and could remember some unusual sights that he had seen along the way.

'Maybe. About two hours north from here. But that logo, it does not refer to the girl you say, but to our captors. They were bragging about becoming rich designers with their clothing range. It's named after them. They are a couple. Like husband and wife. S & J. That means Storm and Johnny.'

THIRTY-SIX
LOVE HER ENOUGH TO LET HER GO

E llis had his foot down on the pedal, hoping some traffic cop wasn't going to be stupid enough to try and slow him down. He was racing to catch up with Billie who had rang to say that she'd got this lead and was already on her way up north. He thought his mind might have exploded out of his head otherwise, trying to get every contact he'd ever known on the blower, coppers, other crime fighters and criminals. Right now he wasn't going to be picky about who he begged for help, but until Billie had rang he had been hitting one dead end after another and time was of the essence.

He'd just whipped around and dropped Maya at work when Billie had made contact. To be truthful, he couldn't take his oldest kid's tears and apologies on top of everything else, so handing her over to Boo had been at least a bit of relief. Boo had always been a calming influence and there had been nothing else Maya could do.

She'd tried ringing that greasy oik, but surprise, surprise, his line had been as dead as a bleeding doornail. Done off with Storm and his little 'un, hadn't he? But if he thought he was going to get away with putting his dirty paws on another of

Ellis's kids, he had another thing coming. He was going to tear his fucking head off when he got hold of Johnny Briggs or whatever he was calling himself today.

Ellis had thanked God out loud, when he had heard Billie's voice with the news. Not that he had ever believed in any big man watching over people, but he'd been going out of his mind until that moment, marching up and down the café area of Freedom Angels.

Boo had finally insisted he sat down, just for a minute, to take a swig from the mug of tea she'd ordered. She'd also called for the biggest slab of cake he'd ever seen, insisting he needed sugar. But he'd been feeling as sick as a parrot. He knew that the situation wasn't so straightforward, what with Storm being Connie's actual mum and the fact that she had been Connie's main carer, until she had just flitted off to who knows where last year, with her latest lover boy, Johnny, by the looks of it. The updated situation going forward of him being his daughter's *sole* carer had been due to be rubber-stamped any day before she had blown back in on an ill wind.

God only knew how it was so difficult for the authorities to understand how serious the situation was, that they shouldn't wait and see, as one or two idiots he had tried to get on the case pronto, had suggested. Storm wasn't going to just come back with Connie after taking her for a quick play in the park. The fact that her crazy boyfriend had arranged a dangerously spiked lunchbox, should have had all alarm bells ringing loud and clear.

Boo had done her best to calm him down. When he had mumbled something about Matt Scalera and Billie having been together the night before when Connie was spiked, he had suddenly remembered Scalera's message to Billie that morning, sealed with a kiss. No wonder he had been so fucking totally wound up. When he'd finished rambling, Boo had grabbed hold of both of his hands and yanked him towards her. She had looked at him with those big brown-black eyes of hers then and had that face she always pulled when she was talking serious business.

'You're going to have to love her enough to let her go, you know...'

'Yeah, yeah, you are right.' He had agreed, just to stop her labouring the point, thinking she was talking about Maya. He knew he had to face up to the fact that his oldest girl needed to do her own thing, maybe go travelling for a bit, rather than be tied down here with her dad on some guilt trip, if God forbid, Connie didn't turn up.

'I'm talking about *Billie* as well as Maya,' Boo had answered, squeezing his hands. Then the next second, the call had come in from Billie herself like she'd pulled off some miracle, right when he was thinking of her, like she'd picked up something telepathically. She was on the case, taking action already, heading for her car with the kid and the old guy in an attempt to find his Connie and all the other kids.

Ellis didn't think he would ever forget that moment. He rammed the car into a low gear now, overtaking three vehicles in a row before rounding a tight bend without braking, instead speeding off like a rocket, leaving Boo's words far behind him. The sooner he caught up with Billie the better. There was absolutely no way he would ever let her go.

THIRTY-SEVEN
BOLD AND BRAVE

Billie had been astonished at Tanko's knowledge of British history and relieved that the quiet whisper with which he had first spoken, had now been exchanged for a more confident tone as he gave recollections of his journey from the place he had fled. She was well aware that it couldn't have been easy to agree to lead them to the spot from which he had so recently needed to run for his life. From what Boo had already told her about the young man, she knew it wasn't for the first time. So in her eyes that made the lad doubly brave.

Jimmy had half turned around in his seat now and then, nodding in encouragement like a proud grandfather, as the youngster had pointed out spots he had recognised. Jimmy was pleased, Billie felt, to be having an extended day out and so far enjoying something of an adventure, the sort that an old war horse didn't get very often these days. Billie only hoped that he wouldn't try to get involved if the going got tough. Bearing in mind the intel and experience she'd had of Storm and Johnny, she guessed that things might get more than a little bumpy before too long.

One of the upsides of the latest information was that Matt

had responded rapidly to her news of having found Tanko. He was splitting off some of his team from the Scottish port, where they were waiting for any sign of a lorry full of people and contraband on the move and sending them closer to the expected location to which Billie was now heading. They would be coming via helicopter so hopefully in the vicinity when Billie arrived with Tanko. She had been given explicit instructions to wait for them to make contact with her before approaching any targets.

As they headed north, she desperately hoped that he could pinpoint the location and that the children were still there. She was also crossing *everything* that Safia and Connie would be safely with them. She also couldn't help hoping, if only secretly to herself, that Matt would be with the team heading her way. They had made no plans, but even so, she wouldn't be averse to seeing him in the flesh again so soon.

'Look, there is the castle on the island!' Tanko had pointed to the island of Lindisfarne, a hauntingly beautiful and ancient location visible from the main road, just as he had described when outlining to Billie the route of his journey south, hanging on to the cab of the lorry whilst it had woven through the main road and towns of 'the place of many castles' as he had called the county of Northumberland. He had already pointed out Alnwick Castle. 'The turrets, full of men,' had been Tanko's description of the striking medieval figures in stone, topping the battlements of the second-biggest inhabited castle in the United Kingdom.

His journey by lorry told via the descriptions of the castles he had seen en route, had made it easy for Billie to work out where they were heading. From Tanko's detailed story of his hitched ride, she had been pretty sure that the kidnapped children had been kept somewhere in the countryside close to the most northern town in England,

Berwick-upon-Tweed. The location lay just before the border with Scotland.

Tanko had described in detail the initial part of his journey south by lorry, which had very soon passed through a town surrounded by ancient stone walls, a Georgian town hall and crossed by a beautiful river heading out to sea. He told how he had looked on in awe as the lorry had crossed the old bridge spanning the river and he had seen a train speeding in the other direction on a sister bridge with many arches. Billie knew and Jimmy had confirmed that there was no other town in Europe, let alone north of the allotment, that shared a similar layout.

Funny, Billie thought, how many people saw the TV news featuring asylum seekers arriving by boat and expected them to be uneducated idiots, in order to take such a crazy and dangerous journey. Instead, she knew that many, like Tanko and Safia, were bright and clever young people with dreams. Simply desperate to start anew in a country that didn't take a wrecking ball to their lives, killing off any chance of success.

It was as they approached the turn-off to Berwick that Tanko went silent, stiffening straight in his seat, staring ahead. Billie glanced at him in her back-view mirror and could see the fear in his eyes. She slowed the car a little, seeing Ellis through the back window. His face was also tense, as he sat behind the wheel of his car following close behind. He was no doubt hoping that he was going to be reunited safely with Connie soon. If she was there, Billie knew that he wouldn't stop until he got her, whatever it might take.

'Look, there's the sign saying Scotland ahead. We're about to leave England.' Jimmy pointed his bony finger at the sign in the distance which stated the approaching change of country. Billie felt her heart sink. Had Tanko been confused about the location after all? But as she drove another half a mile or so further up the road, with the odd whitewashed farm building to one side and a golden field of rapeseed giving way to a spectacular North Sea view on the other, Tanko suddenly gasped.

'There it is. The bridge and the oak tree.' He was pointing now, one of his knees shaking rapidly up and down in anxiety.

'Should we turn off here, son?' Jimmy had asked, but Tanko had fallen deadly silent as though he had suddenly lost his ability to speak again. In any case, Billie was indicating that she was about to leave the main road and Ellis, who had zoomed into view at alarming speed a few miles back and had been tailgating Billie to a point where he'd almost seemed to have been nudging her to drive faster, was following suit. They pulled their cars off and up the slope to a junction.

'There is the rapeseed field where I hid.' Tanko's voice was back but quiet, his breathing heavy, as though he was suffocating. Already the smell of the rapeseed filled the air, densely honeyed, mustardy and musky. Billie quite liked it, although Boo insisted the smell reminded her of dead bodies. It was the sort of smell one loved or hated. It was clear to see which side of the fence Tanko was on right now, as he held his hands to his face, looking up with horror at the broken branch of the large oak tree on the other side of the narrow lane where Billie pulled the car to a halt and got out to survey the view. Tanko pushed open his door.

'That is where the machete man, Johnny, cut the branch away...' He trailed off, a look of horror crossing his face, obviously reliving the rest of that scenario, as a lorry thundered by underneath the road bridge. Ellis had left his car in the lay-by and had jumped out, sprinting over.

'Spotted the gaff yet?' he demanded. A look of fear crossed Tanko's face. He swallowed hard, looking to Jimmy and Billie for help, before shaking his head nervously. 'We are in the right place, yeah?' Ellis persisted. Billie could see why Tanko seemed to have lost his voice once again.

'Give the lad a chance,' Jimmy intervened. 'He's had a bad do at the hands of this lot.'

'Tell me about it. My baby girl is probably in the same shit den right now.' Ellis's face was dark.

'I'm just texting Matt's team. We'd be best to wait for them before we make a move. If Johnny Briggs is handy with a machete and he has like-minded mates, we're only going to get one go at this—'

Ellis cut Billie off in mid-sentence. 'I'm not waiting for anyone. Soon as we pinpoint the spot, I'm in there to get my kid out. I'm not hanging around for some bloody jumped-up cavalry to fly in to the rescue.'

Tanko was scanning the field, desperately. He suddenly pointed.

'The building. It is over there, across the field of rapeseed! I see it now, between the trees when the wind moves the branches,' he suddenly called out anxiously. Billie looked up from where she had been using her mobile. Ellis was already squinting his eyes to see the long, low, ramshackle old farm building visible in the distance through the treeline at the far edge of the field.

'Okay, I'm giving them the co-ordinates, but let's get these cars tucked away.' She knew she was on a hiding to nothing trying to get Ellis to hold back. Truth be told, she didn't want to wait around herself, but there were others to think about too. Tanko had already dropped to a crouching position, clearly terrified at being so close to the place where he had so recently suffered. He had done well to get them to this point. Billie took his arm and gently guided him back up onto his feet. As she turned to Ellis, her voice brooked no argument. 'I want Tanko and Jimmy in a safe place. Then we go in, together.'

The stationary Porkie's Big Eats branded lorry came into view as Billie and Ellis swiftly edged around the back of the old farm building, some of which was tumbling down at the far end. Billie noted that most of the windows were broken or missing and whole areas of the roof appeared to be tile-free. Clearly, Storm and Johnny hadn't taken any trouble to enhance the working conditions of their slave labourers. As Matt had suspected, it looked like this was a short-term working venue. The plan was no doubt to move the latest products along with workers and precious designer of their new fashion range, abroad, removing them completely off the radar of any law enforcers in this country, who might be out searching for the missing youngsters.

Billie had insisted on both Tanko and Jimmy staying put in her car, parked further up the lane just off the road, behind some prickly thorn bushes. But despite the lack of visible guards or any sign of either Johnny or Storm, Billie could feel a sensation of trouble brewing. Had they been spotted already from across the field when they had temporarily parked up, she wondered? It felt way too still. She desperately hoped that Matt's team weren't far away.

'I'm worried it sounds too quiet,' Ellis whispered as they kept their heads down and crept through a copse of trees fringing the back of the farmyard. 'Think they've scarpered already?'

The windows were dark, the only signs of life coming from a loose shutter banging against the wall in the breeze, which carried the scent of the rapeseed even more strongly now, along with a feeling of uncertainty and tension.

'I've brought the lock-picking kit.' Billie damned herself for not being better equipped but the need for speed should the outfit be planning to move on, meant that neither had any time to swing by their office and pick up any further heavy-duty gear.

'Let's do it, now.' Ellis's face was grim. 'Like I said, I'm not waiting around for anyone else, not when Connie's likely to be in there.' Billie was now equally desperate to get inside to suss out the lay of the land. If the place turned out to be empty, then they had no time to lose in attempting to trace both captors and captives elsewhere. They kept within the shadows of the overhanging trees fringing the side of the yard, before breaking free from the copse and running towards the lorry.

They both squatted down, listening. Billie could suddenly hear the faint sound of some sort of machinery now running and whirring.

'I can hear them,' she whispered. 'Sewing machines, by the sounds of it. They're in there.'

Her heart started beating like a drum inside her chest, her fingers brushing against the cold metal of the lock-picking tools which she took from the pocket of her jacket in preparation. Ellis had his gaze fixed on the building with an intensity that matched her own. No sign that anyone was peering at them from behind any of the glass-free windows, the dark spaces like empty eye sockets, blind to the torture inside.

'Let's do this.' Ellis glanced across towards her. Billie gave a silent nod and in unison they moved quickly and silently towards a door at the edge of the building. With practised hands, Billie got speedily to work, feeling adrenaline course through her veins as she worked on the ancient lock, shards of rust falling like shattered autumn leaves onto the ground at their feet. A heavy clunk resonated. They both held their breaths as the door moved open just enough for them to turn sideways and slip inside.

The smell of damp and neglect assaulted Billie's nostrils as she adjusted her eyes to the dim light in the dusty corridor, her ears straining for any noise that might give away the presence of Storm, Johnny or anyone else doing their dirty work, nearby.

Ellis moved ahead, his desperation to find Connie perhaps overriding the need for silence and stealth in their movements, because he suddenly stopped dead. The corridor had opened out into a room full of young people who looked like they had come from all four corners of the world, chained to tables, sewing machines in front of them, fabric all around.

The noise of the sewing machines was louder now, which Billie hoped would be their saving grace, because the figure of a tall broad man, his back to them, blocked their path only a few feet ahead. Ellis reached into a small pouch at his side and brought out what looked like a torch. Billie was momentarily surprised to see the item, as she knew it to be in fact a stun gun, illegal to carry by anyone but police in the UK, which neither of them were these days.

The weapon had been given to Ellis by an American friend, where in almost every state, anyone over eighteen was welcome to walk around with one. But Billie was hardly likely to remind Ellis of the hefty jail sentence if he had been caught with it in his car glove compartment, here in rural Northumberland. It was at that moment a small voice pierced the sound of clacking machinery. Connie was standing in the corner of the room and had spotted Ellis.

'Daddy!' Connie cried out. Billie spotted her next to Safia Jamal. There was desperation in her voice mixed with joy, as she reached out her little arms in Ellis's direction, tripping onto her knees, because shockingly, she, like all of the others, had one tiny ankle shackled to an iron table leg bolted to the floor. 'Daddy!' She cried out in pain now having grazed her knees, her face crumpling into tears. The man in front of Ellis spun around, a baseball bat held in his hand ready to strike, but it was too late. In one swift motion, Ellis delivered a precise jolt of electricity from the stun gun, causing the man's body to convulse before he dropped to the ground.

Ellis rushed across to Connie as Billie reached for the ever-ready handcuffs in one of her pockets, rolling the big guy over and cuffing his wrists behind his back. Racing across to one of the tables, she grabbed a couple of lengths of fabric, tying one around his mouth as a gag and the other around his ankles. He lay trussed up like a turkey as Billie rolled him on one side. She didn't want him in the recovery position, but she wasn't in the business of killing people either. She followed Ellis, who was hugging Connie tightly to him. She was sobbing loudly now, causing her recently cut lip to start bleeding once more.

'The keys to the ankle locks. They are up there!' Safia indicated a bunch of keys hanging up on one wall. Billie ran over to grab them before speedily starting to free the youngsters from their shackles.

'How many of that lot are there?' Billie asked Safia, flicking her head towards the man gagged and bound on the floor.

'One more besides Johnny and Storm. They just left a few minutes ago. I don't know where they were going. There is another storeroom in a building at the far corner of the field. Maybe they went there.'

'Okay. Let's move then. We'll take the lorry,' Ellis announced. He had already carried Connie across the room and had found the lorry keys also hanging on a hook.

'Right, listen up, everyone!' Billie spoke loudly, holding her hands up to stop the rise in noise now the young people were free from their chains. 'Stay quiet. We have to get away from here and quickly. We're going to head for a big lorry outside from which we will be taking you to a place of safety.' Billie turned to Safia who translated her words in several different languages, calming the wide-eyed faces looking their way. Once again Billie marvelled at the hidden talents of so many of these young people. 'Tell them we will roll down the back loading door and lock it, but they will not be prisoners. It's just that we have to take precautions.' Billie didn't add that if Storm, Johnny and their henchman turned up before they made their escape, it could turn out to be a bumpy ride, hence the extra security measure.

When Safia had finished, Billie held her finger to her lips and beckoned the young people to follow her. Ellis reluctantly handed Connie to Safia in order to speedily help Billie load the youngsters on board. They were as silent as mice, well aware of the peril facing them if their captors were alerted to their flight. After all, many of them had been smuggled inside of lorries before, locked up in a tight dark space in fear for their lives, when escaping danger in their own countries.

'Right, let's go.' Ellis banged the padlock shut on the back of the lorry and fastened it with a key attached to the others on the ring.

'Daddy!' Connie cried once more, holding out her arms for Ellis to hug her. *Daddy*, rather than *Mummy* being the preferred call name at long last.

'Give me the keys,' Billie commanded, grabbing them from Ellis's hand as he took Connie from Safia. 'We'll pick up Jimmy and Tanko on the way.'

'So much for Matteo Scalera and his mates swooping in on their white horses to save the day,' Ellis couldn't seem to help saying, Billie thought, as she jumped into the driver's seat and started the engine, backing the massive vehicle out of the farmyard.

The drive back down the lane was tense as Billie got to grips with manoeuvring the huge lorry, whilst Ellis scoured the countryside for any sign that someone was planning to block their escape route. In a matter of minutes Billie had pulled the lorry up alongside the thorn bushes, leaped out and unlocked her car to usher Jimmy and Tanko out. 'What's that noise?' Billie was suddenly alert to the sound of an engine.

'Just that big combine harvester over in the field,' Jimmy advised, as she took him by the arm and propelled him around towards the back seat of the lorry. Tanko jumped in the cab, looking as nervous and agitated as when Billie had first set eyes on him, helping heave Jimmy upwards whilst Billie pushed, slamming the door as soon as he was on board, breathing heavily from the exertion. She raced back around to the driver's side of the vehicle, hopped back up into the seat and then set off again, building up speed as they moved along the lane. Any minute now they would be nearing the road bridge and the turning down onto the main A1 road south and to safety.

'Still no sign of Matt Scalera and the cavalry.' Ellis hadn't got a response to the first comment on the subject. He seemed determined to continue with the subject now. 'Hand me your phone if you like. I can text to say we don't need them.' It was at that very moment that Billie was aware of a movement from the passenger side of the lane, as though a bush was falling in towards them.

'What the fu...' Ellis cried out, as the rest of the line of gorse bushes toppled rapidly towards the vehicle, along with the wooden fence which collapsed like sticks of straw as twelve tonnes of vast red combine harvester smashed through the foliage and into the side of the lorry.

Billie gasped with shock, momentarily stunned. She looked around, trying to make sense of the scene. Connie was screaming and Ellis appeared to be unconscious, whereas Safia, on the far end of the cab nearest the impact, was a shocking sight. Her injuries so severe, that it was clear that her life had been cruelly snuffed out. Billie gave an involuntary whimper as she glanced back to see Jimmy slumped, his hat missing, across

Tanko's lap, his frail body equally decimated. Tanko was looking at him totally aghast.

Suddenly aware of a movement through the hedge, Billie saw Johnny Briggs appear, holding a machete in his hand as was another, younger man behind him. Storm Benbow followed, armed with a rounders bat. Tanko started making a terrified keening sound, like a wounded animal.

'Run!' Billie shouted to Tanko, as she grabbed Connie from Ellis's limp arms and scuttled from the cab. She yanked Tanko's shaking arm. There was no time to gently extricate him from Jimmy's crushed and bleeding corpse. 'Now!' Billie yelled. Tanko finally slid away from under Jimmy, the old man's crushed body toppling into the footwell as Billie dragged the boy determinedly out with one arm. Speedily slamming the doors and clicking on the lock, she could only hope that help arrived before their attackers managed to get inside of the cab or locked unit holding the young people.

'Run as fast as you can!' Billie cried to Tanko, pushing through the foliage on the right of the lane, then starting to sprint across the field beyond. It wasn't easy to pick up speed with a screaming, wriggling five-year-old in her arms and looking back, Billie could see Johnny only a few feet behind and gaining speed. Suddenly she tripped over a rock and hit the ground hard, crying out, 'Run, Connie, run,' as the shocked five-year-old, tears streaming down her face, took fright and raced off screaming, in a random direction. Billie whipped around, trying to grab Johnny's ankle as his nauseating smell enveloped her, but he kicked her hand away, holding the machete high above his head.

Tanko hadn't run. Instead, he had huddled against the hedgerow, rigid with shock at the sight of Jimmy. A fallen soldier dead in the trench between front and back seats. Tanko stared at Jimmy's beret, which had landed on the muddy ground next to his feet. His whole body was shaking now in absolute terror.

Behind him he could hear Storm Benbow and the younger man battling to try to unlock the lorry doors. Tanko knew the padlock on this vehicle might snap with a few strikes of the man's machete. Tanko had been alongside people trying to open doors like that himself enough times when in Calais. Where there was a will, there was always a way, especially with old-fashioned locks. Inside, he could hear the trapped youngsters, screaming in shock or moaning from their injuries.

'Grandfather?' he had whimpered. The sensation of holding a broken bag of pottery in a thin leather bag had washed over him again, in that moment before Billie had dragged him out of the vehicle. Tanko sucked in air, lest he vomit. In the front seat he could see Ellis semi-conscious and moaning, but no one else was here to help. He heard shouting. It was Billie the lioness. Tanko turned in blind panic to see Johnny, a machete in his hand, looming menacingly over the brave and beautiful woman who had tried so hard to save them all, as she attempted to kick him away.

Tanko tried to block the utter terror filling his mind, when he suddenly focused on the machete that Storm's henchman had now dropped on the grass whilst he fumbled with the lock, as directed by Storm's shouted demands as she banged her rounders bat against the back of the loading door in anger. Tanko could hear his own breath loud and ragged, the blood pounding in his ears as he took advantage of the moment, darting out of his hiding place to grab the machete, give a quick sharp chop to the man's arm and even before he fell to the ground screaming in pain, race off at high speed across the field. The lioness was fighting with all of her might, but Tanko knew how evil the man threatening her was. He had already watched him massacre others. He desperately wanted to turn and run away, the adrenaline now pumping through his body directing him to take flight rather than fight, but he had felt this fear before and forced his way through it. He could do it again. He had too.

As he raced forward it took only a swift movement of Tanko's machete to knock Johnny to his knees next to Billie. With a precision that had come from frequent practice since that very first day, when he had seen his family massacred by Boko Haram and then been captured by the group as a new boy soldier, Tanko continued when Johnny hit the ground. He pulled the evil man's ugly head back in a slick movement befitting of the highly trained assassin that in truth, Tanko had become, before slitting him clean across the throat. The lioness had looked totally startled then, as well as colossally relieved.

Tanko had started crying. The last time he had slit anyone's throat it had been his own great-grandfather's. His uncle nearby, was killed by his fellow Boko Haram rebels. That is when he had finally took flight from the horrors of his homeland, vowing never again. But it seemed clear that the ability to kill would never leave him, because cutting the neck of this latest enemy had been as easy as spreading butter on bread. It had become second nature to him. It was time to accept the truth, that he could run away from his past life but he could never run away from his own conscience.

When he had been captured at first, on that terrible day of the initial massacre, after he had hurtled from his school to the market square, too late to save his parents, he had been one of the young boys who had been forced to walk at the front of the Boko Haram raid squads, with the cattle. No matter how many shots had been fired at him, other children captured just like him, falling down all around like skittles, Tanko had simply continued marching forward. Within a year, he had so impressed the group's leaders that he was given his own unit, luxurious living quarters and his pick of captured girls to lie with. No other boy as young as him had achieved such success, but then Tanko's teachers had always said that he was a quick learner.

To survive, he had learned to listen to the Boko Haram chiefs, follow their orders without question and without any show of remorse. They talked of how those who got into bed with the western people and followed their culture, religion and laws were continuing to keep the poorest people in Nigeria in poverty, living with extreme inequality and injustice. The leaders of the west needed to keep major maritime oil shipping routes through the area open and so gave millions of pounds in aid, but instead that desperately needed money was spirited away in a world of corruption. It was time for the ordinary people to fight back.

Before long, Boko Haram had become his new family, so he wholeheartedly believed this. But on that later day, when he had been told to conduct a raid on his great-grandfather's village, he had to join in with the slaughter. Kill or be killed himself, that was the rule of the leaders. It didn't matter if the victims were once friends... or his old family. It had finally sunk into his brainwashed head then that the rebels were just as corrupt as those they claimed to be fighting against. That was the truth and that's why he had to run. But he could never run away from the fact that he had slaughtered his own great-grandfather who had lived so peacefully to such an old age.

'It's okay, it's okay.' The lioness was on her feet now, prising the machete from Tanko's bloodied hands as he dropped to his knees on the ground, ready to strike again if this evil Johnny somehow crazily rose from the dead.

There was more noise now, a car engine roaring to a halt, people tumbling out, crowding around the lorry and the younger wounded attacker, who Tanko could tell them, was one of the two thugs sent out in the van to bring back the young people from the lost children's hotel. They were the ones sent out to do Johnny and Storm's dirty work whilst they pretended in public to be innocents. Just like many of the important people in his own country. Tanko was sorry that these new rescuers had arrived, because otherwise, he would have raced back across the field and finished off the evil man that he had wounded with the machete too. It was in his blood now. He sank his head into his hands in horror at his life.

'Connie!' he heard Billie the lioness call. 'Did you see where Connie went?' She had her hand resting on his shoulder. Did she not realise that she was shouting in the ear of a mass murderer?

'Under the bridge. In the same direction as the devil woman – Storm. I saw her running...' He trailed off as Matt Scalera raced across the field towards them. Tanko held his hands across his head, because this man with a gun at his side would surely kill him for what he had just done.

'This is Tanko. He just saved my life. Take care of him. The others are inside the lorry.' Billie the lioness handed the man the keys to the lorry before wiping away a smear of blood that had splashed across her beautiful face as she scanned the field, looking towards the crumbling tunnel under the small stone bridge. Tanko could see the look of love and admiration in the man's eyes for her. But then she was off, bold and brave and running across the field in the direction that Tanko had pointed.

THIRTY-EIGHT
NOBODY'S GIRL

As Billie raced past the lorry cab, she saw that Ellis was no longer inside and was relieved to spot him sitting looking dazed on the grass, as one of Matt's operatives attended to him. She breathed a sigh of relief, but picked up pace now, aware that on the other side of the bridge under the narrow lane was a bright-yellow rapeseed field and then a cliff, dropping to the sea. The last thing she needed was for Connie to have made it to that point. Just as that thought came into her head, she heard a yelp of surprise and then a cry of fear. It was Connie. Storm Benbow was nowhere to be seen. Billie threw caution to the wind and started shouting.

'Connie, where are you?' Billie had almost crossed the field now, her lungs catching with the musky scent of the rapeseed. After what she had just witnessed, she would now, like Boo, forever link this smell to death. A picture flashed through her mind's eye of Johnny Briggs, a startled expression on his severed head. His body separated by a sod of grass and a lake of blood. She might never forget the scene, but she would be eternally grateful to Tanko for doing what he had done. In fact, being so startlingly efficient at it.

'Connie!' Billie shouted once more, hearing a whimper from down below, as she peered over the spectacular jagged rocks of sandstone and limestone. Her worst fears had come to pass. Connie had fallen over the side and was now lying, terrified, on a ledge a few feet down. It was a short and narrow outcrop and as Connie wriggled in fear she was moving perilously close to the edge.

'Just keep still, sweetheart.' Billie tried to lower her voice, attempting to make herself sound calm and in control, though she felt anything but, right at that moment. 'Remember when we played statues? Well, I want you to stay where you are and stay as still as a statue, while I come and get you.'

'Mummy!' Connie continued to cry, her hand outstretched towards Billie, her terrified gaze fixed upon her. As Billie madly scoured the sheer cliffside, desperately looking for a way to descend and reach the child before she fell to her certain death, she suddenly spotted Storm Benbow emerging from her hiding place, which had been a small cave under the overhang, halfway up the cliff face.

'Mummy's coming,' Storm called in a soothing tone, as she started to pick her way across the cliff towards Connie. Billie ran along the clifftop to an area where it sloped down a little and a ledge ran halfway along the middle of the cliff in the direction that Connie was located. She took that route, hoping that one way or another they could reach the child and stop her from falling.

As the two women edged from different sides, both in danger of slipping to their deaths at any moment, Connie fell strangely silent, perhaps due to shock, Billie wondered. As they clambered nearer to one another, Storm started talking.

'I know this isn't going to end well for me.' Storm was talking breathlessly as she stopped and carefully stretched to the next rock to pull herself across the cliff face. 'But I want you to know that I started off as a good woman, Billie, and maybe, yeah, I *have* done some bad things in my life, because of the way the cards fell for me.'

'You've come out of hiding to save your daughter now though, when you could have gotten away with it.' Billie genuinely meant that. She'd had no idea that there was a cave tucked away in such a seemingly inaccessible spot. All Storm had to do was sit it out then melt away somewhere when the coast was clear. She also wanted to keep Storm calm, because she knew that the way the cliff kept crumbling under her feet as she tested each step, all three of them would be lucky if they ended back safely on solid ground.

Billie reached her foot across onto a rock which suddenly broke free and skittered down to the sea, spraying up salt and foam as the waves crashed against the hard and jutting limestone rocks below. She gripped with all of her might with her fingers on the tiny edge above her, one leg swinging freely for a terrifying moment, until she managed to test another crevice in which to edge her foot, her face turned sideways, her right cheek grazing against the cliff face.

'She's my child. I gave birth to her. Granted, I haven't been the best of mothers. Not confident to stand up to the bastards I've got between the sheets with, that's my problem. But be under no illusions, Ellis is in that camp, whatever romantic hero character he's trying to woo you with right now. Wonder how *that's* going to affect Connie in the future? A dad who can change colours like a chameleon. Trust me. He can be a lovey-dovey daddy one minute and a killer the next.'

Billie decided it wasn't the time or place to broach the subject of Storm's now deceased lover Johnny Briggs, having given Connie a glass-spiked pie. Whatever Connie's mother's shortcomings, it was clear by her actions right now, that she would never have agreed to that. God knows what horrors Johnny might have had in store for Storm in the future, had he survived, and she had one day become surplus to his requirements.

Another rock suddenly tumbled away, this time from under Storm's foot. She let out a little cry, righted herself, then continued moving ever nearer Connie. Billie was making careful progress too. They were almost eye to eye, Connie in between them, just beyond an arm's reach away from both.

'I don't need to tell you how devastating air accidents can be.'

Billie had started to reach out, but stopped and caught her breath at Storm's words.

'No. Not now, Storm. Right now, this is all about Connie.' Was Storm trying to needle her about the unexpected death of her new lover a year earlier, the man who had donated so much money towards Freedom Angels?

'It's about you too, seeing as it's no secret that Ellis is trying to get you all domesticated, playing mummy and daddy with my kid.'

'That's not true.' Billie tried to concentrate on Connie, who was staring at her mother as though she was an interesting stranger. 'Ellis and I are just business associates.' Billie tried to make her voice sound firm, but her body was shaking now as she remembered the shocking news of her close friend's demise. Especially as she had almost been with him on that flight.

'Word in the big bad underworld is that Ellis engineered that little episode. Got friends in high places. It's no secret that he doesn't like his girls being out of his control.'

Billie closed her eyes tightly for a moment. Could Storm's hinted accusation actually be true? She wouldn't respond. She couldn't respond. She had to concentrate on the job in hand.

Spotting a crevice in the rock just before the ledge that Connie was on, Billie managed to wedge her leg in it and twist around with a little stability now that the deep crack in the rock was holding her body in place.

'Now, Connie. Listen to me. Hold your arms out. I'm going to pick you up. Then I want you to wrap your arms around my neck and your legs around my waist tightly, just like when we play koala bears, okay? Can you do that for me?' Connie nodded in response, her little face serious as she held out her arms and Billie leant over and grabbed her tightly to her body. Connie snuggled in to Billie so closely that she could feel her little heart beating. Not as fast as her own, Billie realised as she tried to steady her breathing.

'Take care of my baby,' Storm called shakily, as Billie slowly and hesitantly started to move back along the cliff face. Connie, somehow realising the seriousness of the situation, kept her head snuggled down and her arms and legs limpid-like around Billie.

'Good girl, Connie,' she heard Storm whisper. As she glanced up, she saw tears in the woman's eyes.

When Billie thankfully reached the more gently sloping pathway, away from the cliff face, and made her way to the top, catching her breath, she allowed herself to look back at the perilous scene below, as the wild sea whipped across the base of the cliffs. Storm was slowly trying to pick her way back in the other direction. Right now, Billie didn't care if she managed to get away via a magic cave escape, she simply wanted to get Connie and herself on completely solid ground.

'Well done.' Billie kissed the child on her head as Connie finally dared to look up and smile widely. Billie realised what she was looking at. Ellis had come rushing along the top of the cliff, his face like thunder. 'She's okay. Everything's okay, Ellis. We just need to get help for Storm. It's treacherous down there.' Billie approached him, alarmed that his body was swaying a little when he came to a halt by a large dark and sharp rock. He was staring down. 'Wait for help–' Billie stopped mid-sentence as she noticed Storm looking up into Ellis's eyes, her own were sad and yet a small smile played on the corners of her lips.

'Guess this is it then, Darquie, yeah?' She had the regretful look of someone who had once loved the man.

'I'll catch you up,' Ellis murmured. 'Can you take Connie to the medic man over by the lorry?'

Billie nodded, carrying Connie past. 'I'll get people to come quickly. Just hang on, Storm.' Billie had just started to break into a jog, still holding Connie, when she heard a sudden anguished cry and a huge splash as something large hit the waves that were crashing against the base of the cliff. She spun back in horror, knowing before she even looked, that Storm had fallen.

'Keep your head tucked down, Connie,' Billie instructed. Connie complied, thinking another game was about to start, as Billie, stunned, marched back to the cliff edge. Below, she could see Storm's broken body. She was lying still, her neck at an awkward angle, clearly broken. A wave washed over her face, unseeing eyes gazing up as the foam cleared.

'Got some loose rocks around here.' Ellis shrugged as he looked at Billie. The large rock beside him was no longer there. Billie had already seen it on top of Storm, the waves crashing over it as it pinned her body in place. Billie blinked, remembering Storm's words only a few minutes earlier about Billie's former lover's death. Now this truth was staring her in the face. Was Ellis a good man forced to do bad things due to extreme circumstances, or in truth something much worse?

'She would have destroyed everything, including you. That's the person she was.' Ellis approached, grabbing Connie from her arms. 'I was just protecting my girls – all of them.' Ellis reached out to put his arm around Billie's shoulders, but she pushed him away.

'Get this straight. I'm *nobody's* girl,' she announced forcefully, marching speedily away back towards the tunnel where Matt and the others were now emerging, clearly concerned for their whereabouts. Billie simply kept on walking.

THIRTY-NINE
GONE WALKABOUT

Boo sat next to Billie on Alnmouth beach, the remains of a barbeque before them. Ash was now home with his girls making a magnificent sandcastle at the water's edge on this sleepy, sunny, peaceful afternoon. In the water, Ellis was splashing around with Connie and Andrey the similar-aged son of his new live-in nanny, Daryna, who had recently moved into the penthouse flat in Ellis's house. The one that Maya was vacating today.

Tanko was joining in the high jinks. The young man was making progress slowly but surely. The bungalow that Billie had bought for Jimmy had reverted to her on his death and she had gifted it to Freedom Angels as a halfway home for young asylum seekers who needed to experience family life once more, with a couple of full-time carers in situ. Tanko was the first resident there, along with another former boy soldier, who had also experienced life as both a victim and a perpetrator. Good boys who had done bad things due to extreme circumstances. Kill or be killed. That was the truth of life in war zones the world over.

'Ellis and Daryna seem to be getting on like a house on fire.'

Boo was watching the fun and games. 'Connie seems to love her new virtual family.'

Billie surveyed the scene. It was true that Ellis was calmer of late, seemingly happy to settle down into a life more ordinary, snooping on insurance scammers and wayward spouses, coming home to a happy family-type of scenario at the end of the day.

Billie still couldn't help thinking of Storm though. Maybe she was being naïve, but she had witnessed some motherly love there. Without a doubt she had, in the end, sacrificed her own life to help save Connie. Storm's true mode of death was a secret that Billie had decided she would take to the grave, which wasn't to say that she was happy about that ending. She had killed someone herself once, in self-defence. Maybe that would be Ellis's argument, if they ever chose to speak about it, though that was unlikely. That he had to kill Storm, or be killed by her, eventually.

True, he had been lucky not to have met the same fate as Jimmy the Hat, who had been sitting directly behind him when the combine harvester had ploughed into the lorry. But Billie much preferred a judge and jury to carry out justice, to hear the whole story and work out the narrative that was nearest to the truth. Storm's warning about Ellis had also continued to ring unnervingly in Billie's ears. Could Ellis *really* be a deepfake too, someone who engineered a murder, yet had made it look like an accidental air crash?

'All ready to go then?' Boo turned to Maya who was approaching, a rucksack on her back.

'You bet I am. I'll be in Tina's and her dad's villa this time tomorrow,' Maya trilled. The Porkie's Big Eats sale was already underway. Graham Harper and his daughter had realised that their true dreams, now honestly revealed, were in fact very similar. They were about to launch a combined winery and art exhibition centre in their Spanish home and grounds now that pies were well and truly off their menu. 'Then Thailand after that.' Maya was full of excitement for the year of adventure that she was about to undertake. She headed back towards Billie's house, almost skipping through the gate that led from Billie's garden onto the beach, clearly eager to get underway.

'Taxi's waiting,' Maya called back. 'He's already loaded your rucksack,' she said to Billie, who stood up and brushed the sand from her jeans.

'Not going to wave adios to everyone?' Boo asked.

'I've never been one for long goodbyes.' Billie looked around her raggle-taggle friends, her virtual family, for better and sometimes for worse. 'But I've told Coco where I've left his emergency snacks,' she quipped, referring to the cat that she and Ash had rescued from a murder victim a year earlier. 'And a note for Ellis, breaking the news that I've gone walkabout.'

'Any idea yet where you are heading for your forty days and forty nights in the wilderness?' Boo teased, raising an eyebrow. It had been she who had convinced Billie that she had to get away for a while to clear her head.

'I've got a stopover in Paris tomorrow. Funny, it turns out that Matteo Scalera will be there too.'

'Interesting coincidence.' Boo quietly laughed. 'Keep your wits about you. That man has amazing powers of persuasion.'

'After that, who knows?' Billie shrugged. Where she was heading right now or way into the future, she really wasn't sure. Maybe the National Crime Agency, as she had received a formal offer to join them, or maybe not. But one thing was for certain. She would never forget brave Safia Jamal and her desperate fight to live life on her own terms.

She could see the young woman in her mind's eye right now, on the night that she had spoken before her fashion show at Freedom Angels and then again in Billie's car after fighting off Johnny Briggs. Safia had come to Billie many times in the sleepless nights since that terrible day when she, Jimmy and Storm had lost their lives so tragically. Like a ghost, returning in the small hours. At those times, Billie had finally gotten out of bed and watched the sun rise over the sea right outside of her home, walking for miles along the golden sandy beach, deep in thought.

'I will never forget this opportunity you have given me, to follow my own dreams, not a life that others have chosen for me.' Those had been Safia's words. Billie owed it to that amazing young woman and to all of the other people not free to make such a choice, to be true to herself from now on. It was time at last, to start following her own true dreams.

THE END

ALSO BY MARRISSE WHITTAKER

The Magpie

The Devil's Line

The Mad-Hatter Murders

Buried Dreams

A NOTE FROM THE PUBLISHER

Thank you for reading this book. If you enjoyed it please do consider leaving a review on Amazon to help others find it too.

We hate typos. All of our books have been rigorously edited and proofread, but sometimes mistakes do slip through. If you have spotted a typo, please do let us know and we can get it amended within hours.

info@bloodhoundbooks.com

Printed in Great Britain
by Amazon